ELMORE LEONA[RD]

LaBRAVA

WINNER OF THE EDGAR AWARD FOR BEST NOVEL

"Have I got a book for you. *LaBrava* is a mean-streets romance, laconic and bittersweet, so thoroughly a film noir in novel form that a twenty-five-year-old Holly-wood film noir is itself at the center of the plot. . . . Check it out."

Washington Post Book World

"Elmore 'Dutch' Leonard is more than just one of the all-time greats of crime fiction. He's fast becoming an authentic American icon."

Seattle Times

"Nobody but nobody on the current scene can match his ability to serve up violence so light-handedly, with so supremely deadpan a flourish."

Detroit News

"Terrific . . . Leonard's best book so far."
Philadelphia Inquirer

"The debate over who's the all-time king of the whack job crime novelists just ended. Living or dead, Elmore Leonard tops 'em all."

Ft. Lauderdale Sun-Sentinel

"Many surprises . . . The tone is dry and mordant, the action well-paced, and the voices of the riffraff convincing. . . . *LaBrava* may be the best of Mr. Leonard's books; it is about as good as the form allows . . . a thriller whose conclusion is even more satisfying than the crackling exposition, whose denouement plausibly resolves an ironic plot that was fully thought through."

New York Times Book Review

"A giant among writers of crime fiction."
Columbus Dispatch

"A master of narrative . . . A poet of the vernacular . . . Leonard paints an intimate, precise, funny, frightening, and irresistible mural of the American underworld."

The New Yorker

"A major literary star . . . He defies categorization, and when you do try to categorize him, you are invariably wrong."

Chicago Tribune

"Tough and smart . . . His dialogue is so authentic that it dances off the page. . . . The characters flash on and off in multicolored neon. . . . And the scam that forms the backbone of the novel's plot is intriguingly mystifying."

New York Times

"The Dickens of Detroit . . . He creates colorful characters from the seamier side of life. . . . His style is as strong and personal as Van Gogh's brush strokes. He has perfect pitch for the street talk you might hear from armed robbers who are not very good at armed robbery."

George F. Will

"Elmore Leonard has few peers. . . . His work [is] marked by razor-sharp characterizations, wonderful dialogue, quirky humor, and the sort of seductive plots and movie-style editing that allows little time for questions."

Los Angeles Times Book Review

"Leonard's cinematic grasp of scene and setting, his ability to arouse within us a helpless sympathy for even the lowest of his characters, his quirky pacing and plot twists, and his sly humor and artfully oddball prose sear our eyeballs and keep the pages turning."

Miami Herald

"The best writer of crime fiction alive."
Newsweek

About the Author

ELMORE LEONARD has written more than forty novels and nearly as many short stories, including such best-sellers as *Up in Honey's Room*, *The Hot Kid*, *Mr. Paradise*, *Tishomingo Blues*, *Pagan Babies*, and *Glitz*. Many of his books have been made into movies, including *Get Shorty* and *Out of Sight*. He lives with his wife, Christine, in Bloomfield Village, Michigan.

ALSO BY ELMORE LEONARD

FICTION

Road Dogs

Up in Honey's Room

The Hot Kid

The Complete Western Stories of
    Elmore Leonard

Mr. Paradise

When the Women Come Out to
    Dance

Tishomingo Blues

Pagan Babies

Be Cool

The Tonto Woman and Other
    Western Stories

Cuba Libre

Out of Sight

Riding the Rap

Pronto

Rum Punch

Maximum Bob

Get Shorty

Killshot

Freaky Deaky

Touch

Bandits

Glitz

Stick

Cat Chaser

Split Images

City Primeval

Gold Coast

Gunsights

The Switch

The Hunted

Unknown Man No. 89

Swag

Fifty-Two Pickup

Mr. Majestyk

Forty Lashes Less One

Valdez is Coming

The Moonshine War

The Big Bounce

Hombre

Last Stand at Saber River

Escape from Five Shadows

The Law at Randado

The Bounty Hunters

NONFICTION

Elmore Leonard's 10 Rules of
    Writing

L_ABRAVA

ELMORE LEONARD

HARPER

NEW YORK • LONDON • TORONTO • SYDNEY

HARPER

A hardcover edition of this book was published in 1983 by William Morrow, an imprint of HarperCollins Publishers.

HarperCollins books may be purchased for educational, business, or sales promotional use. For information please write: Special Markets Department, HarperCollins Publishers, 10 East 53rd Street, New York, NY 10022.

FIRST HARPERTORCH EDITION PUBLISHED 2003.
FIRST HARPER PAPERBACK PUBLISHED 2009.

Library of Congress Cataloging-in-Publication Data is available upon request.

ISBN 978-0-06-176769-2

09 10 11 12 13 ID/RRD 10 9 8 7 6 5 4 3 2 1

This one's for Swanie,
bless his heart.

———————————

1

"**HE'S BEEN TAKING PICTURES** three years, look at the work," Maurice said. "Here, this guy. Look at the pose, the expression. Who's he remind you of?"

"He looks like a hustler," the woman said.

"He *is* a hustler, the guy's a pimp. But that's not what I'm talking about. Here, this one. Exotic dancer backstage. Remind you of anyone?"

"The girl?"

"Come on, Evelyn, the shot. The feeling he gets. The girl trying to look lovely, showing you her treasures, and they're not bad. But look at the dressing room, all the glitzy crap, the tinfoil cheapness."

"You want me to say Diane Arbus?"

"I want you to say Diane Arbus, that would be nice. I want you to say Duane Michaels, Danny Lyon. I want you to say Winogrand, Lee Friedlander. You want to go back a few years? I'd like very much for you to say Walker Evans, too."

"Your old pal."

"Long, long time ago. Even before your time."

"Watch it," Evelyn said, and let her gaze wander over the eight-by-ten black and white prints spread out on the worktable, shining in fluorescent light.

"He's not bad," Evelyn said.

Maurice sighed. He had her interest.

"He's got the eye, Evelyn. He's got an instinct for it, and he's not afraid to walk up and get the shot. I'll tell you something else. He's got more natural ability than I had in sixty years taking pictures. He's been shooting maybe four."

Evelyn said, "Let's see, what does that make you, Maury? You still seventy-nine?"

"Probably another couple years," Maurice said. "Till I get tired of it." Maurice Zola: he was five-five, weighed about one-fifteen and spoke with a soft urban-south accent that had wise-guy over-tones, decades of street-corner styles blended and delivered, right or wrong, with casual authority. Thirty-five years ago this red-headed woman had worked for him when he had photo concessions in some of the big Miami Beach hotels and nightclubs. Evelyn Emerson—he'd tell her he loved the sound of her name, it was lyrical, and he'd sing it taking her to bed; though never to the same tune. Now she had her own business, the Evelyn Emerson Gallery in Coconut Grove and outweighed him by fifty pounds.

Evelyn said, "I sure don't need any art deco, impressionistic angles. The kids like it, but they don't buy."

"What art deco?" Maurice looked over the worktable, picked out a print. "He shoots people. Here, the old Jewish broads sitting on the porch—sure, you're gonna get some of the hotel. The hotel's part of the feeling. These people, time has passed them by. Here, Lummus Park. They look like a flock of birds, uh? The nose shields, like beaks."

"Old New York Jews and Cubans," Evelyn said.

"That's the neighborhood, kid. He's documenting South Beach like it is today. He's getting the drama of it, the pathos. This guy, look, with the tattoos . . ."

"He's awful looking."

"Wants to make himself attractive, adorn his body. But you look at him closely, the guy's feeling something, he's a person. Gets up in the morning, has his Cheerios like everybody else."

She said, "Well, he's not in the same league with any number of people I could name."

"He's not pretentious like a lot of 'em either," Maurice said. "You don't see any bullshit here. He shoots barefaced fact. He's got the feel and he makes *you* feel it."

"What's his name?"

"It's Joseph LaBrava."

Evelyn said, "LaBrava. Why does that sound familiar?"

She was looking at Maurice's tan scalp as he lowered his head, peered at her over his glasses, then pushed them up on his nose: a gesture, like tipping his hat.

"Because you're aware, you know what's going on. Why do you think I came here instead of one of those galleries up on Kane Concourse?"

"Because you still love me. Come on—"

"Some people have to work their ass off for years to get recognition," Maurice said. "Others, they get discovered overnight. September the second, 1935, I happen to be on Islamorada working on the Key West extension, Florida East Coast line, right?"

Evelyn knew every detail, how the '35 hurricane tore into the keys and Maurice got pictures of the worst railroad disaster in Florida history. Two hundred and eighty-six men working on the road killed or missing . . . and two months later he was shooting pictures for the Farm Security Administration, documenting the face of America during the Depression.

She said, "Maury, who's Joseph LaBrava?"

He was back somewhere in his mind and had to close his eyes and open them, adjusting his prop, his heavy-frame glasses.

"It was LaBrava took the shot of the guy being thrown off the overpass."

Evelyn said, "Oh, my God."

"Joe had come off the 79th Street Causeway going out to Hialeah. He's approaching I-95 he sees the three guys up there by the railing."

"That was pure luck," Evelyn said.

"Wait. Nothing was going on yet. Three guys, they look like they're just standing there. But he senses something and pulls off the road."

"He was still lucky," Evelyn said, "I mean to have a camera with him."

"He always has a camera. He was going out to Hialeah to shoot. He looks up, sees the three guys and gets out his telephoto lens. Listen, he got off two shots before they even picked the guy up. Then he got 'em, they're holding the guy up in the air and he got the one the guy falling, arms and legs out like he's flying, the one that was in *Newsweek* and all the papers."

"He must've done all right."

"Cleared about twelve grand so far, the one shot," Maurice said, "the one you put in your window, first gallery to have a Joseph LaBrava show."

"I don't know," Evelyn said, "my trade leans more toward exotic funk. Surrealism's big now. Winged snakes, colored smoke . . ."

"You oughta hand out purgatives with that shit,

Evelyn. This guy's for real, and he's gonna make it. I guarantee you."

"Is he presentable?"

"Nice looking guy, late thirties. Dark hair, medium height, on the thin side. No style, but yeah, he's presentable."

Evelyn said, "I see 'em come in with no socks on, I know they've got a portfolio full of social commentary."

"He's not a hippy. No, I didn't mean to infer that." Maurice paused, serious, about to confide. "You know the guys that guard the President? The Secret Service guys? That's what he used to be, one of those."

"Really?" Evelyn seemed to like it. "Well, they're always neat looking, wear suits and ties."

"Yeah, he used to have style," Maurice said. "But now, he quit getting his hair cut at the barbershop, dresses very casual. But you watch him, Joe walks down the street he knows everything that's going on. He picks faces out of the crowd, faces that interest him. It's a habit, he can't quit doing it. Before he was in the Secret Service, you know what he was? He was an investigator for the Internal Revenue."

"Jesus," Evelyn said, "he sounds like a lovely person."

"No, he's okay. He'll tell you he was in the wrong business," Maurice said. "Now he spots an undesirable, a suspicious looking character, all he wants to do is take the guy's picture."

"He sounds like a character himself," Evelyn said.

"I suppose you could say that," Maurice said. "One of those quiet guys, you never know what he's gonna do next . . . But he's good, isn't he?"

"He isn't bad," Evelyn said.

2

"**I'M GOING TO TELL** you a secret I never told anybody around here," Maurice said, his glasses, his clean tan scalp shining beneath the streetlight. "I don't just manage the hotel I own it. I bought it, paid cash for it in 1951. Right after Kefauver."

Joe LaBrava said, "I thought a woman in Boca owned it. Isn't that what you tell everybody?"

"Actually the lady in Boca owns a piece of it. 'Fifty-eight she was looking for an investment." Maurice Zola paused. "'Fifty-eight or it might've been '59. I remember they were making a movie down here at the time. Frank Sinatra."

They had come out of the hotel, the porch lined with empty metal chairs, walked through the lines of slow-moving traffic to the beach side of the street where Maurice's car was parked. LaBrava was patient with the old man, but waiting, holding the car door open, he hoped this wasn't going to be a long story. They could be walking along the street, the old man always stopped when he wanted to tell something important. He'd stop in the doorway of Wolfie's on Collins Avenue and people behind them would have to wait and hear about bust-out joints where you could get rolled in the old days, or how you could tell a bookie when everybody on the beach was wearing resort outfits. "You know how?" The people behind them would be waiting and somebody would say, "How?" Maurice would say, "Everybody wore their sport shirts open usually except bookies. A bookie always had the top button buttoned. It was like a trademark." He would repeat it a few more times waiting for a table. "Yeah, they always had that top button buttoned, the bookies.

"Edward G. Robinson was in the picture they were making. Very dapper guy." Maurice pinched the knot of his tie, brought his hand down in a smoothing gesture over his pale blue, tropical sports jacket. "You'd see 'em at the Cardozo, the whole crew, all these Hollywood people, and at the dog track used to be down by the pier, right on First Street. No, it was between Biscayne and Harley."

"I know . . . You gonna get in the car?"

"See, I tell the old ladies I only manage the place so they don't bug me. They got nothing to do, sit out front but complain. Use to be the colored guys, now it's the Cubans, the Haitians, making noise on the street, grabbing their purses. *Graubers*, they call 'em, *momzers, loomps*. 'Run the *loomps* off,

Morris. Keep them away from here, and the *nabkas*.' That's the hookers. I'm starting to sound like 'em, these *almoonas* with the dyed hair. I call 'em my bluebirds, they love it."

"Let me ask you," LaBrava said, leaving himself open but curious about something. "The woman we're going to see, she's your partner?"

"The lady we're gonna rescue, who I think's got a problem," Maurice said, looking up at the hotel; one hand on the car that was an old-model Mercedes with vertical twin headlights, the car once cream-colored but now without lustre. "That's why I mention it. She starts talking about the hotel you'll know what she's talking about. I owned the one next door, too, but I sold it in '68. Somebody should've tied me to a toilet, wait for the real estate boom."

"What, the Andrea? You owned that, too?"

"It used to be the Esther, I changed the name of both of 'em. Come here." Maurice took LaBrava by the arm, away from the car. "The streetlight, you can't see it good. All right, see the two names up there? Read 'em so they go together. What's it say?"

There were lighted windows along the block of three- and four-story hotels, pale stucco in faded pastels, streamlined moderne facing the Atlantic from a time past: each hotel expressing its own tropical deco image in speed lines, wraparound corners, accents in glass brick, bas relief palm trees and mermaids.

"It says the Andrea," LaBrava said, "and the Della Robbia."

"No, it don't say *the* Andrea and *the* Della Robbia." Maurice held onto LaBrava's arm, pointing now. "Read it."

"It's too dark."

"I can see it you can see it. Look. You read it straight across it says Andrea Della Robbia. He was a famous Italian sculptor back, I don't know, the fourteen, fifteen hundreds. They name these places the Esther, the Dorothy—what kind of name is that for a hotel on South Miami Beach? I mean back then. Now it don't matter. South Bronx south, it's getting almost as bad."

"Della Robbia," LaBrava said. "It's a nice name. We going?"

"You say it, Della *Robbia*," Maurice said, rolling the name with a soft, Mediterranean flourish, tasting it on his tongue, the sound giving him pleasure. "Then the son of a bitch I sold it to—how do you like this guy? He paints the Andrea all white, changes the style of the lettering and ruins the composition. See, both hotels before were a nice pale yellow, dark green letters, dark green the decoration parts, the names read together like they were suppose to."

LaBrava said, "You think anybody ever looks up there?"

"Forget I told you," Maurice said. They walked back to the car and he stopped again before getting in. "Wait. I want to take a camera with us."

"It's in the trunk."

"Which one?"

"The Leica CL."

"And a flash?"

"In the case."

Maurice paused. "You gonna wear that shirt, uh?"

LaBrava's white shirt bore a pattern of bananas, pineapples and oranges. "It's brand new, first time I've had it on."

"Got all dressed up. Who you suppose to be, Murf the Surf?"

There was a discussion when LaBrava went around the block from Ocean Drive to Collins and headed south to Fifth Street to get on the MacArthur Causeway. Maurice said, we're going north, what do you want to go south for? Why didn't you go up to Forty-first Street, take the Julia Tuttle? LaBrava said, because there's traffic up there on the beach, it's still the season. Maurice said, eleven o'clock at night? You talk about traffic, it's nothing what it

used to be like. You could've gone up, taken the
Seventy-ninth Street Causeway. LaBrava said, you
want to drive or you want me to?

They didn't get too far on I-95 before they came
to all four lanes backed up, approaching the 112
interchange, brake lights popping on and off as far
ahead as they could see. Crawling along in low
gear, stopping, starting, the Mercedes stalled twice.

LaBrava said, "All the money you got, why don't
you buy a new car?"

Maurice said, "You know what you're talking
about? This car's a classic, collector's model."

"Then you oughta get a tune."

Maurice said, "What do you mean, all the
money I got?"

"You told me you were a millionaire one time."

"Used to be," Maurice said. "I spent most of my
dough on booze, broads and boats and the rest I
wasted."

Neither of them spoke again until they were beyond Fort Lauderdale. They could sit without talking and LaBrava would be reasonably comfortable;
he never felt the need to invent conversation. He
was curious when he asked Maurice:

"What do you want the camera for?"

"Maybe I want to take a picture."

"The woman?"

"Maybe. I don't know yet. I have to see how she is."

"She a good friend of yours?"

Maurice said, "I'm going out this time of night to help somebody I don't know? She's a very close friend."

"How come if she lives in Boca they took her to Delray Beach?"

"That's where the place is they take them. It's run by the county. Palm Beach."

"Is it like a hospital?"

"What're you asking me for? I never been there."

"Well, what'd the girl say on the phone?"

"Something about she was brought in on the Meyers Act."

"It means she was drunk."

"That's what I'm afraid of."

"They pick you up in this state on a Meyers Act," LaBrava said, "it means you're weaving around with one eye closed, smashed. They pick you up on a Baker Act it means you're acting weird in public and're probably psycho. I remember that from when I was here before."

He had spent a year and a half in the Miami field office of the United States Secret Service, one of five different duty assignments in nine years.

* * *

He had told Maurice about it one Saturday morning driving down to Islamorada, LaBrava wanting to try bonefishing and Maurice wanting to show him where he was standing when the tidal wave hit in '35. LaBrava would remember the trip as the only time Maurice ever asked him questions, ever expressed an interest in his past life. In parts of it, anyway.

He didn't get to tell much of the IRS part, the three years he'd worked as an investigator when he was young and eager. "Young and dumb," Maurice said. Maurice didn't want to hear anything about the fucking IRS.

Or much about LaBrava's marriage, either—during the same three years—to the girl he'd met in accounting class, Wayne State University, who didn't like to drink, smoke or stay out late, or go to the show. Though she seemed to like all those things before. Strange? Her name was Lorraine. Maurice said, what's strange about it? They never turn out like you think they're going to. Skip that part. There wasn't anything anybody could tell him about married life he didn't know. Get to the Secret Service part.

Well, there was the training at Beltsville, Maryland. He learned how to shoot a Smith & Wesson .357 Magnum, the M-16, the Uzi submachine gun, different other ones. He learned how to disarm and theoretically beat the shit out of would-be assassins with a few chops and kicks. He learned how to keep his head up and his eyes open, how to sweep a crowd looking for funny moves, hands holding packages, umbrellas on clear days, that kind of thing.

He spent fifteen months in Detroit, his hometown, chasing down counterfeiters, going undercover to get next to wholesalers. That part was okay, making buys as a passer. But then he'd have to testify against the poor bastard in federal court, take the stand and watch the guy's face drop—Christ, seeing his new buddy putting the stuff on him. So once he was hot in Detroit, a familiar face in the trade, they had to send him out to cool off.

He was assigned to the Protective Research Section in Washington where, LaBrava said, he read nasty letters all day. Letters addressed to "Peanut Head Carter, the Mushmouth Motherfucker from Georgia." Or that ever-popular salutation, "To the Nigger-loving President of the Jewnited States." Letters told what should be done to the President of the USA, "the Utmost Supreme Assholes" who believed his lies. There was a suggestion, LaBrava said, the President ought to be "pierced with the prophet's sword of righteousness for being a goddamn hypocrite." Fiery, but not as practical as the one that suggested, "They ought to tie you to one of those MX missiles you dig so much and lose your war-lovin ass."

Maurice said, "People enjoy writing letters, don't they? You answer them?"

LaBrava said usually there wasn't a return address; but they'd trace the writers down through postmarks, broken typewriter keys, different clues, and have a look at them. They'd be interviewed and their names added to a file of some forty thousand presidential pen pals, a lot of cuckoos; a few, about a hundred or so, they'd have to watch.

LaBrava told how he'd guarded important people, Teddy Kennedy during the Senator's 1980 presidential campaign, trained to be steely-eyed, learned to lean away from those waving arms, stretched his steely eyes open till they ached listening to those tiresome, oh my, those boring goddamn speeches.

Maurice said, "You should a heard William Jennings Bryan, the Peerless Prince of Platform English, Christ, lecture on the wonders of Florida—sure, brought in by the real estate people."

LaBrava said he'd almost quit after guarding Teddy. But he hung on and was reassigned to go after counterfeiters again, now out of the Miami field office, now getting into his work and enjoying it. A new angle. He picked up a Nikon, attached a 200-mm lens, and began using it in surveillance work. Loved it. Snapping undercover agents making deals with wholesalers, passers unloading their funny money. Off duty he continued snapping away: shooting up and down Southwest Eighth Street, the heart of Little Havana; or riding with a couple of Metro cops to document basic Dade County violence. He felt himself attracted to street life. It was a strange feeling, he was at home, knew the people; saw more outcast faces and attitudes than he would ever be able to record, people who showed him their essence behind all kinds of poses—did Maurice understand this?—and trapped them in his camera for all time.

He got hot again through court appearances and was given a cooling-off assignment—are you ready for this?—in Independence, Missouri.

After counterfeiters?

No, to guard Mrs. Truman.

A member of the twelve-man protective detail. To sit in the surveillance house watching monitors or sit eight hours a day in the Truman house itself on North Delaware. Sit sometimes in the living room looking around at presidential memorabilia, a picture of Margaret and her two kids, the grandfather's clock that had been wired and you didn't have to wind—which would have been something to do—listening to faint voices in other rooms. Or sit in the side parlor with Harry's piano, watching movies on TV, waiting for the one interruption of the day. The arrival of the mailman.

"Don't get me wrong, Mrs. Truman was a kind, considerate woman. I liked her a lot."

The duty chief had said, "Look, there guys

would give an arm and a leg for this assignment. If you can't take pride in it, just say so."

He glanced at Maurice sitting there prim, very serious this evening. Little Maurice Zola, born here before there were roads other than a few dirt tracks and the Florida East Coast Railway. Natty little guy staring at this illuminated interstate highway—giant lit-up green signs every few miles telling where you were—and not too impressed. He had seen swamps become cities, a bridge extended to a strip of mangrove in the Atlantic Ocean and Miami Beach was born. Changes were no longer events in his life. They had happened or they didn't.

One of the green signs, mounted high, told them Daytona Beach was 215 miles.

"Who cares?" Maurice said. "I used to live in Daytona Beach. First time I got married, October 10, 1929—wonderful time to get married, Jesus—was in Miami. The second time was October 24, 1943, in Daytona Beach. October's a bad month for me. I paid alimony, I mean plenty, but I outlived 'em both. Miserable women. In '32, when I worked for the septic tank outfit and wrestled alligators on the weekends? It was because I had the experience being married to my first wife."

"What about the lady we're going to see?"

"What about her?"

"You ever serious with her?"

"You're asking, you want to know did I go to bed with her? She wasn't that kind of girl. She wasn't a broad you did that with."

"I meant did you ever think of marrying her?"

"She was too young for me. I don't mean she was too young you wanted to hop in the sack with a broad her age, I mean to get married and live with. I had all kinds of broads at that time. In fact, go back a few years before that, just before Kefauver, when I had the photo concessions and the horse book operation. I'll tell you a secret. You want to know who one of the broads I was getting into her pants was at the time. Evelyn, at the gallery. She was in love with me."

"I don't think you've introduced me to any who weren't."

"What can I say?" Maurice said.

"How old's the woman we're going to see?"

"Jeanie? She's not too old. Lemme think, it was '58 I gave her a piece of the hotel. Or it might've been '59, they were making that movie on the beach. Frank Sinatra, Edward G. Robinson . . . Jeanie was gonna be in the picture, was why she came down. But she didn't get the part."

"Wait a minute—" LaBrava said.

"They wanted her, but then they decided she

looked too young. She was in her twenties then and she was gonna play this society woman."

"Jeanie—"

"Yeah, very good-looking girl, lot of class. She married a guy—not long after that she married a guy she met down here. Lawyer, very wealthy, use to represent some of the big hotels. They had a house on Pine Tree Drive, I mean a mansion, faced the Eden Roc across Indian Creek. You know where I mean? Right in there, by Arthur Godfrey Road. Then Jerry, Jerry Breen was the guy's name, had some trouble with the IRS, had to sell the place. I don't know if it was tax fraud or what. He didn't go to jail, anything like that, but it cost him, I'll tell you. He died about oh, ten years ago. Yeah, Jeanie was a movie actress. They got married she retired, gave it up."

"What was her name before?"

"Just lately I got a feeling something funny's going on. She call me last week, start talking about she's got some kind of problem, then changes the subject. I don't know if she means with the booze or what."

"You say she was a movie actress."

"She was a star. You see her on TV once in a while, they show the old movies."

"Her name Jeanie or Jean?"

"Jean. Jean—the hell was her name? You believe it? I'm used to thinking of her as Jeanie Breen."

Maurice pointed. "Atlantic Boulevard. See it? Mile and a half. You better get over." Maurice rolled his window down.

"Jean Simmons?"

"Naw, not Jean Simmons." Maurice was half-turned now, watching for cars coming up in the inside lane. "I'll tell you when."

"Gene Tierney?" *Laura.* He'd watched it on television in Bess Truman's living room. "How's she spell her name?"

"Jean. How do you spell Jean? J-e-a-n."

Jean Harlow was dead. LaBrava looked at the rearview mirror, watched headlights lagging behind, in no hurry. "Jeanne Crain?"

"Naw, not Jeanne Crain. Get ready," Maurice said. "Not after this car but the one after it, I think you can make it."

3

THEY PARKED IN THE REAR and walked around to the front of the one-story building on Northeast Fourth Street, Delray Beach. From the outside the place reminded LaBrava of a dental clinic: stucco and darkwood trim, low-cost construction; a surface that appeared to be solid but would not stop a bullet. A laminated door that would not stop much of anything. LaBrava, former guardian of presidents and people in high places, automatically studying, making an appraisal. Oh, man, but tired of it. In an orange glow of light they read the three-by-five card taped to the door.

CRISIS CENTER
South County Mental Health
EMERGENCY SCREENING SERVICE

They had to ring the bell and wait, Maurice sighing with impatience, until a girl about twenty-one with long blond hair opened the door and Maurice said, "I come to get Mrs. Breen."

"You're Mr. Zola, right? Hi, I'm Pam."

She locked the door again and they followed her—broad hips compacted within tight jeans—through an empty waiting room and hallway, LaBrava looking around and judging this place, at the low end of institutional decor. He had never seen so many stains and burns. Like people came in here to throw up or set the place on fire with cigarettes. There were cracks and broken holes in the dull-yellow drywall, fist marks. He could see people trying to punch their way out. They came to a doorway, the room inside was dark.

"She's in here. Asleep."

Maurice stuck his head in. "She's on the floor."

"There's a mattress," Pam said. "She's fine, didn't give us a bit of trouble. The cops that brought her in described her condition as staggering, speech slurred, I guess she didn't know where she was."

Maurice said, "Was there a problem, a disturbance of any kind?"

"Well, not really. I mean there's no charge against her. She was walking down the street with a drink in her hand."

Maurice frowned. "A drink? Outside?"

"They said she came out of a bar, on Palmetto.

They saw her on the sidewalk with the drink and when they pulled over she threw it at them. Not the glass, the drink. I guess she was, you know, so bombed they thought they better bring her here." Pam looked at the doorway. "Why don't you go in with her? Let her wake up to a familiar face."

"Why don't I get her out of here," Maurice said. He went in the room.

LaBrava followed Pam. They came to a room filled with fluorescent light that was about fifteen-by-twenty: a metal desk standing between two mattresses on the floor, a line of metal chairs along the inside wall and a back door wtih double locks. The stains and burn marks seemed magnified in here. LaBrava saw skinny legs with dried sores, a light-skinned black girl asleep on the mattress in front of the desk. He saw a drunk, dirty from living in doorways, that familiar street drunk, soft mouth nearly toothless, cocking his head like a chicken. The drunk sat in the row of folding chairs. Next to him an elderly man sat rigid, his shirt collar buttoned, hands flat on bony thighs. He said to LaBrava, "You ever see an eagle?"

Pam, sliding behind the metal desk that was covered with forms and scrawled notes, said, "Walter—"

LaBrava said, "Yeah, I've seen an eagle."

The rigid man said, "Did it have hair?"

"The one I saw had feathers."

The rigid man said, "Oh." He looked at Pam now. "You ever see an eagle?"

Pam said, "Excuse me, Walter, but I have to finish with Earl first. Okay? Be nice." She glanced down at a clipboard. "Earl, if I call this person Eileen, will she come and get you?"

"She don't keep up her house," the drunk said. "You go in the kitchen . . . I tell her, Jesus Christ, get some wash powder. I can't live in a place like that."

Pam looked up at LaBrava in the doorway. "Sit down. Make yourself at home."

He took the end seat, two metal chairs away from the drunk hunched over his crossed legs, the drunk staring, trying to focus, saying, "Do I know you?"

"I don't know," LaBrava said, "we might've met one time. How you doing?"

"See, I don't want to go to court drunk. I don't want to go in there, maybe get sick."

Pam said, "Earl, I told you, there no charges against you." She said, "You ever drink anything like aftershave?"

"No, not ever. Just some home brew, some wine. Eileen, if I'm staying over there, she fixes these toddies are nice. Bourbon and ice cubes, you sprinkle some sugar on top. 'Bout a teaspoonful's all . . ."

A scream came from a room close by, a wail of obscenities that rose and died off, and LaBrava looked at Pam, expecting her to get up.

"It's okay. One of our consumers," Pam said. "She's catharting, sort of working it out on her own. But there's someone with her, don't worry."

"Consumer," LaBrava said.

The girl had a nice smile, very natural; she seemed too young and vulnerable to be working here. Psych major no more than a year out of college. "That's what we call the people we screen. They're not, you know, patients technically till they're admitted somewhere. This's just a temporary stop more or less."

The drunk said, "Then I'm leaving." He got up, stumbling against the rigid man, pushed off and tilted toward the girl lying on the mattress before finding his balance. He reached the back door and began working at the locks.

Pam said, "Come on, Earl, sit down and be good. You have to stay here till you've sobered up and you're a little more appropriate."

Earl turned from the door, falling against it. "More *pro*priate? Shit, I'm 'propriate."

"You are not," Pam said, a young schoolteacher at her desk. "Please sit down so we can finish."

The drunk fell against the chairs, almost into the rigid man whose hands remained flat on his thighs. The girl with sores on her legs moaned and rolled from her side to her back, eyes lightly closed, lids fluttering in the overhead light.

LaBrava was looking at her and Pam said, "She's Haitian. She got stoned and walked out on the Interstate. A car had to swerve out of the way and hit another car and one of the drivers, I don't know which one, had to have twenty stitches in his head."

The drunk said, "Shit, I was at Louisville Veterans, they put sixty-four stitches in my leg. Boy jammed a bottle, broke it off, jammed the end of it in my leg. See? Right there. Sixty-four stitches. Doc said he stopped counting."

"It's a beauty," LaBrava said. "Cut you good, didn't he?" He saw the drunk look up.

LaBrava turned. Maurice was standing over him.

"Get the camera."

LaBrava kept his voice down. "You sure you want to? Maybe they won't like it."

Maurice said to the girl, "Sweetheart, would you do something for my friend here? Unlock the door? He's got to get a camera outta the car."

Pam let him out the back telling him to knock and she'd open it again.

What Maurice wanted to do—LaBrava was sure now—was take a picture of his friend smashed, bleary-eyed, then show it to her tomorrow. "See

what a beauty you are when you're drunk?" Shame
her into sobriety. But if the woman had a problem
with booze it would be a waste of time. He
wouldn't mind, though, getting a shot of Earl. Earl
showing his scar. Shoot it from down on the floor.
The guy's leg crossed, pants pulled up, shin in the
foreground, shiny crescent scar. Earl pointing with
a dirty fingernail. Grinning near toothless, too
drunk not to look proud and happy.

Bending over in the trunk LaBrava felt inside the
camera case, brought out the Leica CL and attached a wide-angle lens.

Headlights flashed on him, past him. By the time
he looked around the car had come to a stop parallel to the building, its dark-colored rear deck standing at the edge of the floodlit area that extended out
from the back door. LaBrava felt in the case again
for the flash attachment. He straightened, slam-
ming the trunk closed.

A young guy was out of the car. Big, well-built
guy in a silver athletic jacket, blue trim. Banging on
the door now with the thick edge of his fist, other
hand wedged in the tight pocket of his jeans.
LaBrava came up next to him. The guy grinned, fist
still raised, toothpick in the corner of his mouth.

"How you doing this evening?" Slurring his
words.

He was thick all over, heavily muscled, going at
least six-three, two-thirty. Blond hair with a green-

ish tint in the floodlight: the hair uncombed, clots
of it lying straight back on his head without a part,
like he'd been swimming earlier and had raked it
back with his fingers. The guy wasn't young up
close. Mid-thirties. But he was the kind of guy—
LaBrava knew by sight, smell and instinct—who
hung around bars and arm-wrestled. Homegrown
jock—pumped his muscles and tested his strength
when he wasn't picking his teeth.

LaBrava said, "Not too bad. How're you doing?"

"Well, I don't idle too good, but I'm still running." With a back-country drawl greasing his
words. "You gonna take some pitchers?"

"I'm thinking about it."

"What of, this pisshole? Man, I wouldn't keep
goats in this place."

"I imagine they don't have much of a budget, run
by the county," LaBrava said. Hearing himself, he
sounded like a wimp. He had the feeling he would
never agree with this guy. Still, there was no sense
in antagonizing him.

"Palm Beach County, shit, they got more money'n any county in the state of Florida. But you
look at this pisshole kind of shack they put people
in—I mean nice people—you'd never know it,
would you? You don't see none of that Palm Beach
crowd brought in here. They can be pissing on the
squad car, cop'll go, 'Get in, sir. Lemme drive you

home, sir.' Shit . . . Hey, you want a take my pitcher? Go ahead, I'll let you."

"Thanks anyway," LaBrava said.

"What paper you with?"

LaBrava paused. He said, "Oh," a pleasant, surprised tone. It was not recognition of himself, LaBrava the street shooter, but it was recognition of a sort. "What makes you think I'm a news photographer?"

The guy said, "I guess 'cause all you assholes look alike." He turned away as they heard the locks, the door opening.

LaBrava saw Pam's expression change, startled, the girl tiny next to the silver jacket. She said, "Hey, what're you doing—" The guy was taking her by the arm as he entered.

"I come on official business, puss. How you doing? You're new here, huh? I ain't seen you before."

LaBrava edged past them with the camera, walked toward the hall and heard the locks snapping again behind him, heard the guy's bullshit charm hard at work. "Here, shake hands. I'm Richard Nobles, puss, with the police hereabouts." He heard Pam say, "Wait a minute. What police hereabouts?" He heard the rigid man say, "You ever see an eagle?" And heard Richard Nobles say, "You kidding me, papa? I've cooked and *ate* a eagle . . ."

* * *

Maurice was waiting in the hall by the doorway.

"Go in get a shot of her. Wait, what've you got, the Leica? Okay, go on."

"She awake?"

"I'm getting her outta here. Shoot straight down on her. What do you have it set at?"

"I don't know yet." LaBrava walked into the room. He saw bare legs in the shaft of light from the hall, sandals with medium heels. Slim legs, one of them drawn up. She was lying on her side, wearing a light-colored dress, her shoulders bare, an arm extended, partly covering her face. Maurice stooped down to move her arm, gently. LaBrava went out to the hall to make his adjustments. When he came back in and stood over the woman on the mattress, framing her in the viewfinder, dark hair against pale skin, Maurice said, "What'd you set it at?"

"Sixtieth at eight."

"I don't know . . ."

LaBrava didn't wait. The flash went off as he triggered the camera tight to his right eye, cocked it with his thumb, shot the second time, cocked and shot again.

"Set it lower and get another one."

"That's enough," LaBrava said.

"I want to be sure we got something."

"We got it," LaBrava said. "Take her out the front and I'll bring the car around."

There was another girl in the office now who seemed only a few years older than Pam but more grown up, in charge. Coming into the room again LaBrava heard her tell Nobles she was the supervisor and wanted to see some identification or there would be nothing to discuss. Right away LaBrava liked her confidence. He liked her slim build in jeans standing with long legs apart, arms folded, brown hair waved to her shoulders. A good-looking girl who knew what she was doing.

Nobles dug a wallet out of his back pocket, turning sideways and brushing his silver jacket open so they would see the checkered walnut grip of a revolver stuck in the waist of his jeans. Saying, "Boca police brought this lady here happens to be a friend of mine. See, I checked with them and they said it would be okay to release her to my custody. They said fine, go ahead." He flipped open the wallet to show a gold shield on one side, an I.D. card bearing his photograph on the other. "See what it says there? Palm Beach County."

The slim girl took a half step, extending her hand and he flipped the wallet closed. She said, "Palm

Beach County what? If the Boca Police said it was okay, they'd have called to let us know. That's how it works."

Nobles shook his head, weary. "Look, I'm doing you a favor. Lemme have the lady and we'll say nighty-night, let you all go on back play with your nuts."

"No one leaves without authorization," the slim girl said, standing right up to him.

"I'm *giving* you authorization. Jesus Christ, I just now showed it to you."

LaBrava said, "Excuse me. Would somebody like to open the front door?"

Nobles gave him a look, cold, with no expression, and the slim girl said, "Show me identification or get out. That's the way it is. Okay?"

LaBrava watched Nobles sigh, shake his head—not so drunk that he couldn't put on an act—and flip open the wallet again. "What's that say? Right there? Palm Beach County authorization." Giving her a flash of official wording and flipped the wallet closed.

He's not a cop.

LaBrava would bet on it. He heard the girl say, "That's not PBSO or any badge I've ever seen before."

Nobles shook his head again. "Some reason you got your ass up in the air. Did I say I was with the Palm Beach sheriff's office? You don't listen good,

do you? See, long as I got credentials as to who I am
and Boca PD says it's fine with them, then tell me
what your problem is, puss, cause I sure as hell
don't see it."

Sounding drunk, but with a swagger that was
part the guy's brute nature and would not be contained for long; his size, his eighteen-inch neck giving him permission to do as he pleased. LaBrava
had known a few Richard Nobles.

The guy was no cop.

He might've been at one time; he had a service revolver and the official off-duty look of a small-town
cop taken with himself, but he wasn't one now.

The slim girl had already assumed as much. She
was looking at Pam, telling her, "Get Delray Police,
276-4141."

Nobles said, "Hey, come on," watching Pam
dial. "Look, this lady you got happens to be a friend
of mine. Officer at Boca name of Glenn Hicks says
they brought her in here. See, I was even with her
earlier tonight, having some drinks." He watched
the slim girl step to the side of the desk and take the
phone from Pam. "Ask her. Go on . . ."

The slim girl said into the phone, "This is South
County on Fourth Street. There's a gentleman here
who's been asked to leave and refuses. I'd like you
to send somebody to escort him the fuck out of
here, right now . . . Thank you very much." She
looked at Pam again. "Unlock the back door."

Pam edged around the desk, all eyes as she looked at Nobles standing in front of her, in the way. She said, "There *is* a Boca officer named Glenn Hicks. He's been here before."

The slim girl said, "I don't care who he knows or if he's with the FBI. This guy's got no business being here."

LaBrava was falling in love with her. He watched her look directly at Nobles again.

"You've got about two minutes to get out of here or you're gonna be in deep shit."

Nobles said, "All I need, puss." He reached for her. The slim girl pulled her arm away without giving ground, glaring at him.

LaBrava said, "Let's take it easy, okay?" Trying to sound reasonable, an observer, but knowing he was getting into it.

Nobles, close to where the drunk and the rigid man sat watching, turned to LaBrava, raised a fist with a finger pointing out of it. A clot of blond hair hung down in his eyes. He said, "I'll put you through the wall you fuck with me, you little son of a bitch."

An ugly drunk. Look at the eyes. Ugly—used to people backing down, buying him another drink to shut him up. Look at the shoulders stretching satin, the arms on him—Jesus—hands that looked like they could pound fence posts. LaBrava, with the camera hanging from his neck, did not see anything close by to hit him with.

The slim girl picked up the phone again. Nobles reached for it as she started to dial, yanked the phone out of her hands and gave her a shove. The slim girl yelled out. Nobles raised the phone over his head, as a threat or to club her with it, LaBrava wasn't sure.

He stepped in, said, "Hey—" as he raised the camera with the flash attached, put it in Nobles' face and fired about a hundred thousand candles in the guy's eyes, blinding him, straightening him for the moment LaBrava needed to hit him in the ribs with a shoulder, drive him into clattering metal chairs, close to the drunk and the rigid man. LaBrava got Nobles down on his spine, head hard against the wall to straddle his legs. Worked free the bluesteel revolver stuck in his jeans, a familiar feel, a .357 Smith. Held him by the hair with one hand and slipped the blunt end of the barrel into his open mouth. Nobles gagged, trying to twist free.

LaBrava said, "Suck it. It'll calm you down."

They got him into a room, Nobles rubbing the back of his neck, looking around before they pulled the door closed, saying, "Hey, who the hell you suppose to be?"

LaBrava said, "The asshole photographer," and locked the door.

They locked the gun in the desk. He told the slim

girl he hoped the guy didn't try to bust the place up before the cops came; he'd stay if she wanted him to. She said it had been busted up before, look at it. God. She said thanks, really, but he'd better get out of here or he might be hanging around all night, the cops playing games with him. They might be the guy's buddies. She said she wouldn't be surprised if they let the guy out and all laughed their ass off. Cops really thought they were funny. Some of them anyway. Talking, nervous now that it was over. She was some girl. Supervisor here, but forced to work all hours, the slim girl's name was Jill Wilkinson.

He asked her what she thought Nobles did. She said he was probably a rent-a-cop, he acted like one.

That's what he was, too. LaBrava checked the dark-blue Plymouth sedan parked out in back before going to the Mercedes. There was a gold star on the door and the inscription *STAR SECURITY SERVICE, PALM BEACH COUNTY, FLORIDA.*

He drove around front to see Pam and Maurice coming out with the woman, Jeanie Breen, the woman with her head lowered but as tall as Maurice and as pale as her dress, letting him help her with his arm around her waist. They got in back, Maurice saying to him, "What were you doing, shooting the drunks?"

Maurice told him they were going to stop in Boca, pick up some of Mrs. Breen's things. Mrs.

Breen was coming back to South Beach with them, stay at the hotel a while.

After that Maurice's tone was soft, soothing, and LaBrava would look at the mirror to be sure it was Maurice back there. The little bald-headed guy, his glasses catching reflections, the woman a pale figure curled up in his arms. Maurice calling her sweetheart, telling her a change would be good . . . talk to your old pal . . . whatever's bothering you. Get a new outlook. LaBrava heard the woman say, "Oh, shit, Maury. What's happening to me?" Worn out. Still, there was an edge to her tone. Life in there. Anger trying to break through the self-pity.

What was her problem—living in a luxury condominium on the ocean—if her hair wasn't falling out or she didn't have an incurable disease?

Maybe living in the luxury condominium on the ocean. By herself.

It did not occur to LaBrava until later—cruising at seventy, the dark car interior silent—that the woman in the back seat could be the same one Nobles had tried to take out of there. A woman he'd been drinking with earlier in the evening.

4

LABRAVA DID HIS PORTRAIT WORK in an alcove off the Della Robbia lobby that Maurice said had originally been a bar: the area hidden now by a wall of cane screening nailed to a frame and clay baskets of hanging fern.

This morning he was working with the Leica, wide-angle lens and strobes, shooting the young Cuban couple, Paco Boza and Lana Mendoza, against a sheet of old, stiff canvas that gave him a nothing background. Paco sat in his wheelchair wearing a straw hat cocked on the side of his head, one side of the brim up, the other down, cane-cutter chic. Lana stood behind the wheelchair. She wore a cotton undershirt that was like a tank top and would stretch it down to show some nipple in the thin material. Pretty soon, LaBrava believed, she would pull the undershirt up and give him bare breasts with a look of expectation. The two of them were fooling around, having fun, stoned at 11 A.M.

LaBrava said, "Don't you want to look at each other?"

"At him?" the girl said. "I look at him and wish I never left Hialeah."

"Why don't you go home then?" Paco said, looking straight up over his head.

The girl looked down at him. "Yeah, you wouldn't have nobody to push you. He sit in this thing all day."

LaBrava released the shutter and went down to his knees, eye level. "Come on, this's supposed to be young love. You're crazy about each other."

"Like *The Blue Lagoon*, man," Paco said, looking bland, cool, not reacting when the girl punched him on the back of the neck.

"He's crazy all right," she said.

"That *Blue Lagoon*, man, you see that? Why did it take them so long, you know, to get it on? Man, they don't do nothing for most of the movie."

The girl punched him again. "They kids. How do they know how to do it, nobody tell them."

"I knew," Paco, the lover, said, grinning. "It's something a man is born with, knowing how to do it."

"You the creature from the blue lagoon," the girl said, "tha's who you are." Stretching now, bored.

LaBrava got it, the girl's upraised arms, the yawn hinting at seduction.

But he was losing it, hoping for luck. He had be-

gun with a good feeling and it would be in the first
two head-on shots if he got it. Now he was moving
around too much. He felt like a fashion photographer snicking away as the model throws her hair
and sucks in her cheeks, getting split moments of
the model pretending to be someone who wanted
to go to bed with the photographer or with the
lights or with whatever she saw out there. He didn't
want Boza and Mendoza to fall into a pose unless
he could feel it was natural, something they wanted
to do. But they were showing off for him now.

LaBrava said, "I think that'll do it."

Paco said, "Man, we just getting loosey goosey."

The girl said, "Hey, I got an idea. How about . . .
one like this?"

In the Della Robbia lobby, close to the oval front
window, the old ladies would nod and comment to
each other in Yiddish, then look at the young,
frizzy-haired girl again to listen to her advice.

"It saddens me," the girl said, and she did sound
sad, "when I see what neglect can do to skin. I'm
sure you all know there's a natural aging process
that robs skin of its vitality, its lustre." If they didn't
know it, who did? "But we don't have to hurry the
process through neglect. Not when, with a little
care, we can have lovely skin and look years and
years younger."

The girl was twenty-three. The youngest of the ladies sitting in the rattan semi-circle of lobby chairs had lived for at least a half century before the girl was born. But what did they know about skin care? Rub a peeled potato on your face, for sunburn.

She told them that extracts of rare plants and herbs were used in Spring Song formulations to fortify and replenish amniotic fluids that nourish the skin. The old ladies, nodding, touched mottled cheeks, traced furrows. They raised their faces in the oval-window light as the girl told them that women have a beauty potential at every age. She told them it gave her pleasure to be able to provide the necessities that would help them achieve that potential. It was, in fact, this kind of satisfaction, making women of all ages happy, proud of their skin, that being a Spring Song girl was all about.

She gave the ladies a pert smile, realigned the plastic bottles and jars on the marble table to keep moving, busy, as she said, "I thought for this first visit I'd just get you familiar with the Spring Song philosophy. Then next time I'll give a facial, show you how it works."

A voice among the women said, "You don't tell us how much it is, all this philosophy mish-mosh."

"We'll get into all that. Actually," the girl said, "I came to see the manager. What's his name again?"

"Mr. Zola," a woman said. "A nice man. Has a cute way."

There were comments in Yiddish, one of the
ladies referring to Maurice as a *k'nocker*, Mr. Big
Shot. Then another sound, in the lobby, tennis
shoes squeaking on the terrazzo floor. The girl
turned to look over her shoulder.

"Is that Mr. Zola?"

"No, that's Mr. LaBrava, the *loksh*. He's like a
noodle, that one."

"He's a cutie, too," a woman said. There were
more comments in Yiddish, voices rising with
opinions.

"Listen, let me give you an exercise to start
with," the girl said. "Okay? Put the tips of your fingers here. That's right, in the hollow of your
cheeks . . ."

LaBrava checked his mail slot on the wall behind
the registration desk. Nothing. Good. He turned to
see the girl coming across the lobby. Weird hair: it
looked tribal the way it was almost flat on top,
parted in the middle and frizzed way out on the
sides. Pretty girl though, behind big round tinted
glasses . . .

She said, "Hi. You don't work here, do you?"

Violet eyes. Some freckles. Smart-looking Jewish
girl.

"You want Maurice," LaBrava said. "He should
be down pretty soon. He's visiting a sick friend."

"You know if there's a vacancy?"

"I think somebody just moved out."

"You mean somebody died," the girl said. "I want a room, but I don't plan to stay that long."

"You want a one-bedroom or a studio? The studio's only three and a quarter." LaBrava looked over at the women, their mouths open saying "ohhhhh," as they stroked their cheeks in a circular motion.

"Studio, that's a hotel room with a hot plate," the girl said. "I've been there. In fact I just left there. I'm at the Elysian Fields and I need more space."

"What're they doing? The ladies."

"Working the masseter. That's the muscle you masticate with."

"You think it'll do 'em any good?"

"Who knows?" the girl said. "They're nice ladies. I figure those that weren't raped by Cossacks were mugged by Puerto Ricans. It won't do them any harm."

"You're the Spring Song girl," LaBrava said. "I've seen you on the street, with your little kit. How you doing?"

"I'm up to my ass in cosmetic bottles, nine kinds of cream by the case. Also, I've got tubes of paint, sketch pads, canvases all over my room, I've got shitty light and I need more space."

"I was at the Elysian Fields for a week last summer," LaBrava said. "This place's much better. Cleaner."

"Are you saying there no roaches?"

"Not as many. You see a loner once in a while. Think of it as a palmetto bug, it doesn't bother you as much. You paint, uh?"

"Some oil, acrylics mostly. I'm getting ready to do Ocean Drive, figure out my views before they tear it all down."

"Who's tearing it down?"

"Progress. The zoners are out to get us, man, cover the planet like one big enclosed shopping mall. We're getting malled and condoed, if you didn't know it. Gray and tan, earth tones. The people that designed these hotels, they had imagination, knew about color. Go outside, all you see is color and crazy lines zooming all over the place. God, hotels that remind you of ships . . ."

"I'm glad you explained that," LaBrava said. "I've always liked this neighborhood and I never was sure why." She gave him a sideways look, suspicious. Really weird hairdo but he liked it. "I mean it. I feel at home here and I don't know why."

"Because it's cheap," the girl said. "Listen, you don't have to know why. You feel good here, that's reason enough. People always have to have reasons instead of just feeling." She said, "You're the photographer, aren't you?"

Recognition. LaBrava leaned on the cool marble-top counter: artist relaxed, an unguarded moment. "Yeah, I guess so."

"Aren't you sure?"

"I'm just starting to get used to the idea."

"I saw your show over at the Emerson Gallery, it's dynamite. But all the color here—why aren't you into color?"

"I don't know how to use it. I feel safer with black and white."

"You selling anything?"

"A few more street shots than portraits."

"Well, what do they know. Right? Fuck 'em. You have to do what you do."

"You have to get mad?"

"If it helps. Why not? It's good to be hungry, too. You do better work."

She had a healthy build, tan arms, traces of dark hair. She would go about one-twenty, LaBrava judged; not the least bit drawn, no haunted, hungry-artist look about her. Gold chain. Rings. The white blouse was simple and could be expensive. But you never knew. He said, "You want some lunch? We can go across the street, the Cardozo. They got a nice conch salad, good bread."

"I know, I've seen you over there. No, first I have to see about new digs. I'm not going back to that fucking cell I've been living in. You have to go in sideways."

LaBrava looked up at the sound of the elevator cables engaging, the electric motor whining. He said, "You may be in luck," staring across the lobby at the elevator door, a gold sunburst relief. The door opened and he said, "You are. That's the manager."

Maurice said, even before reaching the desk, "Where the prints? They didn't come out, did they? What'd I tell you last night? I said stop it down."

"I've got an idea," LaBrava said. "Why don't you take care of this young lady—she's looking for a respectable place, no roaches, no noise—and I'll go see about the negatives I got hanging in the dryer."

"How they look?"

"Just tell me if you want 'em printed soft or crisp."

"I want 'em *now* is what I want. While she's still hung-over, ashamed, kicking herself."

LaBrava said to the girl, "Did I tell you he was a sweet old guy?"

"You didn't have to," the girl said, smiling at Maurice. "Mr. Zola, it's a pleasure. I'm Franny Kaufman."

A pair of dull amber safelights recessed in the ceiling gave the darkroom form, indicated shapes, but nothing more. LaBrava hit the negative with a squirt of Dust Chaser, slipped it into the enlarger and paused. He added a yellow filter, feeling sympathy for the woman upstairs in 304, Maurice's guest suite. The exposure was timed for twelve seconds.

He moved to the long section of the L-shaped stainless steel sink, dropped the exposed eight-by-ten sheet into the first of three trays.

An image began to appear, lights and darks, the curve of a woman's shoulder, arm touching the lower part of her face. He had not seen her clearly through the viewfinder; only a glimpse in that part of a moment as the flash exploded. He didn't know what she looked like and was intrigued now, the way he had been curious about her in the car last night.

LaBrava lifted the print from the solution, dipped it into the second tray, the stop bath, drew it through and placed it face up in the third tray, in the clear liquid of the fix solution. He leaned his arms on the narrow edge of the sink, low and uncomfortable, hunched over to study the face, the eyes staring at him through water and amber darkness.

Someone he had seen before.

But he wasn't sure. It might be the look, an expression he recognized. He couldn't see her features clearly.

He lifted the print from the tray, staring as water ran from it, dripped from it, became single drops in the silence, and he was aware of a curious feeling: wanting to turn on the light and see the woman's face, but hesitant, cautious, on the verge of discovery and wanting the suspense of these moments to last a while longer. Then thought of a way.

He set the eight-by-ten aside and printed the second and third exposures of the woman's arm and face against the mattress, this time without the softening effect of the yellow filter, and ran them through the baths. When there were three images, three pairs of eyes set in pale white staring at him from the counter top, he walked to the door, turned on the light and walked back . . .

He stopped and could do nothing but stare at the familiar gaze, knowing why darkness, before, had given him a feeling of recognition.

Because he had seen her only in the dark. Had watched her, how many times, in the black and white dark of movie theaters, up on the screen.

Jean Shaw.

Dark hair parted in the middle, the awareness in her eyes even half awake. Why hadn't he thought of her in the car yesterday? He had seen her for a moment in his mind, without a name, and by then they were looking for Northeast Fourth Street.

She had changed. Well, yeah, in twenty-five years people changed, everybody changed. She hadn't changed that much though. The hair maybe, the way it was styled. But she was pale in black and white as she had been on the screen and the eyes— he would never forget her eyes.

Jean Shaw. Upstairs, right now.

The movie star he had fallen in love with the first time he had ever fallen in love in his life, when he was twelve years old.

5

CUNNO REY SAID TO NOBLES, "Let me ask you something, okay? You ever see a snake eat a bat? Here is a wing sticking out of the snake's mouth, the wing, it's still moving, this little movement like is trying to fly. The snake, he don't care. You know why? Because the other end of the bat is down in the snake turning to juice, man. Sure, the snake, he don't even have to move, just lay there and keep swallowing as long as it takes. He don't even have to chew," Cundo Rey said, watching Richard Nobles eating his Big Mac and poking fries in his mouth a few at a time, dipped in ketchup. "Mmmmmmm, nice juicy bat."

They were in the McDonald's on Federal Highway, Delray Beach, the place crowded with local people having lunch. Nobles had on his two-tone-blue Star Security uniform, but not the hat. Here he was from a family whose men spent their lives outdoors and wore their hats in the house and he hated 'em. No, he liked to leave his golden hair free and run his fingers through it from time to time. Give it a casual look.

He said, mouth full of hamburger, "I ate a snake. I've ate a few different kinds. You flour 'em, deep-fry 'em in some Crisco so the meat crackles, they're pretty good. But I never ate a bat. Time you skin it what would you have?"

There—if the Cuban was trying to make him sick he was wasting his time. If the Cuban had something else in mind and was leading up to it, Nobles did not see it yet.

Ah, but then the Cuban said, drinking his coffee, not eating anything, "You understand what I'm saying to you?"

So, he would be making his point now. Fucking Cuban hotshot with his wavy hair and little gold ring in his ear. Cundo Rey was the first nigger Richard Nobles had ever seen with long wavy hair. It was parted on the right side and slanted down across his forehead over his left eye. The hair and his gold chains and silk shirts gave Cundo Rey his hot-shit Caribbean look. The way they had met last summer, ten months ago:

Nobles was making night rounds in the company Plymouth with the official Star Security stars on the doors—cruising past shopping malls and supermarkets, shining the spot into dark areas of parking lots, dying to see some suspicious dark-skinned character in his beam so he could go beat

on him—came to the Chevy dealership out Glade
Road and got out of the car. It was one of the
places he had to go inside, turn off the alarm with
a shunt key they gave him, and look around. This
night when he came out there was this dinge
standing by the Plymouth. The dinge goes, "What
about you leave the door open, sir, so I can get my
car keys?" Telling Nobles he was supposed to pick
up his car in for the free five thousand mile
checkup before the place closed but didn't make
it. See, all he needed was to get his keys—telling it
to Nobles in this Cuban nigger accent like Nobles
was a fool. Nobles had slapped his cowhide sap
against the palm of his hand a few times, but then
had to grin. Which must have given the dinge confidence, for then he goes, "And if you don't believe
that, sir, how you like to put five hundred dollars
in your pocket and drive yourself the fuck out of
here?"

Nobles admired all kinds of nerve and this
Cuban was polite and had fun in his eyes.

What Cundo Rey would do usually he'd wire a
brand new car out on the lot and put on stolen
plates, then drive it down to South Miami or
Homestead, nighttime garages he knew, and sell the
car for parts. Once or twice a month make a mini-
mum twenty-five hundred a car. Also, couple nights
a week dance go-go. Get sweaty, man, lose yourself, have some fun and make a few hundred bucks.

This had confused Nobles at first. Wait a minute. Dance *go-go?*

Yeah, Cundo Rey danced go-go as a pro in a little leopard jockstrap, let the ladies reach up on their bar stools and stuff money in there, let them have a feel, spin around and shake a finger, naughty-naughty, if they tried to grab his business. Sure, dance go-go, bump and grind to salsa riffs, sometimes steel drum, have a time, work clubs Ladies' Night from West Palm down to South Beach where he appeared at a gay bar once in a while, Cheeky's; though he would have to work up his nerve for that scene, stuff his nose good with coke, because it was the freak show at the end of the world, that place.

Was he a queer? At first, usually when they were sitting in the Plymouth looking over a car dealership, Nobles had half-expected Cundo to reach over and try to cop his joint; but he had not tried it yet and he did talk about ass like he got his share of it; so Nobles decided Cundo was straight. Just weird.

But why would a man, even a Cuban, act like a queer if he wasn't one? "What do you do it for?" he asked Cundo Rey, and Cundo Rey said, "I steal cars in darkness, I dance in lights." Nobles had seen him dance only one time. It was a place out by Miami International and Nobles had felt his own body moving as the ladies reached for Cundo Rey's crotch and Cundo Rey squirmed and writhed above them to that booger music, mouth full of white teeth sucking and smacking. Jesus. That one time was enough. Nobles believed it would take more nerve to get up there and act crazy than it would to break and enter.

They had a deal going now. Nobles would go in a dealership and get a key, Cundo Rey would start a car with it and Nobles would hang the key back up on the board—later scratch his head with everybody else, squint and kick gravel at how new cars were disappearing off the lots. He was making an extra grand a month for a few minutes' work on dark nights.

"The snake I saw, is only this long," Cundo Rey said, moving his hands apart in the air and looking from one to the other. "What is that? Less than two meters. The snake lay in the sand and swallowed for three hour, still you see the tip of the bat's wing sticking out of is mouth. Taking his time . . . the snake isn't going nowhere."

Nobles said, "Yeah?"

"What does the snake have? Patience. What's the hurry? Now with the lady, you know you going to score good there, uh? Sure, so be cool, let it happen."

Nobles said, "I'm gonna get a present, like on

my birthday? I want to know what it is. I pick the box up and shake it. I was a little kid I used to do that. You give me a hard time, partner, I'll pick you up and shake *you*."

Cundo Rey sipped his coffee—very poor coffee, like water—watching Nobles wiping his big thick hands on a golden arch napkin, sucking at his teeth. The Monster from the Big Scrub, with a neck so red it could stop traffic. Cundo Rey had come ashore in Dade County only a few years ago, boat-lifted out of Cambinado del Este prison and had worked hard to learn English—asking the girls why they didn't correct him and the girls saying, because he talked cute. Richard Nobles had come down out of some deep woods only a few hours by car to the north. And yet there was no doubt in Cundo Rey's mind that he was the American, a man of the city, and Nobles the alien, with mud between his toes. Nobles, with his size, his golden hair, his desire to break and injure, his air of muscular confidence, was fascinating to watch. A swamp creature on the loose.

Cundo Rey said, "You threaten me?" Yes, he liked to watch Nobles and he liked to annoy him, too, sometimes. Without getting too close. "I don't have to do this thing with you."

"I'm kidding," Nobles said. "You're my little helper, aren't you?"

Let him believe it. "If this is a good idea," Cundo

Rey said, "I don't see why you can't wait for her to come home."

"Man, I got to get going *now*, take off this goddamn uniform and get into something sporty. I mean *all* the time, not just off-duty. That drunk asshole I work for, he's gonna go broke any minute the shape he keeps things. Hires a bunch of scudders barely out of high school, they got as much brains as a box of rocks, I'm out there humping like a four-horse weed chopper, keeping the son of a bitch in booze."

Cundo Rey was staring at him, squinting, fooling with his gold earring. "I don't know what you talking about."

"I'm saying I want to get out of there, *now*, is what I'm saying. Clean out your ears. Take that girlish goddamn thing off while you're doing it. I'm embarrassed to be seen with you."

"Yes, but you don't have the plan yet," Cundo Rey said, not the least self-conscious, fishing now, pulling the line in slowly. "You got this woman has a big place, very expensive, you been with her, what, a few times . . ."

"I was with her last night."

"Okay, she's got a big place, a car . . ."

"Cadillac Eldorado."

"Some jewelry maybe . . ."

"You spook, we ain't gonna rob her."

"No? What we going to do?"

"We gonna hang her up and flat skin her."

Cundo Rey began fooling with his earring again. "Hang her up and skin her. Flat?"

"Only first, right now, we got to find out where she went."

"You don't want to wait for her to come home."

"When's that? She in a hospital, a rest home or what?"

Nobles paused, squeezed his eyes to slits and grinned, show the Cuban he had his number along with great admiration. "Be easy to find out. Man as nervy as you are. Be fun, too. What else you got to do?"

Three young girls with trays came by. Cundo Rey, fooling with curly ends of his raven hair now, working in his mind but always aware, looked up idly as they passed the booth. Nobles didn't say a word to them, didn't reach out or make a grab. He was serious today, all business.

He had started out, with his first hamburger, talking about a guy he wanted to stomp, a guy he didn't know but wore a shirt with bananas and different fruit on it. Some guy who had . . . "sandbagged" him? He wanted to know where the guy lived. But first he wanted to find the woman who had been a film actress.

"You don't have a feeling for this woman?" the Cuban asked.

Nobles said, "I want a feel I pick one about

twenty years younger. This here is old meat. Good looking, you understand, but aged." Nobles hunched over the table. "Come on. Ain't any of us getting any younger."

"I'll tell you what it is," the Cuban said, "why I hesitate. I don't like to get drunk."

"You have about five rum and Cokes, get you a little glassy-eyed's all. So it looks real. I Meyers-Act you in there and you find the record book first chance, see where they took her. Glenn says it's like a blue notebook. Be on one of the desks but not in that back office, the office to the west side of the building, in there. Bear right as you go in the front door. Blue notebook, it's got the record of where everybody's sent, whether they went to detox or the shelter or if they left with somebody, the name and address of the party."

Cundo Rey said, "Glenn knows where the book is, why don't he do it? Go in and ask where she went."

"No, Glenn ain't the person I thought he was. See, they was to ask him why he wants to know, Glenn, he'd start to sweat like he's got little bugs up his ass, become twitchy, afraid they'd call Boca Police and check him out. No, Glenn ain't casual enough for this type of deal."

"Yes, but you bring him into this . . ."

"No. No, I haven't. I come out of the bar last night looking around—was Glenn told me where they took her, that's all. See, Glenn's from Umatilla originally, me and him go way back. But this here's not any kind of deal for old Glenn." Nobles winked and grinned. "I got you, partner, what do I need anybody else for?"

"I still don't like to get drunk," Cundo Rey said.

"Hey, no, just get feeling good's all."

"I got another idea," Cundo Rey said. "You finished?"

They left the McDonald's and got in Nobles' official dark blue star-decorated Plymouth.

"One time I was picked up," Cundo Rey said, "it was up in Volusia County, strange place, man. I don't know what I was doing there, making a special delivery, 'Vette to some guy ran whiskey, I think. Everyone there talk like you."

Nobles grinned at him. "Sure, that's close to my neck of the woods. Fact I know several boys ran booze." He saw Cundo's shirt unbuttoned, Cundo leaning forward to take it off. "The hell you doing?"

"I was in the jail there, they say plead guilty, man, go to Apalachee for a year, I think was the place they tole me."

Christ, raising his skinny butt to slip his pants off now. Nobles would look from Cundo to the Federal Highway and back again, moving along north in light traffic. "Apalachee Correctional," Nobles said, deciding to be cool. "I think it's for juveniles, but I guess a squirt like you could get sent there."

"So I tore my clothes off," Cundo Rey said.

"You did?"

He had his clothes off *now*, pants and silk shirt, sitting there in skimpy red jockeys as he unfastened his gold chains.

"I told them there were all these little invisible creatures crawling all over me and I screamed and scratched myself enough to bleed."

"Invisible creatures," Nobles said, grinning. "Shit."

"So they sent me up to this place, Chatahoochee, instead. You know where it is?"

"You bet I do. Nuthouse right up there by the Georgia line."

"Yes, so one night I walked out, stepped across that line to freedom. I'm going to leave my shoes on."

"I would." Nobles turned onto Northeast Fourth, let the car coast as it approached the stucco mental health facility up on the left. There were cars at a gas station farther on, but none on the street.

"I'm going to trust you with my jewelry. So don't sell it."

"No, I'll take good care of it. Listen, I ain't walking in with you bareass."

"It's okay, they let me in. A blue notebook, uh?"

Nobles braked gently to a full stop and pointed. "Be in the office that end of the building there."

"Okay, I'll call you later," Cundo Rey said, opening the door.

Nobles said, "Wait a sec. There's a broad works in there, I think she's the supervisor. Brown wavy hair, these real long legs, nice high butt. See if you can find out where she lives or if she just works nights or what."

"Man, you don't want much, do you?" Cundo Rey got out, slipped off his red briefs and dropped them in through the window. "Hide these . . . where? So I can find them."

"I'll put 'em in a paper sack, in the bushes back there where they park. Then you come on over the public beach, nobody'll think you're strange."

"Okay. I see you."

Jesus. Nobles couldn't believe it. He watched Cundo walk around past the front of the car— bareass as the day he was born back of some sugarmill, except for his tan socks and white shoes—watched him cross the street and walk up to the mental health place, cheeks of his ass pale moons, lighter than his dusky skin and it surprised Nobles. Look at the son of a bitch, like he was out for a stroll. As Cundo turned half around and waved Nobles mashed the gas pedal and got out of there.

6

HE FOUND MAURICE IN 304, the guest suite facing the ocean, the room filled with sunlight and old slip-covered furniture. Maurice took the prints without comment, began studying them as he moved toward the closed door to the bedroom. LaBrava came in, followed him part way. He was anxious, but remembered to keep his voice low.

"Why didn't you tell me who she is?"

"I did tell you."

"That's Jean Shaw."

"I know it's Jean Shaw. I told you that last night."

"She's supposed to be an old friend—you couldn't even think of her name."

"I like this one, the expression. She doesn't know where the hell she is." Maurice looked up from the prints, eyes wide behind his glasses. "What're you talking about, I couldn't think of her name? Twenty years she's been Jeanie Breen. I told you she left the picture business to marry Jerry Breen, her husband. I remember distinctly telling you that."

"How is she?"

"Not suffering as much as I hoped."

"You bring her some breakfast?"

"What do you think this is, a hotel?" Maurice turned to the bedroom, paused and glanced back with his hand on the door. "Wait here." He went in and all LaBrava saw was the salmon-colored spread hanging off the end of the bed. The door closed again.

Wait. He moved to one of the front windows, stood with his hands resting on the air-conditioning unit. He thought he knew everything there was to know about time. Time as it related to waiting. Waiting on surveillance. Waiting in Mrs. Truman's living room. But time was doing strange things to him now. Trying to confuse him.

What he saw from the window was timeless, a Florida post card. The strip of park across the street. The palm trees in place, the sea grape. The low wall you could sit on made of coral rock and gray cement. And the beach. What a beach. A desert full of people resting, it was so wide. People out there with blankets and umbrellas. People in the green part of the ocean, before it turned deep blue. People so small they could be from any time. Turn the view around. Sit on the coral wall and look this way at the hotels on Ocean Drive and see back into the thirties. He could look at the hotels, or he could look at Maurice's photographs all over his apartment, be reminded of pictures in old issues of *Life* his dad had saved, and feel what it was like to have lived in that time, the decade before he was born, when times were bad but the trend, the look, was to be "modern."

Now another time frame was presenting pictures, from real life and from memory. A 1950s movie star with dark hair parted in the middle, pale pure skin, black pupils, eyes that stared with cool expressions, knowing something, never smiling except with dark secrets. The pictures brought back feelings from his early teens, when he believed the good guy in the movie was out of his mind to choose the other girl, the sappy one who cried and dried her eyes with her apron, when he could have had Jean Shaw.

There were no sounds from the other room. No warning.

The door opened before he was ready. Maurice came out and a moment later there she was in a navy blue robe, dark hair, the same dark hair parted in the middle though not as long as she used to wear it and he wasn't prepared. He hadn't thought of anything to say that would work as a simple act of recognition, acknowledgment.

Maurice was no help. Maurice said, "I'll be right back," and walked out, leaving him alone in the same room with Jean Shaw.

She moved past the floral slipcovered sofa to the

other front window, not paying any attention to him. Like he wasn't there. He saw her profile again, the same one, the same slender nose, remembering its delicate outline, the soft, misty profile as she stood at the window in San Francisco staring at the Bay. Foghorn moaning in the background. *Deadfall*. The guy goes off the bridge in the opening scene and everybody thinks it's suicide except the guy's buddy, Robert Mitchum. Robert Mitchum finds out somebody else was on the bridge that night, at the exact same time. A girl . . .

He saw the movie—it had to have been twenty-five years ago, because he was in the ninth grade at Holy Redeemer, he was playing American Legion ball and he went to see the movie downtown after a game, a bunch of them went. She did look older. Not much though. She was still thin and her features, with that clean delicate look, always a little bored, they were the same. He remembered the way she would toss her hair, a gesture, and stare at the guy very calmly, lips slightly parted. Robert Mitchum was no dummy, he grabbed her every chance he had in *Deadfall*, before he ended up with the dead guy's wife. That was the only trouble with her movies. She was only grabbed once or twice before the good guy went back to Arleen Whalen or Joan Leslie. She would have to be at least fifty. Twelve years older than he was. Or maybe a little more.

He didn't want to sound dumb. Like the president of a fan club. *Miss Shaw, I think I saw every picture you were ever in.*

She said, without looking at him, "You don't happen to have a cigarette, do you?"

It was her voice. Soft but husky, with that relaxed, off-hand tone. A little like Patricia Neal's voice. Jean Shaw reminded him a little of Patricia Neal, except Jean Shaw was more the mystery-woman type. In movies you saw Jean Shaw at night, hardly ever outside during the day. Jean Shaw could not have played that part in *Hud* Patricia Neal played. Still, they were somewhat alike.

"I can get you a pack," LaBrava said. He remembered the way she held a cigarette and the way she would stab it into an ashtray, one stab, and leave it.

"Maury said he'll bring some. We'll see."

"I understand you're old friends."

"We were. It remains to be seen if we still are. I don't know what I'm suppose to do here, besides stare at the ocean." She came away from the window to the sofa, finally looking at him as she said, "I can do that at home. I think it's the same ocean I've been looking at for the past . . . I don't know, round it off, say a hundred years."

Dramatic. But not too. With that soft husky sound, her trademark.

He said, "You were always staring at the ocean

in *Deadfall*. I thought maybe it was like your conscience bothering you. Wondering where the guy was out there, in the water."

Jean Shaw was seated now, with the *Miami Herald* on her lap. She brought a pair of round, wire-framed glasses out of the robe and slipped them on. "That was *Nightshade*."

"You sound just like her, the part you played."

"Why wouldn't I?"

"I think in *Deadfall* you lured the guy out on the bridge. You were having an affair, then you tried to blackmail him . . . In *Nightshade* you poisoned your husband."

She hesitated, looking up at him, and said very slowly, "You know, I think you're right. Who was the guy in the bridge picture?"

"Robert Mitchum."

"Yes, you're right. Mitchum was in *Deadfall*. Let me think. Gig Young was in *Nightshade*."

"He was the insurance investigator," LaBrava said. "But I think he grew flowers, too, as a hobby."

"Everybody in the picture grew flowers. The dialogue, at times it sounded like we were reading seed catalogues." She began looking at the front page of the *Herald*. Within a few moments her eyes raised to him again.

"You remember those pictures?"

"I bet I've seen every picture you were in."

There. It didn't sound too bad. She was still looking at him.

She said, "Really?" and slipped her glasses off to study him, maybe wondering if he was putting her on. "On television? The late show?"

"No, in movie theaters, the first time." He didn't want to get into ages, how old he had been, and said, "Then I saw some of them again later. I'm pretty sure about *Deadfall* and *Nightshade* because I saw 'em both in Independence, Missouri, just last year."

"What were you doing in Independence, Missouri?" With that quiet, easy delivery.

"It's a long story—I'll tell you sometime if you want. What I could never figure out was why you never ended up with the guy in the movie, the star."

She said, "I was the spider woman, why do you think? My role was to come between the lead and the professional virgin. But in the end he goes back to little June Allyson and I say, 'Swell.' If I'm not dead."

"In *Deadfall*," LaBrava said, "I remember I kept thinking if I was Robert Mitchum I still would've gone for you instead of the guy's wife, the widow."

"But I was in on the murder. I lured what's his name out on the bridge. Was it Tom Drake?"

"It might've been. The thing is, your part was always a downer. At least once in a while you should've ended up with the star."

"You can't have it both ways. I played Woman as Destroyer, and that gave me the lines. And I'd rather have the lines any day than end up with the star."

"Yeah, I can understand that."

"Someone said that the character I played never felt for a moment that love could overcome greed. The only time, I think, I was ever in a kitchen was in *Nightshade*, to make the cookies. You remember the kitchen, the mess? That was the tip-off I'm putting belladonna in the cookie batter. Good wives and virgins keep their kitchens neat."

"It was a nice touch," LaBrava said. "I remember he takes the cookies and a glass of milk out to the greenhouse and practically wipes out all of his plants in the death scene, grabbing something to hold onto. Gig Young was good in that. Another one, *Obituary*, I remember the opening scene was in a cemetery."

She looked up as he said it and stared at him for a moment. "When did you see *Obituary?*"

"Long time ago. I remember the opening and I remember, I think Henry Silva was in it, he was your boyfriend."

She was still watching him. She seemed mildly amazed.

"You were married to a distinguished looking gray-haired guy. I can sorta picture him, but I don't remember his name."

"Go on."

"And I remember—I don't know if it was that picture or another one—you shot the bad guy. He looks at the blood on his hand, looks down at his shirt. He still can't believe it. But I don't remember what it was about. I can't think who the detective was either, I mean in *Obituary*. It wasn't Robert Mitchum, was it?"

She shook her head, thoughtful. "I'm not sure myself who was in it."

"He seems like a nice guy. Robert Mitchum."

She said, "I haven't seen him in years. I think the last time was at Harry Cohn's funeral." She paused and said, "Now there was a rotten son of a bitch, Harry Cohn, but I loved him. He ran Columbia. God, did he run it." She looked up at LaBrava. "I haven't been interviewed in years, either."

"Is that what this is like?"

"It reminds me. Sitting in a hotel room in a bathrobe, doing the tour. Harry would advise you how to act. 'Be polite, don't say *shit*, keep your fucking knees together and don't accept any drink offers from reporters—all they want is to get in your pants.' Where in the hell is Maurice?"

LaBrava glanced toward the door. "He said he'd be right back."

There was a silence. He had been in the presence of political celebrities and world figures. He had stood alone, from a few seconds to a few minutes, with Jimmy Carter, Nancy Reagan, George Bush's wife Barbara, Rosalynn Carter and Amy, not Sadat but Menachem Begin at Camp David, Teddy Kennedy a number of times, nameless Congressmen, Tip O'Neill was one, Fidel Castro in New York, Bob Hope . . . but he had never felt as aware of himself as he did now, in front of Jean Shaw in her blue bathrobe.

"I was trying to think," LaBrava said, "what your last movie was."

She looked up from the paper. "Let's see, I made *Let It Ride* at Columbia. Went to RKO for one called *Moon Dance*. A disaster . . ."

"The insane asylum."

"I quit right after that. I tested for a picture that was shot right around here, a lot of it at the Cardozo Hotel. I thought sure I was going to get the part. Rich widow professional virgin, my first good girl. But they gave it to Eleanor Parker. It didn't turn out to be that much of a part."

"Frank Sinatra and Edward G. Robinson," LaBrava said, impressing the movie star.

She said, "That's right, *A Hole in the Head*. Frank Capra, his first picture in I think seven years. I really wanted to work with him. I even came here on my own to find out what rich Miami Beach widows were like."

"I think you would've been too young."

"That's why Frank gave it to Eleanor Parker. Before that, half the scripts I read had Jane Greer's prints all over them." She said then, "No, the last one wasn't *Moon Dance.* I went back to Columbia—oh my God, yeah—to do *Treasure of the Aztecs.*"

"Treasure of the Aztecs," LaBrava said, nodding. He had never heard of it.

"Farley Granger was Montezuma's bastard son. In the last reel I'm about to be offered up to the gods on top of a pyramid, have my heart torn out, but I'm rescued by Cortez's younger brother. Remember?"

"The star," LaBrava said. "I can't think who it was."

"Audie Murphy. I took the first flight I could get out of Durango and haven't made a picture since."

"I imagine a lot of people liked it though."

"You didn't see it, did you?"

"I guess that's one I missed. How many pictures did you make?"

"Sixteen. From '55 to '63."

He could think of four titles. Maybe five. "I might've missed a couple of the early ones too," LaBrava said, "but I saw all the rest. I have to tell you, whether it means anything to you or not, you were *good.*"

Jean Shaw raised her eyes to his, giving him that cool, familiar look. "Which one was your favorite?"

7

AT 8:10 P.M. JILL WILKINSON told Pam and Rob, the crisis center night staff, she was getting out before anything else happened. Three consecutive shifts without sleep was about it for hanging in and being a loyal South County employee. She said if she didn't go home to bed within the next hour, they'd be admitting her to Bethesda Memorial for intensive rehabilitation due to social-service burnout. South County would have to scrounge around for another wide-eyed, dedicated supervisor willing to work a seventy-hour week. Good luck. They didn't stay wide-eyed long. During the past twenty-four hours:

First there was the big blond creep with the Mickey Mouse badge and the very real gun. (The Delray cops were good guys; they did think it was sort of funny, but only after informing Mr. Richard Nobles that if he ever came in here and bothered Jill again they would fucking break his jaw on both sides of his you-all mouth and that was a promise.)

Then Earl, smoking, had set fire to a mattress during the night—after they were absolutely sure he had no cigarettes or matches on him. Walter continued to drive them nuts asking if they'd ever seen an eagle, until he was finally shipped off to Crisis Stabilization. A girl who had shaved her hair back to the top of her head, shaved off her eyebrows too, locked herself in the john most of the morning while two alcoholics threw up in wastepaper baskets. A consumer waiting to be interviewed got into the case of john paper stored in the counseling office (there was no room for it anywhere else) and streamed several rolls of it around the office. And then there was the smiling Cuban who gave his name as Geraldo Rivera and walked into the center naked except for sporty perforated shoes and tan silk socks. He was sort of cute.

At first he said he had no English. Jill picked up the phone to request a bilingual Delray Police officer and he said wait, some English was coming back to him. He said perhaps he was suffering from amnesia. He remembered dressing to go to the jai alai, but must have forgotten to put his clothes on. He said this is the fronton where they play, isn't it? Jill told him they played just about everything in here except jai alai. She left him for a minute and he wandered through the offices, God, with his limp dong hanging free. The new girl, Mary Elizabeth, said wow, she had never seen one like that before, so dark compared to the rest of him. The drunks opened watery eyes to watch without comment. What else was new? Walter, who had not yet been shipped off when Geraldo arrived, asked him if he had ever seen an eagle. The Cuban said yes, in fact his mother was an eagle. He said he had been stolen by an eagle when he was a small baby, taken to its nest and fed the regurgitated meat of rabbits. They wrapped the Cuban in a sheet, which he seemed to like, rewrapping himself different ways until he settled on leaving one arm free, toga-fashion. He seemed to quiet down.

Then their twenty-year-old potential suicide, manic depressive, climbed up on a file cabinet and punched through the screen to shatter the glass of the ceiling-high window in the main office. They brought him down bloody, blood smearing the wall, an arm gashed from wrist to elbow. Sometime while the paramedics were taking him out to the van, the naked Cuban disappeared.

They called Delray Police to report a missing consumer who might or might not be running around their catchment area wrapped in a South County bed sheet and might or might not answer to the name Geraldo. They would take him back whoever he claimed to be.

There was no positive response from the police.

About five o'clock, when first Jill fantasized going home at a normal hour, seeing herself barefoot, alone, sipping chilled Piesporter, she discovered her wallet and ring of something like a dozen keys missing from her bag. The only person she could think of responsible was the naked Cuban.

Mary Elizabeth left about 6:45. She came back in with Jill's ring of keys and wallet, the wallet empty. Found them, she said, right out in the middle of the parking lot. She had kicked the keys, in fact, walking to her car.

Something was strange. Jill had looked outside earlier, front and rear. If the keys and wallet weren't there a few hours ago, how could they be there now?

Well, if the guy was chronically undifferentiated enough to walk naked into South County thinking it was a jai alai fronton ... yes? ... play with a bed sheet, rip off her wallet and keys ... who knows, he could have sneaked back during a lucid period, basically a nice guy, thoughtful, knowing she would need her keys, her driver's license ...

It was a guess that she could accept.

Until she was driving home to Boynton Beach— FM top-forty music turned low, the dark, the muted sound relaxing—and began to wonder if there might not be more to it.

What if that whole number, the guy walking in naked, had been an act? To get her keys, find out where she lived ... imagining the naked, possibly-

undifferentiated Cuban now as a thoughtful bur-
glar. Did that make sense?

None.

Still it was in her mind, the possibility, as she
mounted the circular cement stairway to the second
floor, moved along the balcony walk past orange
buglights at the rear doors of the apartments and
came to 214.

Would it be cleaned out?

Jill held her breath opening the door. She had
paid almost seven hundred for the stereo and
speakers, God, over three hundred for the color
television set. Her two-hundred-dollar bike was on
the front balcony . . .

The apartment was dark. A faint orange glow in
the kitchen window showed the sink and counter.
She moved past the kitchen, along the short hallway to the living room. Saw dim outside light framing the glass door to her private balcony. Saw her
bike out there. Felt the television set sticking out of
the bookcase. She let her breath out in a sigh, feeling exhaustion, relief. Thought, Thank you, Jesus.
Not as a prayer but a leftover little-girl response.
And sucked her breath in again, hard, and said out
loud, "Jesus!" Still not as a prayer. Said, "What do
you want!" with her throat constricted. Seeing part

of an outline against the glass door. Only part of the figure in the chair, but knowing it was a man sitting there waiting for her.

She turned to run out. Got to the hallway.

And a light came on behind her.

A lamp turned on in her own living room. The goddamn deceiving light that made her stop and turn, feeling in that moment everything would be all right because, look, the light was on and the unknown figure in darkness would turn out to be someone she knew who would say gee, hey, I'm sorry and offer an incredible explanation . . .

She knew him all right. Even in the two shades of blue uniform. The blond hair . . . Coming toward her, bigger in this room than he had looked last night, not hurrying. Still, it was too late to run.

Nobles said, "Bet you're wore out. I swear they must work you like a nigger mule at that place, the hours you put in. See, I figured you wouldn't want me sitting out in the car, so I come on in. I been waiting, haven't had no supper . . ." He stretched, yawning. "I was about to go in there, get in the bed. How'd that a been? You come home, here I'm under the covers sleeping like a baby."

That thin coat of syrup in his tone.

Jill concentrated. All the words, the dirty words, the sounds in her mind, screaming obscenities, she kept hold of them as he spoke, as he grinned at her; she knew words would be wasted. She concentrated instead, making an effort to breathe slowly, to allow the constriction in her body to drain, and said nothing. She would wait. As she had waited nearly a half hour for the police while a psychopath dumped over file cabinets, tore up her office . . . She knew how to wait.

Nobles said, "Yeah, you're wore out, aren't you? Come on sit down over here"—taking her to the sofa, easing her down—"I'll get you a cold drink. I notice you have a bottle of something there in the icebox. Look like piss in a green bottle, but if it's your pleasure . . ." Standing over her now, towering. "How's that sound?"

She stared at his hips, at dark blue, double-knit material worn to a shine, a belt of bullets, a holstered revolver. She said nothing.

Nobles said, "Cat got your tongue? . . . Hey, you mad at me? Listen, I'm the one should be angry here, way I got treated last night. I'd had a few, but I wasn't acting nasty or nothing, was I? Just fooling around, giving you a flash of my I.D. I was about to show it to you and this boy I never seen before whomps me a good'n, blindsides me while I ain't looking. All I see's this flash of light, wham bam. I still don't know what it was he hit me with. Must a been like a two-b'-four."

Nobles waited. There was a silence. He hooked his thumbs in his gunbelt, looked about the room idly, taking his time, and came back to Jill.

"Who was that boy, anyway? Friend of yours?"

She said nothing.

"I know he said he was with one of the newspapers. I was wondering which one he worked for."

She said nothing.

"Hey, I'm asking you a question."

Jill eased back against the cushion. She looked up at Nobles. Saw his expression, the lines along both sides of his nose drawn tight. His face seemed to shine.

Sociopathic, if not over the edge.

She said, "You know more about him than I do."

"What's his name?"

Low impulse control.

"I don't know. He didn't tell me."

"Well, what was he doing there?"

Anger threshold you could poke with an elbow.

"I really don't know. I think he came with someone."

"With who?"

"We have people in and out all day. I don't remember their names. I don't meet half of them."

"You see what that scudder hit me with?"

It caught her by surprise. She said, "He didn't hit you with anything, he put you down and sat on you," and wanted to bite her tongue.

Seeing his expression again, the sheen of anger. She saw him draw his revolver and saw his knuckles and the round hole of the barrel come toward her face, close, almost touching her.

He said, "Open your mouth."

"Why do you want to do that?"

He said, "Open your goddamn mouth!"

Hunched over her to grab a handful of hair as she tried to turn her face, yanked her up tight against the cushion. With the pain she gasped, wanting to cry out, and he slipped the tip of the revolver into her open mouth.

His expression changed, the grin coming back. He said, "Hey, puss, you give me an idea."

8

THEY HAD DINNER AT PICCIOLO'S on South Collins, Maurice telling them what it used to be like before the lower end of Miami Beach went to hell; LaBrava watching Jean Shaw raise her fork, sip her wine, coming to believe she was more attractive now than she had been in black and white, on the screen.

Picciolo's, Maurice said, height of the season you couldn't get near the place, the cars lined up outside. Now you could shoot a cannon off in here, maybe hit a waiter. Notice they still wore black tie. LaBrava studying her profile as she looked off across empty tables, head held high, purity of line against the dark color of the booth done up as a gondola, head turning in time back to Maurice next to her; he would shoot her in profile, either side flawless in restaurant light, this lady who had played spider women, enticed second leads to their death and never got the star. Maurice saying Picciolo's and Joe's Stone Crab were the only places left on the south end, the neighborhood taken over by junkies, muggers, cutthroats, queers, you name it. Cubans off the boat-lift, Haitians who had swum ashore when their boats broke to pieces, old-time New York Jews once the backbone, eyeing each other with nothing remotely in common, not even the English language. The vampires came out at night and the old people triple-locked their doors and waited for morning. Ass-end of Miami Beach down here.

Remember the pier? Look at it. Used to be nice. They sell drugs out there now, any kind of pills you want, take you up or down. (The old man of the street speaking.) Bar around the corner there, guys dress up like girls. Lovely place. "I'm telling you," Maurice said, telling them, giving his friend Jean Shaw a slow tour of the old neighborhood on the thirteen-block drive from the restaurant to the Della Robbia Hotel. The three of them in the front seat of the Mercedes. LaBrava inhaling without sound but deeply, his thigh touching hers, filling himself with her scent.

"You remember the kind of people use to come down for the season? Now we got three hundred bums, count 'em, three hundred, show up every winter. Look. Over there on the bench, look, the bag lady. That's Marilyn. Says she used to be a movie star, a singer and a gourmet cook. Look at her. She's got a shopping cart she pushes down Lincoln Road Mall, it's fulla plastic bags, bottles, old copies of *The Wall Street Journal*. Marilyn. Maybe you knew her back when."

"Go slower," Jean Shaw said. "Where does she live?"

"You're looking at it, on the bench. They live in alleys, the bums, they live in empty buildings. The respectable people, they work in a garment loft forty-five years, come down here, put their life savings in a co-op and have to triple-lock their doors. Afraid even to look out the window.

"They were suppose to start redeveloping the whole area ten years ago, put in canals, make it look like Venice. Nobody's allowed to fix up their property, they got to wait for the big scheme. Only the big scheme went bust, never happened. The boat-lifters and dopers come in, half the neighborhood's already down the toilet.

"I know a guy lives in a place called the Beachview on Collins. Listen to this, Collins Avenue, he pays four hundred seventy-five bucks-a-year rent. You know why? He's got a seven-by-ten room, no bath, newspapers on the floor, no air, no stove even. Joe, is that right? Joe took some pictures of the guy in his room he'll show you. Looks like a gypsy wagon, all the crap piled up in there. Four-seventy-five a year on Collins Avenue, you think it hasn't changed?

"Show her the La Playa."

Why would she want to see a run-down fleabag hotel?

"We already passed it."

"Show her," Maurice said.

There, corner of Collins and First. Two blocks from the Miami Beach Police station, they had over two hundred assaults, shootings, knifings, rapes, ripoffs and what have you in that one hotel alone last year. You believe it? Look. What're we on? Washington Avenue. They got video cameras mounted up on cement poles, close-circuit TV, so the cops can watch the muggings, the dope transactions, and not have to leave the station. Look. Right before our eyes, two young girls beating the shit outta each other on the street. Nice? I'm telling you . . .

But *why* was he telling her? His good friend the once-famous movie star. To frighten her? So she'd stay in the hotel and never go out alone?

No, LaBrava decided. It was to impress her. The old man was showing off. Letting her know, yeah, it was a rough place, but he knew his way around. Ballsy little eighty-year-old guy. What it came down to, Maurice loved South Beach.

Jean Shaw said she would join them in a few minutes, she wanted to change. LaBrava watched her walk down the hall to the guest suite.

She had long thin legs, still a good figure. He had liked blonds with coppery tans but was coming to prefer dark hair parted in the middle, pale skin.

He took off his sport coat following Maurice into his apartment, the gallery, a photographic record of what Maurice had witnessed in his life covering most of three walls. The rest of the room was crowded with hotel-lobby furniture, a sectional sofa, Maurice's La-Z-Boy recliner. Maurice went to his bar, a credenza by the formal dining-room table, and got ready to pour their nightcaps. Tighteners. LaBrava hung his coat on the back of a dining-room chair and, as he always did, began looking at photographs.

The way it went most times, Maurice would pretend not to notice. LaBrava would study a row of framed black-and-white prints. And finally Maurice would say:

"Terpentine camp, wood smoke and backyard cauldrons, men working that sticky mess for a dollar a day . . . and dance with their women at a jook place called the Starlight Patio, way in the piney woods . . . Sniff, you can smell the coal-oil lamps, look at the eyes shining, dirt rings on the neck of that lovely woman . . ."

LaBrava would move a step, concentrating, not looking around, and Maurice would say:

"Georgia road gang, 1938. They wore stripes till '42. That's the captain there. Gene Talmadge, used to be governor, said, 'You want a man knows how to treat convicts, get you somebody who has et the cake.' Somebody once a convict himself. Eugene believed in whipping and the use of the sweatbox."

LaBrava would move on, gaze holding, and Maurice would say:

"That's Al Tomani, known as the next-to-tallest man in the world. His wife was born without legs and together they were billed as the World's Strangest Couple. About 1936."

And LaBrava would move on to be told about men digging mole drains in canefields, migrants cutting palmetto, boy sitting under a tung tree, Miccosuki Indians drinking corn beer, called *safki* . . .

But not this evening.

Maurice came out of the kitchen with an ice tray, glanced over to say, "Arrival of the Orange Blossom Special, January 1927 . . ." and got a surprise. LaBrava stood with his back to the Florida East Coast Railway shots.

He said to Maurice, "I don't think she has a problem at all. She had two drinks before dinner, couple of Scotches, she didn't finish the second one. I think all she had was one glass of wine . . ."

Maurice slid the ice cubes into a bowl. "What're you talking about?"

"You said in the car yesterday, going to get her, she had a problem."

"I told you she called me up . . ."

"You said she sounded strange."

"I said she sounded funny. She tells me she's got a problem, I ask her what it is, she changes the subject. So I don't know if it's booze or what."

"You seemed to think it was."

"Well, it still could be. You throw a drink at a cop car, that's not exactly having it under control. But today she's fine."

"You ask her why she did it?"

"She says she was in a bad mood, should a stayed home. The cop gets out of the car, says something smart . . . she throws the drink."

"Yeah, but what was she doing out on the sidewalk with a drink in the first place?"

"Getting some air—who knows. She was a movie star, Joe. They're all a little nuts."

She sat with them in Maurice's living room wearing slacks and a white cotton sweater now, sandals; she sipped her Scotch with a squirt of soda and struck LaBrava as a person who was courteous and a good listener. But then what choice did she have once Maurice got started?

He was showing off tonight:

". . . Neoga, Española, Bunnell, Dupont, Korona, Favorita, Harwood, National Gardens, Windle, Ormond, Flomich, Holly Hill, Daytona Beach,

Blake, Port Orange, Harbor Point, Spruce Creek, New Smyrna, Hucomer, Ariel, Oak Hill, Shiloh, Scottsmoor, Wiley, Jay Jay, Titusville, Indian River City, Delespine, Frontenac, Hardee's, Sharpes, City Point, Spratt's, Dixon's, Ives, Cocoa, Rock-ledge, Williams, Garvey's, Paxton's, Bonaventure, Pineda . . ."

On his way to naming every stop on the Florida East Coast line from Jacksonville to Key Largo, reciting the names without a pause, as he had learned them back in the early thirties.

This evening Maurice had to get off at Vero Beach to go to the bathroom and LaBrava and Jean Shaw looked at each other.

"The first time I met him," Jean Shaw said, "we were having dinner with a group. I think it was a place called Gatti's."

"It's right over here. Not far."

"He did his train stops. Exactly the same way, the same pace."

LaBrava said, "But how do we know he's not leaving some out?"

She said, "Would it make any difference?"

There was a silence. LaBrava looked toward the bathroom, then at Jean Shaw again. "I'd like to ask you something I've been wondering."

"Go ahead. About the movies?"

"No, it's about a guy named Richard Nobles. Do you know him?"

She sure did. It was in and out of her eyes.

When she said nothing, but continued to stare at him, he felt like a sneak. "Big guy with blond hair. About six-two."

"He's six-three and a half," Jean Shaw said. "He's a security cop and he thinks every woman he meets falls in love with him."

LaBrava felt relief, and a little closer to her.

She was frowning slightly. "How do you know him?"

"He came to that clinic in Delray last night, while we were there."

"Really?" She showed only mild surprise.

"He was pretty drunk." LaBrava offered it as a cue, wanting her to begin talking about Nobles, but it didn't prompt much.

All she said was, "I can believe it."

LaBrava tried again. "He said he was with you earlier. I mean he said he'd been with the person he came to pick up. He didn't mention anyone by name."

She was nodding, resigned. "The reason I left the bar was to get away from him." Her eyes returned to LaBrava. "I suppose you heard what I did."

"Got a little upset with a policeman."

"It was that flashing light. I didn't need help, I wanted to be alone. But they wouldn't leave, or turn off those goddamn blue lights."

"It can be irritating," LaBrava said. "Yeah, I

wondered about this fella Nobles . . . He said you were friends."

"He did, huh. I'm surprised he didn't say we were more than that."

"Military Park, Melbourne, Hopkins, Shares, Palm Bay, Malabar," Maurice said, coming out of the bathroom, "Valkaria, Grant, Micco, Roseland, Sebastian . . . Comfort stop. Who's ready for another drink? . . . Nobody?"

Jean Shaw said, "Maury, why didn't you tell me about the guy last night, looking for me? Richard Nobles."

"What guy?"

"He didn't see him," LaBrava said. "Maurice was with you the whole time."

"Did he get rough? Threaten to punch anybody?"

"Well, the girl in charge called the police . . . He calmed down. No, I just wondered if you were the one he came to get. I had a feeling."

"*What* guy?"

"Maury, sit down, rest your engine," Jean Shaw said. "We're talking about someone I met a few months ago, a security cop in Boca."

Maurice said, "You're going with a security cop now?" He eased into the La-Z-Boy, his body stiff; he seemed swallowed by the chair's contour, laid his head on his shoulder to look at Jean past his pointy shoes. "What happened to the bartender and the guy works at Hialeah?"

"I'm not *going* with anyone. I met him, I was nice to him . . . I mean I didn't tell him to get lost. But that might've been a mistake." She glanced at LaBrava.

Maurice said, "Wait a minute. How do you know this guy?"

"He works for the security service the building hired. I happened to meet him one night. I was out taking a walk. He was making his rounds." Choosing her words with care. "We started talking . . ."

Maurice said, "Yeah?" Sounding suspicious.

"You have to understand, first of all," Jean Shaw said, "he has a way about him. Very friendly, comes on with a certain country-boy charm. If you know the type I mean."

"Looks up at the condos with his mouth open," Maurice said, "scratching his ass."

"He looks you right in the eye, and he grins," Jean Shaw said. "He grins quite a lot. And he stands right on top of you when you're talking. He comes on like he's trying to be friendly, a nice guy, you know? But there's something intimidating about him. He's a little scary."

Maurice said, "I never saw the guy in my life I can tell you what his game is, Christ."

LaBrava listened.

"All the rich broads that live down here, lonely, don't know what to do with themselves . . ."

"Thanks a lot," Jean said.

"Not you. But even you, you gotta be careful."

"The ladies in the building think he's cute."

"Yeah? *You* think he's cute?"

"In a way, I suppose. He's attractive . . . He's awfully big though."

LaBrava did not think Nobles was cute in any way, by any supposition or measurement. He believed Nobles was dangerous, that you could look at him funny and set him off. But he said nothing. He listened.

"They come in all shapes and sizes looking for a score," Maurice said. "Find 'em in all the classier lounges."

Jean Shaw said, "Maury, I think I can spot a snake faster than you can. Don't worry about it."

"Then what're we talking about?"

"I haven't said this guy's out for anything in particular." She paused. "Other than what they're usually out for."

LaBrava saw her eyes come to him and hold for a moment as she sipped her drink. A familiar look from long ago, the calm dark eyes. A screen gesture . . . Or was it real?

"So what's his game?" Maurice said.

"He's a little too . . . familiar. That's all."

"He call you? Want to go out?"

"I did meet him a couple of times. Just for a drink."

"Jesus Christ," Maurice said.

"I didn't encourage him, I was being friendly. I'm not a snob."

"I'll tell you something," Maurice said. "At times you're not very smart either. Guys you get mixed up with."

She said, "Let's keep it simple, all right? I've never had trouble dealing with men, because I don't play games with them. I'm not a tease."

LaBrava listened. He didn't like the sound of "dealing with men." For a moment, thinking of her with other men, he was uncomfortable.

"But you happen to let this guy get too close," Maurice said. "That why you called me last week? You tell me you have a problem, then you don't want to talk about it." He glanced at LaBrava for confirmation.

She said, "Oh," and nodded with that look of resignation. She said, "Well, I was beginning to get a little scared. So I called you. But then as we were talking I thought, no, you're going to think I sound dumb. You're going to say all the things you've been saying, I'm a big girl and should know better. So I kept quiet . . . It's not your problem anyway."

LaBrava could close his eyes and listen and see

her on the screen. The easy delivery, the slight husk-
iness in her voice, serious but calm, almost off-
hand about it.

Maurice said, "So what happened you got
scared?"

"He was in my apartment that afternoon, the
day I called you." She seemed to be picturing it. "It
was the way he made himself right at home. Like he
was taking over."

Maurice said, "Wait a minute. He was in your
apartment. You let him in?"

LaBrava listened.

"Months ago, like the first or second time we
talked, I promised I'd show him one of my pictures."

Maurice said, "One of your movies."

"See, the way it started, he didn't believe I was
an actress. We were talking about it and, in a weak
moment, I promised I'd run one of my pictures for
him. I have video cassettes of a couple. I think the
only two available."

Maurice looked at LaBrava. "You catch that 'in
a weak moment'?"

LaBrava was wondering which movies she had.

"I didn't invite him," she said, "he just came. I
opened the door, there he was."

"Forced his way in."

"He talked me into it."

"Musta taken at least ten fifteen seconds," Maurice said, "talk a movie actress into showing one of her hits. So what would you say it was outweighed common sense? You miss being a celebrity? What?"

"He's standing there at the door, hat in hand. Grinning."

"Hat in hand—so you sit him down, just the two of you. The place is dark—"

"It was the middle of the afternoon."

"You show the movie, there you are, the star, bigger than life on the silver screen."

"On a television set, Maury."

"He sees you putting the make on Robert Mitchum, Robert Taylor, whoever, with that sexy come-hither look . . . Okay, the picture ends, lights're still low, the guy tries to climb all over you and you wonder why."

"That's not what I'm talking about," Jean Shaw said. "I can handle that end of it."

LaBrava listened.

"I'm talking about his attitude. The way he walks around the apartment, looks at my things. He's possessive and he's intimidating, without saying a word. He wants something and I don't know what it is."

"He wants *you*," Maurice said. "Guy like that, doesn't have any dough. What's he make? He wants you to keep him, buy him presents."

"I don't think so," she said. "He would've given

me a few hints by now. Like he can't afford new
clothes on his salary, wouldn't mind having a new
car." Her eyes moved to LaBrava. "His sister's a
cripple and needs an operation."

High Sierra, LaBrava thought.

"What he's doing, he's sneaking up," Maurice
said.

Humphrey Bogart and Ida Lupino, LaBrava
thought. He couldn't think of the name of the girl
with the clubfoot.

"Doesn't want to move too fast and blow it,"
Maurice said. "Only he's too dumb to realize you
can see it coming a mile away."

"See *what* coming?"

Maurice said, "Jeanie," taking his time, "is this
guy in love with you? Is that a possibility?"

"He's in love with himself."

"Okay. Then he's looking for a free ride. Dinner
at the club, some new outfits, little spending
money . . . That's how those guys operate. They
been around Miami Beach since the day they built
the bridge."

"Maybe," she said. "But I think he's got something else in mind."

LaBrava said, "I do too."

Jean Shaw looked over. Maurice looked over.

"I don't think he has a particular lifestyle in
mind," LaBrava said. "Dinner at the club . . . I

think what he wants, if he's after anything at all, is a whole lot of money."

"Then there's nothing to worry about," Jean Shaw said, "because I don't have any."

On a stool in the darkroom LaBrava sat hunched over contacts of the stoned Cuban couple, Boza and Mendoza, who had posed for him this morning, moving a magnifier down the strips of miniature prints, deciding Lana had had the right idea ("How about one like this?"), the shot of her exposing herself was the best one. Not because of her bared chest, but because of her eagerness to show breasts that were lifeless and seemed too old for her, and because Paco, sitting below her in the wheelchair, didn't know what was going on. LaBrava felt sorry for the girl; he saw ambition but little about her that was appealing and believed she would be hard to live with.

He could look at this girl, Lana Mendoza, barely a name to him, and know her, while his mind was still upstairs with Jean Shaw, wondering.

Trying to see her clearly.

He caught glimpses of her in black and white from the past and now in soft color, the same person, pale features, the lady in lamplight, dark eyes coming to rest on him. Her eyes could do things to him without half trying. He believed she was beautiful. He believed she was vulnerable. He believed she looked at him in a different way than she looked at Maurice.

He had walked her down the hall to 304. In the doorway she said, "I'm glad I came here." She kissed him on the cheek. She said, "Thank you," and was still looking at him as she closed the door.

Was that familiar? Seeing her eyes and then the door closing, filling the screen. He wasn't sure.

Why did she thank him?

He didn't do anything, offer advice. He listened.

He listened to her tell Maurice she was serious. She didn't have any money. Really. Not money as you thought of having *money*. She wasn't living on Social Security. But, she said, she didn't have that much to begin with. Jerry hadn't exactly left her set for life. Not after the IRS got through with him. Three audits in a row. LaBrava listened. All of his tax shelters disallowed. They had to sell the house on Pine Tree. Then his stock portfolio went to hell, he took a bath there. LaBrava listened. Between the government and the market Jerry was almost into bankruptcy when he died. That's what killed him, Jean Shaw said. Maurice didn't say much. He listened, watching her almost sadly, and seemed to nod in sympathy. He did ask her how she was fixed. She said well, she had the income from her piece of the hotel, she had a few stocks, she could sublease the apartment and move to a cheaper place. She said, with that dry delivery, she could always make appearances at condominium openings. "Screen Star Jean Shaw in Person." A developer had suggested it one time. Or, she said, if things got really bad she could team up with Marilyn, the bag lady, work up a routine. Maurice, serious, said come on, don't talk like that. He told her not to worry about her financial situation, not as long as he was around. There was no mention again of Richard Nobles.

Now, in the darkroom, Joe LaBrava wondered which of her movies she had showed Nobles. He wondered why she had said, "The way he walks around the apartment, looks at my things." Like Nobles had visited her more than that one time, to see the movie.

He wondered about her eyes, too, if she used them in a studied, theatrical way. Twice, while Maurice was speaking, he had felt her eyes and turned to see her watching him. He saw her eyes as she sipped her drink . . . as she closed her door.

I'm glad I came here.

And heard a girl's voice say, "Boy, you put in long hours, don't you?"

Franny Kaufman stood in the doorway. He smiled, glad to see her. He liked her, with the strange feeling they were old friends. "The Spring Song girl. You moved in?"

"Sorta. A friend of mine has a van helped me with the heavy stuff, the boxes. I still have some junk to get tomorrow."

"What room're you in?"

"Two-oh-four. It's not bad, I get morning light. I haven't seen any bugs yet." She wore jeans and a gas-station shirt that said *Roy* above the pocket, intricate silver rings on her fingers. She turned, looking around. "I didn't know you had all this."

"It's the old man's, really."

"I was just nosing around, seeing what's here." She came over to the counter. "Can I look?"

"Here, use the loupe," he moved aside, off the stool.

Franny took off her round glasses, bent over to study the contacts through the Agfa magnifier, inching it over the pictures, stopping, moving on. He looked at her strange hair that he liked, frizzed out on both sides—it seemed part of her energy— and looked at the slender nape of her neck, the stray hairs against white skin.

She said, "I've seen him around, but I haven't seen her. Which ones're you gonna print? No, wait. I bet I know the one you like the best. The one, the girl showing her tits. Am I right?"

"I think so," LaBrava said. "I'm gonna play with it, print it different ways, see what I get."

"It's sad, isn't it?" Franny said. "Except I get the feeling she's a ballbuster. I feel sorry for her, you know? But only up to a point. Was the pose your idea?"

"No, hers."

"What's her name?"

"Lana."

"Oh, that's perfect."

"Yeah, Lana gets the credit."

"But it didn't turn out the way she thought it would. You got something better. You do good work, Joe."

"Thank you."

"You do any nudes?"

"I have. A lady one time had me shoot her sitting on a TV set naked."

"Coming on to you?"

"No, she wanted her picture taken."

"Far out."

"It wasn't bad. She started with a fur coat on. Then she says, 'Hey, I got an idea.' Lets the coat fall open, she's got nothing on under it. They always say that, 'Hey, I got an idea,' like they just thought of it."

"I got an idea," Franny said. "Shoot me nude, okay? I want to do a self-portrait in pastels, send it to this guy in New York. I'm thinking life-size, re-clined, very sensual. What do you charge for a sitting? Or a lying."

"You can buy lunch sometime."

"Really? But you have to promise not to send it

to *Playboy*. This is for art, like Stieglitz shooting Georgia O'Keeffe in the nude. You ever see those?"

"They were married then."

She said, "They were?" surprised. She said, "You know what you're doing, don't you?"

"Sometimes."

"Are you tired? I mean right now."

"Not especially."

"Let's go outside, look at the ocean. That's the only reason to live here, you know it? The ocean and these weird hotels, both of them together in the same place. I love it."

They walked through the empty lobby.

"Yeah, I think reclined. Unless you've got some ideas."

"It's your painting."

"I'm gonna render myself about twelve pounds lighter and straighten my hair. See if I can turn the guy on."

They crossed the street past locked parked cars.

"I like your hair the way it is."

"Really? You're not just being nice?"

"No, I mean it."

And crossed the grass to the low wall made of cement and coral where she raised her face to the breeze coming out of darkness, off the ocean. "I feel good," Franny said. "I'm glad I came here."

"Somebody else told me that, just a little while ago." He sat down on the wall, facing the Della

Robbia, looked up at the windows. Faint light showed in 304. "I'll tell you who it was. Jean Shaw."

Franny turned from the ocean, her face still raised. "Who's Jean Shaw?"

"You never heard of Jean Shaw?"

"Joe, would I lie to you?"

"She was a movie star. She was in pictures with Robert Mitchum."

"Well, obviously I've heard of Robert Mitchum. I love him."

"And some others. She was my favorite actress."

"Wow, and she's a friend of yours, uh?"

"I met her today."

"Is she the one, dark hair, middle-aged, she came out of the hotel this evening with you and Mr. Zola? We were in the van, we'd just pulled up."

"We went out to dinner." He thought about what he was going to say next and then said it, before he changed his mind. "How old you think she is?"

Franny said, "Well, let's see. She looks pretty good for her age. I'd say she's fifty-two."

"You think she looks that old?"

"You asked me how old I think she is, not how old I think she looks. She's had a tuck and probably some work done around the eyes. She *looks* about forty-five. Or younger. Her bone structure helps, nice cheekbones. And her complexion's great, you can tell she stays out of the sun, and I'll bet she buys protein fiber replenishers by the case. But her actual age, I'd have to say fifty-two."

"You think so?"

"Joe, you're talking to the Spring Song girl."

"Okay, how old am I?"

"You're thirty-eight."

He said, "You're right."

"But you don't look a day over thirty-seven."

Cundo Rey was driving his black Pontiac Trans Am that he had bought, paid for, black with black windows that Nobles said you couldn't see for shit out of at night, lights looked real weak, yellowish and you couldn't read signs at all. Cundo Rey let him bitch. He loved his Trans Am, he loved going slow in it like they were doing now even better than letting it out, because you could hear the engine rumble and pop, all that power cooking under the hood. Cundo was wearing blue silk with a white silk neckerchief, one of his cruising outfits. Nobles was still wearing his uniform, blue on blue, both the shirt epaulets hanging, the buttons torn off. Nobles said somebody had tried to give him a hard time. Cundo said, "It look like they did, too."

They were creeping along south on Ocean Drive, the strip of Lummus Park and the beach on their left, the old hotels close on their right, the other side of the bumper-to-bumper parked cars. "Netherland," Cundo Rey said, hunched over the steering wheel, looking up at signs. "Cavalier . . . There, the Cardozo. See? On that thing sticks out."

"The awning," Nobles said. "Okay, slow down."

"I'm going slow as this baby can go." He pushed in the clutch and gave it some gas to hear that rumble, get a few pops out the ass end.

A man and a girl with strange electric hair, crossing the street in the headlight beams, looked this way.

"There it is, on the corner. Della Robbia. I don't see a number but that's it," Nobles said, "where her friend took her." And then said, "Jesus Christ—" turning in his bucket seat, both hands moving over the door. "Where's the goddamn window thing?"

Cundo Rey glanced at him. "What's your trouble now?"

"Open the goddamn window."

"Man, I got the air on."

"Open the fucking window, will you! Turn around."

"Hey, what's the matter with you?" Cundo scowling.

Guy acting like he was going crazy, like he was trapped, clawing at the door.

"That's the *guy*, the fucker 'at hit me."

"Where? That guy with the girl?"

"Turn the fuck around, *now*."

They had to go down to Twelfth. Cundo backed into the street and came out to move north on Ocean Drive.

"Put your window down."

"I can see okay. Be cool. Why you want to get excited for?"

"I don't see 'em." Nobles hunched up close to the windshield.

"There," Cundo Rey said. "On the porch."

Nobles turned to look past Cundo, and kept turning.

"Guy is opening the door with a key," Cundo Rey said. "So he must live there too, uh? Is that the guy?"

"That's the guy," Nobles said, calm now, looking out the back as they crept past the Cardozo. "That's him." He didn't straighten around until they came to Fifteenth, where Ocean Drive ended and they had to go left over to Collins.

"I didn't see him too good in the dark," Cundo Rey said. "You sure is the guy?"

Nobles was sitting back now, looking straight ahead. He said, "Yeah, that's him. That's the guy."

"You want me to go back?"

"No, I don't want you to go back just yet."

Looking at him Cundo Rey said, "You sound different."

9

THERE WAS SUNLIGHT in the window. LaBrava picked up the phone next to his bed and the girl's voice said, "I woke you up, didn't I? I'm sorry." He recognized the voice now. She said, "I don't know what time it is and the goddamn nurse won't come when I call . . ."

He drove past the hospital thinking it was a resort motel or it might be a car dealership with all the glass and had to U-turn and come back for another pass before he saw the sign, *Bethesda Memorial*.

Jill Wilkinson was alone in a semi-private room. She looked different, smaller and younger, out of character as victim. She had been diagnosed as having a slight concussion and was under twenty-four-hour observation, chewing on crushed ice when LaBrava came in.

"This is all I've had to eat since yesterday afternoon. You believe it? They won't give me anything else till I'm all better."

"You look pretty good."

"Thanks. I've always wanted to look pretty good."

He leaned over the bed, close to her, looking into her face clean of makeup. Her eyes were brown looking at his, waiting. "You look great. How's that?"

"Better."

"You fish for compliments?"

"I don't have to, usually."

"Your head hurt?"

"It's a little fuzzy. I feel dragged out. Used up."

"That what he did, he used you?"

"He tried to. He had ideas. God, did he have ideas."

"What stopped him?"

"*I* did. I said, 'You put that thing in my mouth I'll bite it off, I swear to God.'"

"Oh."

"He had to think about that. I told him I might be dead, but he'd be squatting to take a leak for the rest of his life."

"Oh."

"He put his gun in my mouth—and you know where he got that. And then *that* gave him the other idea."

"He hit you?"

Two people talking who knew about violence.

"He pushed me around. I tore his epaulets and he got mad. I tried to run in the bathroom and lock the door, but he came in right behind me, banged the door in, and I fell over the side of the tub and cracked my head against the tile."

"He had his uniform on."

"Yeah . . ."

"Were you knocked out?"

"I was sort a dazed, you know, limp, but I wasn't out all the way. He put me on the bed and sat down next to me—listen to this—and held my hand. He said he was sorry, he was just goofing around."

"Did he look scared?"

"I don't know, I wasn't all there." She shook the ice in the paper cup, raised it to her mouth and paused. "Wait a minute. Yeah, he tried to take my blouse off, he said he'd put me to bed, and I grabbed one of his fingers and bent it back."

"Then what?"

"Nothing, really."

"He touch you?"

"Did he give me a feel? Well, sorta. He gave it a try."

"You tell the police that part?"

She hesitated and he thought she was trying to remember.

"I didn't tell them anything."

"You didn't call the cops?"

"I called South County, my office. I got Mr. Zola's name and number and I called, but there was no answer. Last night."

"How'd you get my number?"

"I had your name. I took a chance you lived in South Beach, near Mr. Zola, so I called Information, this morning."

"You haven't told the cops anything."

"No."

He waited a few moments. "Why not?"

Now Jill waited. "He really didn't *do* anything. I mean you have to consider the kind of creepy stuff I run into every day, at work. A guy making a pass isn't all that much."

"How'd he get in your apartment?"

"I don't know."

"You don't think he broke in."

"No."

"What he did comes under attempted sexual battery. In this state it can get you life."

She said, "How do you know that?"

"But you say he really didn't do anything. What would he have to do?"

"You want to know the truth?"

"I'd love to."

"I'm going to Key West for ten days. It's my big chance to get out of that place and nothing's gonna stop me."

"What do you think he wanted?"

"I sign a complaint, I know damn well what'll happen. Get cross-examined at the hearing—didn't I invite him over? Offer him a drink? I end up looking like a part-time hooker and Mr. America walks. Bull *shit*. I've got enough problems." She coaxed ice into her mouth from the paper cup, paused and looked up at him. "What did you ask me?"

"What do you think he wanted?"

"You mean outside of my body? That's why I called—he wants *you*. 'Who *was* that boy, anyway?'" Giving it the hint of an accent. "'What newspaper he with?' About as subtle as that crappy uniform he had on. He's a classic sociopath, and that's giving him the benefit of the doubt. I know his development was arrested. He probably should be too."

"But you're going to Key West."

"I've *got* to go to Key West. Or I'll be back in here next week playing with dolls. I don't think that asshole should be on the street, but I have to put my mental health first. Does that make sense?"

LaBrava nodded, taking his time, in sympathy.

She said, "He thinks you hit him with something."

"I should've," nodding again, seeing Mr. America in his silver satin jacket. The shoulders, the hands. "But there wasn't anything heavy enough."

"I told him you didn't hit him, you put him down and sat on him."

"Oh."

"That's when he got mad. I should've known better."

"Well, I don't think it would take much . . . Let me ask you, did he mention Mrs. Breen? The lady we picked up."

"No, I don't think so . . . No, he didn't."

LaBrava was at ease with her because he could accept how she felt and talk to her on an eye-to-eye level of understanding without buttering words to slip past emotions. She was into real life. Tired, that's all. He wouldn't mind going to Key West for a few days, stay at the Pier House. But then he thought of Jean Shaw and saw Richard Nobles again.

"How did he get in your apartment?"

"If I tell you I think somebody gave him the key, then we're gonna get into a long story about a naked Cuban who thinks he's Geraldo Rivera."

"Well," LaBrava said, "even Geraldo Rivera thinks he's Geraldo Rivera. But I could be wrong."

"Do my eyes look okay?"

"They're beautiful eyes."

"I see giant red things all over your shirt."

"I think they're hibiscus," LaBrava said. "What naked Cuban?"

*　*　*

Joe Stella said to Joe LaBrava, in the Star Security office on Lantana Road, across from the A. G. Holley state hospital, "You believe you can walk in here and start asking me questions? You believe I'm some wore-out cop's gonna roll over for you? I put in seventeen years with the Chicago Police, eight citations, and I've been here, right here, seventeen more. So why don't you get the fuck outta my office."

"We got two things in common," LaBrava said. "I'm from Chicago too."

Joe Stella said, "We aren't over in some foreign country on our vacation. Gee, you're from Chicago, uh? How about that, it's a small fucking world, isn't it? I run into people from around Chicago every day and most of 'em I just as soon not. You could be, all I know, from the license division, Secretary of State, come in here you don't have nothing better to do, see what you can shake loose."

"I'm not from the state, not Florida," LaBrava said. "I'm asking about one guy, that's all."

"See that?" Joe Stella said, the spring in the swivel chair groaning as he leaned back, motioned over his shoulder at the paneled wall.

LaBrava thought he was pointing to the underexposed, 5:00 P.M. color photo of a bluish Joe Stella standing next to a blue-black marlin hanging by its tail. The marlin looked about ten feet long, nearly twice the length of the man, but the man was about 100 pounds heavier.

"That's my license to run a security business," Joe Stella said, "renewed last month."

LaBrava's gaze moving to the framed document hanging next to the fish shot.

"I've posted bond, my insurance is paid up, I know goddamn well I am not in violation of any your fucking regulations 'cause I just got off probation. I spend a whole week running around, get the stuff together, make the appearance before the license division . . . I gotta show cause on my own time why they're full a shit and ought never've put me on probation. I have to show 'em it wasn't my fault the insurance lapsed *one* week, that's *all*, and long as I'm there show 'em in black and white all my guys are licensed, every one of 'em. Fine, they stamp a paper, I'm pardoned of all my sins I never committed. I'm back in business. I'm *clean*. So why don't you get the fuck out and leave me alone, okay? Otherwise I'm gonna have to get up and kick you the fuck out and I'm tired this morning, I had a hard night."

LaBrava got ready during Joe Stella's speech. When the man finished, sitting immovable, a block of stone, LaBrava said, "The other thing we have in common, besides both of us being from the Windy City, we'd like to keep the Director of Internal Revenue happy. Wouldn't you say that's true?"

Joe Stella said, "Oh, shit," and did sound tired.

"You're familiar with form SS-8, aren't you?"

"I don't know, there so many forms"—getting tireder by the moment—"What's SS-8?"

LaBrava felt himself taking on an almost-forgotten role—Revenue officer, Collection Division—coming back to him like hopping on a bike. The bland expression, the tone of condescending authority: I'm being nice, but watch it.

"You file payroll deductions, withholding, F.I.C.A.?"

"Yeah, a course I do."

"You never hire guards as independent contractors? Even on a part-time basis?"

"Well, that depends what you mean . . ."

"You're not aware that an SS-8 has ever been filed by a former employee or independent contractor? It's never been called to your attention to submit a reply?"

"Wait a minute—Jesus, you know all the forms you gotta keep track of? My bookkeeper comes in once a week, payday, she's suppose to know all that. Man, I'm telling you—try and run a business today, a bonded service. First, where'm I gonna get anybody's any good'd work for four bucks an hour to begin with? . . . Hey, you feel like a drink?"

"No thanks."

"You know who I get?"

"The cowboys."

"I get the cowboys, I get the dropouts, I get these guys dying to pack, walk around the shopping mall in their uniform, this big fucking .38 on their hip. Only, state regulation, they're suppose to pin their license—like a driver's license in a plastic cover—on their shirt. But they do that they look like what they are, right? Mickey Mouse store cops. So they don't wear 'em and the guy from the state license division sees 'em and I get fined a hunnert bucks each and put on probation ninety days. I also, to stay in business, I gotta post bond, five grand, and I gotta have three-hundred-grand liability insurance, a hunnert grand property damage. The insurance lapses a week cause the fucking insurance guy's out at Hialeah every day and it's my fault, I'm suspended till I show cause why I oughta not get fucked over by the state of Florida where I'm helping with the employment situation. I'm not talking about the federal government you understand. You guys, IRS, you got a job to do—keep that money coming in to run the government, send guns to all the different places they need guns, defend our ass against . . . you know what I'm talking about. Fucking Castro's only a hunnert miles away. Nicaragua, how far's that? It isn't too far, I know."

"Richard Nobles," LaBrava said, "he ever been arrested before?"

Joe Stella paused. "Before what? Jesus Christ, is that who we're talking about? Richie Nobles? Jesus, you can have him."

"You know where I can find him?"

"I think he quit. I haven't seen him in three days. Left the car, no keys, the dumb son of a bitch. All those big good-looking assholes, I think they get hair instead of brains. What's the matter, Richie hasn't paid his taxes? I believe it."

"What I'm curious about—guy applies for a job, you ask him if he's ever been arrested, don't you?"

"I did I'd be in violation of your federal law, invasion of privacy. I can't ask if the guy was ever a mental patient either. I can ask him, have you ever been convicted of a felony, or have you ever committed one and didn't get caught? But I can't ask him if he's ever been arrested."

"You did issue him a handgun."

"They buy their own."

"So he's got a license."

"You apply, you want to be an armed guard, you gotta get clearance through the FBI and the State Department of Law Enforcement. The guy—it takes months—he gets his license or he gets a certified letter in the mail saying he's turned down. But they don't notify me, ever."

"Have you seen his license?"

"Yeah, he showed it to me."

"Then he must be clean, uh? They checked him out."

Joe Stella said, "You ready for a drink now?"

LaBrava nodded. "Sounds good."

He watched Joe Stella push up from his desk. The man moved with an effort to get a bottle of Wild Turkey and glasses from a file cabinet, ice and a can of Fresca from a refrigerator LaBrava had thought was a safe. Pouring double bourbons with a splash of Fresca Joe Stella said, "First one today. What time is it? Almost ten-thirty, that's not bad. Long as you had breakfast." He handed a drink to LaBrava and sat down with the bottle close to him on the desk.

LaBrava took a good sip.

"Nice drink, huh?"

"Not bad."

"Refreshing with a little bite to it." Joe Stella took down half his drink. Poured another ounce or so of bourbon into it, and added a little more. He said, "Ahhh, man . . ."

"I bet he's been arrested," LaBrava said, "but never convicted, uh?"

Joe Stella said, "Richie's from upstate. Some of the boys here call him Big Scrub when he's in a good mood, call him Big Dick he'll grin at you. Otherwise nobody talks to him. You understand the type I mean?"

"I know him," LaBrava said.

"He was arrested up there, you're right, for destruction of government property. The son of a bitch shot an eagle."

"I understand he ate it," LaBrava said.

"I wouldn't be surprised. Richie'll eat anything. He'll drink al*most* anything. He came to work here he gave me a half gallon of shine with peaches in it, whole big peaches . . . That's a good drink, isn't it?"

"Nice."

"He shot the eagle he was living up around Ocala, the Big Scrub country. Richie was a canoe guide, he'd take birdwatchers and schoolteachers back in the swamp, show 'em nature and come out somewhere up on the St. Johns River. He wasn't doing that he'd run supplies for a couple of moonshiners, few hundred pounds a sugar a trip. These two brothers he knew had a still in there. So when he got busted for the eagle he traded off, gave the feds the two brothers and they got two to five in Chillicothe. I asked him, didn't it bother him any to turn in his friends? He says, 'No, it weren't no hill to climb.'" Joe Stella drank and topped it off again, the color of his drink turning clear amber in the window sunlight. "No, it weren't no hill to climb. He's around here more'n ten minutes I start to sound like a fucking cracker." Joe Stella took another drink and sat back. "You ever hear of Steinhatchee?"

"Sounds familiar."

"Way up on the Gulf side, where the Stein-hatchee River comes out. Sleepy little place, the people there, they cut timber for Georgia-Pacific or fish mullet outta the river, use these skiffs they call bird-dog boats, make ten thousand a year, top. Till they saw their first bale of marijuana and found out they could make ten thousand a *night*—buy it offa shrimp boats'd come in there and wholesale it. These hardshell Baptists, all of a sudden they're getting rich in the dope business. They never smoked it, you understand, they just ran it. Well, Richie Nobles had a relative living over there and found out about it. So what do you think Richie does?"

"If he got rich," LaBrava said, "I know he didn't declare it."

"No, Richie believes marijuana is for sissies. But it bothers him these people that don't know shit're making all that money. So he tells the DEA and they send him in, see if he can join the business."

"Professional snitch," LaBrava said.

"Kind you people love, huh?" Joe Stella said. "Once he was in tight there, part of the deal, the feds wired him. Richie comes back with enough to bust all his new friends. Testified against 'em in Jacksonville federal court, change of venue to protect his ass, and put enough on his own rela-tive, some cracker name Buster something, to send

him up to Ohio for thirty-five years. Second flop's
the long one, the first time the guy only drew
three."

"What's Richard get out of it?"

"Enemies. He knows anything he knows how to
piss people off." Joe Stella hesitated, about to
drink. He stared over the rim of his glass. "None of
that's familiar?"

"Why would it be?"

"You don't know an old guy name Miney, huh?
Miney"—looking over his desk, picking up a scrap
of notepaper—"Combs. Father of Buster Combs,
the one was sent up."

"Don't know 'em," LaBrava said.

"See, you're not the first one come looking for
Richie. He's a popular boy."

"I can see why."

"This old guy was in here, talk just like Richie.
He's the one told me about Steinhatchee. I asked
Richie—it was only like a week ago—if it was true.
He says, 'Yeah, I done more'n one favor for my Un-
cle Sam.' "

LaBrava said, "So he left the Big Scrub, came
down here to work . . ."

"Came down to Dade with a federal recommen-
dation, wanting to join the police. Miami and
Dade-Metro he says wouldn't even talk to him. He
was a gypsy cop for a while, worked for Opa-
locka, Sweetwater, Hialeah Gardens, got fired for

taking bribes, one thing or another, and came to work for me."

"Where's he live?"

"Same thing the old guy asked. I don't know. I never was able to reach him on a number he gave me. A woman'd answer and say, 'No, he ain't here and I hope I never see the son of a bitch again.' Words to that effect, they'd say it different ways and hang up."

"Any of the women sound . . . older or educated, like they were well off?"

"I don't know how *well* off, I know they were *pissed* off."

"Why'd you keep him on?"

"I thought I explained it, Christ, try and get help aren't all misfits or retirees, old geezers . . . You want another drink? I think I'll have one."

"No, I'm fine."

Joe Stella pushed up to get himself another ice cube and the can of Fresca, stumbled against the desk as he came back and sat down again. "I think you laid a smoke screen on me. You aren't with the IRS, are you? . . . Gimme that Windy City shit, I bet you never even been to Chicago."

"I passed through it once," LaBrava said, "on my way to Independence, Missouri. It looked like a pretty nice town."

"Passed through it . . . You know, I was thinking," Joe Stella said, pouring. "Guy like you—I could fire three of my dumbbells, pay you twelve bucks an hour and give you just the cream, supervisory type work. What would you say to that?"

10

AGAIN HE EXPERIENCED the strange sense of time. Having lunch on the front porch of the Cardozo Hotel with a movie star out of his memory. She wore dark glasses, round black ones, and a wide-brimmed Panama straight across her eyes. He watched her.

He watched her take dainty bites of marinated conch, raising the fork in her left hand upside down, her moves unhurried. He watched her break off a piece of French bread, hold it close to her face, elbow resting on the table, wrist bent, staring out of shade at the ocean in sunlight, then slowly bring the piece of bread to her mouth, not looking at it, and he would see her lips part to receive the bread and then close and he would see the movie star's masseter begin to work, still unhurried. He wasn't sure where the masseter was located, Franny hadn't told him that. Franny said the movie star used some kind of secret cream, placenta tissue extract, and very likely said Q and X with exaggerated emphasis in front of mirrors and wore sunglasses till sundown so she wouldn't get squint wrinkles. His gaze would shift briefly from Jean Shaw and he would see:

Franny sitting on the wall in the strip of ocean-front park across the street, taking Polaroid shots of the hotels. Franny in cutoffs cut so high they must be choking her.

Della Robbia women in lawn chairs talking about Medicare and Social Security.

Maurice coming along Ocean Drive with a grocery sack, skinny legs, faded yellow shorts that reached almost to his knees.

Cars with tourists passing slowly, sightseeing.

A young Cuban guy talking to Franny now. The guy fooling with his ear, Franny laughing. The guy posing, hand on his hip, seductive, strange, as Franny aimed her Polaroid at him.

And his eyes, behind his own sunglasses, would slide back to the movie star's face, pale but in full color. The skin was smooth, without a trace of what might appear to be a tuck, a lift. He believed it didn't matter even if she'd had one. He believed he was in love with her face.

She would turn her head to him and seem to smile, used to being looked at. He wanted to see her eyes but would have to wait.

She said, "You know, that's a lovely shirt." Then surprised him, lowered her sunglasses to the slender tip of her nose, letting him see in daylight a line beneath each of her eyes, slightly puffed, a look that he liked, a slight imperfection. She replaced her glasses as she said, "I don't believe I've ever called a man's shirt lovely before, but it is. I love hibiscus." She said, "I almost married a man who wore only dark brown shirts and always with a dark brown necktie. Odd? . . . Maybe not. He made three thousand dollars a week as a screen writer, he kept an apartment at the Chateau Marmont and died of malnutrition." She said, "I want to see more of your work, I think it's stunning. Will you show me?"

He said, "I want to photograph you."

"I've been photographed."

"Maybe you have . . ."

Maurice said, "Well well *well*," on the street side of the stone-slab porch railing, stepping up on the base to look at their table. "What're you having, conch? You ever see it they take it out of the shell? You wouldn't eat it. Gimme a bite." He lowered the grocery sack to the railing and leaned over it, face raised waiting as Jean Shaw speared a piece of conch and offered it.

"Another? You can have the rest, I'm finished."

"I don't want to wreck my appetite. We're eating in tonight, fried steak and onions, railroad-style. Gimme a sip—whatever it is."

She offered her glass. "Plain old Scotch."

"How many you had?"

She looked at LaBrava. "How many, six, seven?"

Maurice said, "It's three o'clock in the afternoon!"

"We've had two, Maury. Don't have a heart attack." In that quiet, unhurried tone. He left them and she said, "Do you like his shorts? They have to be at least twenty years old. He may be the most eccentric guy I know. And I've known a few, I'll tell you."

"Well, he's different," LaBrava said.

He saw Franny, alone now, farther down the beach . . . Paco Boza coming along the sidewalk in his wheelchair, a ghetto blaster in his lap; it looked like an accordion.

"Joe, when you're as well off as Maury and you choose to live in a place like the Della Robbia, that's eccentric."

"He said he used to have money, but I don't know that he has that much now."

She said, "Oh," and paused.

He said, "That was my understanding. Had it and spent it." He could hear Paco's blaster now, turned up all the way. "In fact the other night, he was telling me when he sold the hotel next door, the Andrea, he could've kicked himself for not waiting, get a better price."

She said, "Does he confide in you?"

"I wouldn't say he confides."

"But you're close. I know he likes you, a lot."

"Yeah, we get along. We argue all the time, but that's part of the routine."

"He's an actor, Joe. He plays the crabby but loveable retired bookie, hangs out at Wolfie's, Picciolo's, all those places from the old days."

"That's his age—he lives in the past."

"He's a fox, Joe. Don't ever sell him short."

He wanted to say, Wait a minute, what're we talking about exactly? But now Paco Boza was rolling toward them, his ghetto box playing soul against his body, Paco letting it run up through his shoulders and down his arms to turn the silver wheels of the wheelchair wired to the beat, no hurry or worry in the world.

"Hey, the picture man. When do I get my pictures, man?"

LaBrava told him maybe in a few days. Maybe sooner. Come back when you're not busy.

Paco Boza left them, taking his sound down the street, soul with a kick that got into LaBrava sitting there in his sunglasses drinking Scotch with a movie star on the porch of the Cardozo Hotel.

She said, "The poor guy. He's so young." He told her there was nothing wrong with Paco. He had stolen the chair from Eastern Airlines, had his girlfriend push him out of Miami International in it because he didn't like to walk and because he thought it was cool, a way for people to identify him. She said, "What does he do?" and he told her about two-hundred-dollars worth of cocaine a day. She said, "You're part of this, you feel it." She said, "I love to watch you. You don't miss anything, do you?" He did not move or speak now. Close to him she said, "You think you're hidden, but I can see you in there; Mr. LaBrava. Show me your pictures."

"At Evelyn's gallery they sip wine and look at my photographs . . ."

Looking at them now spread over the formica table, Jean Shaw picking up each print and studying it closely—in his rooms on the second floor of the Della Robbia. 201. He paid for the rooms, he had been living here eight months, but there was nothing of him in the rooms. They were rooms in a hotel. He had not got around to mounting or hanging any of his prints, or was sure there were any he cared to look at every day. There were other prints in envelope sleeves in the bookcase and among magazines on the coffee table. He told her *Aperture* magazine had contacted him about doing a book. Call it *South Beach*. Get all the old people, the art deco look. He was working on it now. No, he was thinking about it more than he was working on it. He wanted to do it. He wouldn't mind having a coffee-table book on his coffee table. It seemed strange though—ask thirty or forty dollars for a book full of pictures of people who'd never see it, never be able to afford it.

"At the gallery they sip wine and look at my pictures. They say things like, 'I see his approach to art as retaliation, a frontal attack against the assumptions of a technological society.'

"They say, 'His work is a compendium of humanity's defeat at the hands of venture capital.'

"They say, 'It's obvious he sees his work as an exorcism, his forty days in the desert.' Or, another one, 'They're self-portraits. He sees himself as dispossessed, unassimilated.'

"The review in the paper said, 'The aesthetic subtext of his work is the systematic exposure of artistic pretension.' I thought I was just taking pictures."

Jean Shaw said, "Simplicity. It is what it is." Then paused. "And what it isn't, too. Is that what you're saying?"

He didn't want her to try so hard. "I heard one guy at the gallery—it was his wife or somebody who said I was dispossessed, unassimilated, and the guy said, 'I think he takes pictures to make a buck, and anything else is fringe.' I would've kissed the guy, but it might've ruined his perspective."

Jean Shaw said, studying a print, "They try to pose, and not knowing how they reveal themselves."

He liked that. That wasn't bad.

"Your style is the absence of style. Would you say?"

He said, "No tricky angles," because he didn't know if he had a style or not. "I'm not good at tricky angles."

"Some of them look like actors. I mean like they're made up, costumed."

"I know what you mean."

"When you're shooting them, what do you see?"

"What do I see? I see what I'm shooting. I wonder if I have enough light. Or too much."

"Come on. Tell me."

"I see 'images whose meanings exceed the local circumstances that provide their occasion.'"

"Who said that?"

"Walker Evans. Or somebody who said he did."

"What do you think about when you look at your own work?"

"I wonder why I can't shoot like Stieglitz."

"How long have you been doing it?"

"Or why I'll never be able to. I wonder why my people don't look at me the way August Sander's people looked at him. I wonder if I should have moved in closer, taken one step to the right or left."

There was a silence.

"What else do you see?"

"But it isn't what I see, is it? It's what I wonder

when I look at the picture. I wonder if I'll ever have enough confidence."

She said, "Yes? What else?"

"I wonder, most of all I wonder what the people are doing now. Or if they're still like that, the way I shot them."

He heard her say, in the quiet afternoon apartment, "What do you see when you look at me?"

And almost answered, turning from the table of black and white prints. Almost. But as soon as he was facing her, close to her, he knew better than to speak, break the silence and have to start over. No, they were now where they wanted to be, if he could feel or sense anything at all. So he touched the face he had watched on the screen, bringing up one hand and then the other just before he brought his mouth to hers and felt her hands slide over his ribs.

They went into the bedroom and undressed without a word to make love in dimmed silence, to make love as soon as they were in bed and she brought him between her legs, Joe LaBrava believing this was unbelievable. Look at him. He was making love to Jean Shaw, he was honest-to-God making love to Jean Shaw in real life. He didn't want to be watching, he wanted to be overwhelmed by it, by Jean Shaw, making *love* to her, but he didn't want to just do it either, he wanted the overwhelming feeling of it to take hold and carry them away. But her eyes were closed and maybe she was just doing it, doing it with him, moving with him, but she could be doing it without him because he didn't know where she was with her eyes closed so tight. He wanted to see her eyes and he wanted her to see *him* . . . so close to her face, her hair, her skin and not a blemish, not a trace of a tiny scar . . . He had to stop thinking if he was going to be overwhelmed. He had to *let* himself be overwhelmed . . .

It wasn't something he would tell anyone. He would never do that. Though it seemed like the kind of thing you might tell a stranger on a train without naming names. On a *train?* Come on. He was making an old-time movie out of it looking for a way to tell it. Or maybe write it in a diary. Though he could never imagine, under any circumstances, even in solitary confinement, writing or talking to himself.

No, he would never be able to tell anyone there was more to making love to a movie star than just . . . making love. Or, maybe he should qualify it. Say, making love to a movie star the first time . . . there was more to it than just making love. The idea of it, the anticipation, the realization, was more overwhelming than the doing of it. Although he could not say that would be true of all movie stars.

What he had almost said to her when she said, "What do you see when you look at me?" was:

"The first woman I ever fell in love with, when I was twelve years old."

But the mood, something, had saved him from maybe getting pushed out the window. He was able to move through the next steps letting heavy breathing bring them along, into the bedroom to the act itself. But you see, with all the anticipation, thinking back twenty-five years to the first time you saw her and were knocked out by her, finally when you're there and it's happening, it's almost impossible to quit thinking about how great it's going to be, how unbelievable, and do it without watching yourself doing it.

The movie star smoked a cigarette after. In bed. She actually smoked a cigarette. He went in the kitchen, fixed a couple of light Scotches and brought them back. The movie star acted a little like a kitten. She seemed much younger with her clothes off, not at all self-conscious. She gave him those secret looks, sly smiles that were familiar. (But did she have secrets? Now?) She asked him how he would photograph her. He said he'd like to think about it.

What he thought about though, what he was most aware of, was a feeling. It was not unlike the way he felt and wondered about things when he was looking at his photographs.

He felt—lying in bed with Jean Shaw, after—relief. There, that was done.

And wondered if he had learned anything about illusions, since that time when he was twelve years old and first fell in love.

There were other feelings he had that he would save and look at later. All things considered, he felt pretty good. The movie star was a regular person. Underneath it all, she was. Except that she was never a regular person for very long.

She said, "You're good for me, Joe. Do you know that?"

Familiar. But he didn't know the next line, what he was supposed to say, and the words that came to mind were dumb. So he smiled a tired smile and patted her thigh, twice, and left his hand there.

She said, "I have a feeling you're the best thing that could happen to me, Joe."

Another one, so familiar. He sipped his Scotch. He looked at the ceiling and a scene from *Deadfall*, early in the picture, began to play in his mind. Jean Shaw saying to Robert Mitchum, "I have a feeling you're the best thing that could happen to me . . . Steve."

And Robert Mitchum, giving her that sleepy look, said . . .

11

THERE WAS THE Had a Piece Lately Bar. There was the Play House, the Turf Pub. There was Cheeky's. "Don't go in there without me," Cundo Rey said. "They liable to tear you to pieces, fight over you."

"Queers," Nobles said. "I love queers. Jesus."

There was Pier Park. Go in there at night and get anything you want, light up your head.

Nobles said, "Those guys have dough, huh, that sell it."

Cundo Rey said, "Yes, is true." Low behind the wheel of the Trans Am, holding the beast in as they cruised, he said, "But they got guns."

Nobles said, "Shit, who hasn't."

They cruised Collins Avenue and Washington, staying south of the Lincoln Road Mall, Nobles peering through smoked glass at the activity along the streets, all the little eating places and stores and bitty hotels, every one of the hotels with those metal chairs out front. Nobles said, "You ever see so many foreigners in your life?" After a few more blocks of sightseeing he said, "I think I'm having an idea."

Cundo Rey was learning not to say anything important unless he was sure Nobles was listening. Nobles didn't listen to very much. Sometimes Cundo wanted to tie him to a chair and press a knife against him and say, "Listen to me!" Shout it in the man's ear.

He said, "I thought you had an idea already."

"I got all kinds of 'em."

He was listening. Talk about him, he listened.

"The woman is still there," Cundo Rey said. "I saw her again. The guy is there, I think. I didn't see him good to know what he look like, but he's there. Why wouldn't he be, if he live there?"

"I'm waiting on the spirit to move me. It ain't the same as heisting cars, Jose. You gotta be in tune." Nose pressed to the side window. "You know what it's like down here, you read the signs? It's like being in a foreign country."

"You want to hear my idea?" Cundo Rey said.

"I want to get something to eat, partner. My tummy says it's time."

"Listen to my idea."

"Well, go ahead."

"Shoot the guy," Cundo Rey said. "You want to shoot him, shoot him. You want to shoot him in the back, get it over with, it's okay. You want to use a knife, you want to push him off a roof—any way you like, okay."

"That's some idea, chico."

"No, that's not the idea. That's to get him out of the way, so you can think of the woman."

"Watch the road. I don't want us having a accident."

"Okay, you want the woman? You know how to get her?"

"I'm certainly anxious to hear."

"You save her life."

"I save her life. Like out swimming?"

"Listen to me, all right? You listening?"

"Go ahead."

"She gets a call on the telephone or she gets a letter that say, *Pay me some money or I'm going to kill you*. A hundred thousand, two hundred thousand—how much has she got? You have to figure that out, how much you want to ask for. Okay, then you find the guy that sent her the letter and kill him. You her hero and she loves you. She say, take me, take my money, anything you want, baby, I'm yours."

"I find the guy sent her the letter . . ."

"Exactly."

"What guy?"

"Any guy. What difference does it make? Go in the La Playa Hotel, down the end of this street, is full of guys you can use. Set the guy up—don't you know anything? Make it look like he's the guy, see. Tell him to come to her room in the hotel—somebody want to buy some poppers from him. He goes up there, you shoot him. The woman say, 'Oh, my hero, you save my life.' She give you anything you want."

"That's how you do it, huh?"

"Listen, maybe even you use the guy you want to shoot anyway. Is it possible? If he's on drugs maybe?"

"Little shit, he's gonna need something for pain, anyhow."

"But the best part—"

"That's if I don't put him all the way outta his misery."

"You listening to me?"

"I thought you was through."

"The best part," Cundo Rey said, "see, the woman is so ascared she *pays* the money. She leaves it some place the letter tells her. You comprehend? See, *then* you shoot the guy. The guy is dead and the police, nobody, they look in the guy's place, but *nobody can find the money*. You like it?"

Nobles said, "You been reading the funnypaper, haven't you? I love to hear boogers like you talking about setting people up and shooting 'em—Lord have mercy, like you done it all and taken the midnight train more'n once, huh? Cundo, you little squirt, let's go get us something to eat."

A place called Casa Blanca looked fine to Cundo. Nobles said he didn't feel like eating Mex. Cundo tried to tell him it was a Cuban place, there was a big difference. Nobles said dago chow was dago chow. He picked Eli's Star Deli on Collins near Fourteenth, saying he had never ate any Jew food before, he'd like to give her a try.

So they went in. Nobles had a Henny Youngman on rye, said hey, boy, sucking his teeth, and ordered a Debbie Reynolds on pumpernickel. He told Cundo, watching him pick at his cole slaw, he ate like a goddamn owl. He picked—why didn't he *eat?*

Cundo Rey tried Nobles with, "See, they all in the yard, all around the embassy of Peru, all these thousands of people waiting to leave Havana when it first started, when Fidel decided okay. But they don't have no food. So you know what they ate? They ate a papaya tree, man. The whole tree. Then they ate a dog. You know what else they ate? They ate cats, man. They killed and ate the cats."

Nobles said, "Yeah?" admiring the thickness of his Debbie Reynolds, tucking in the fat ends of corned beef hanging out.

There was no way to make him sick, to make

him even stop to make a face. Look at him, sucking his teeth, waving at the man in the apron behind the meat counter, telling him he wanted a dish of potato salad.

Cundo Rey said, "Would you pay thirty dollars for a chicken? A cooked one?"

"Fried or roast chicken?"

"If you were starving?"

"Would I get biscuits and gravy?"

"At Mariel it was like a parking lot of boats waiting to leave, a thousand of them, it was so crowded with all kinds of boats. We sitting there for days and days, everybody running out of food and water. Now this boat is like a cantina comes to you. Is painted blue. The man on it offer you a cooked chicken for thirty dollars. Black beans, ten dollars a pound. Bottle of rum, eighty dollars."

"Where's this at?"

"I just *tole* you. Mariel. You never hear of Mariel?" Almost gritting his teeth, Christ, trying to talk to this guy. "The name don't mean nothing to you?"

"Yeah, I heard of it. You're talking about your boatlift back—when was that, three four years ago, brought all you boogers up here. Yeah, shit, I'd had me a boat I'd a gone down there made some dough."

"You know what it cost to leave Havana? What they charge people? Thousand dollars. More than that—some of them, they think you have the money, they charge you ten thousand dollars."

"It's what I'm saying. Get a old beat-up shrimper cheap, pack about five hundred of you squirts aboard—shit, you could retire, never work again long as you live."

"If you don't get fined, put in jail by the Coast Guard when you come back from there," Cundo Rey said. "Listen, they put twenty of us on a cruiser, a charter-boat, a nice one about ten meters with the name Bar*bar*a Rose on the back. From Key West."

"That's *Barb*'ra Rose, you spook."

"The captain, this tough guy, say he only suppose to pick up five people, that's all he was paid for. See, he got their names, given to him by their people in Miami. They came down to Key West to hire the boat. Thousands of people were doing that, to get their relatives. But see, the G-two man from Fidel say to the captain, you think so, but you going to take four for one, twenty people. See, so the rest of us on the boat, with this family that was paid for, we all from Cambinado. Brought to Mariel in a truck."

"What's Camba-nato?"

"Jesus Christ, it's the prison, Cambinado del Este. I told you I was in there—I picked up a suitcase in a hotel I find out belong to a Russian. I sell his big Russian shoes for ninety dollars—is how bad it is in Cuba, man—and a shirt, you know, that kind with the reptile on it. Where did the Russian get it? I don't know, but I sell it for fifty dollars. They give me life in prison."

"You poor little bugger, I thought they put you away for being queer."

"They put plenty of them in Cambinado, yes, and plenty of them come here, too."

"Let's go find some," Nobles said, "and kick the shit out of 'em." He licked mustard from his fingers. "Yeah, I wish I had me a boat that time."

"Not if you talk to the captain of the Bar*bara* Rose," Cundo said. "He look at twenty people crowded in his boat, no food, a hundred and ten miles of ocean and if he reaches here he's going to make five thousand dollars."

"I don't know if I'd get seasick or not. I doubt it, but I don't know. Biggest boat—you might not believe this—I ever been in's a canoe."

"You hear what I'm telling you? The captain, this tough guy, don't like it. So all he does is complain."

"No, I been in a bird-dog boat, too, up on the Steinhatchee. But it wasn't no bigger'n a canoe."

"Listen, the captain of the boat is complaining, he's saying, 'Oh, I could go to jail. I could be fined. I could lose my business, this sixty-thousand-dollar boat because of you people. Why did I come here? Look at the ocean, the choppiness all the way.' Man, all he did was complain."

"Yeah, but he took you to Key West, didn't he? And he made out pretty good."

"First we had to lock him up in the below part, while we waiting for the approval to leave."

"You did?"

"Then, it's time to go, he say it's a mutiny, he wants to leave the boat. No, first call the Coast Guard on the radio, then leave the boat. But then, finally, we leave."

"He saw the light."

"He saw the knife we got holding against his back. We leave Mariel, but still he complain, never shut up. He complain so much," Cundo Rey said, "we come to think, this is enough. So we throw him in the ocean and take his boat up to a place, it isn't too far from Homestead, and run it in the ground, in the sand. We have to walk, oh, about a hundred meters in the water to get to shore, but is okay, we make it."

Nobles said, "Well, you little squirt, you surprise the hell outta me."

Cundo was staring back at him, giving Nobles his nothing-to-it sleepy look.

"Why you think I was in Cambinado del Este?"

"You said you stole a suitcase, belonged to a Russian."

Cundo had Nobles' attention now, Nobles hooked, hanging on, wanting to know more.

"I took it out of his room, yes."

"And the Russian got a good look at you, huh?"

"Yes, of course. Why else would I have to kill him?"

The little Cuban dude kept staring right at him, playing with his earring in his girlish way, nose stuck up in the air like he was the prize.

It took Nobles a few moments to adjust—wait a sec here, what's this shit he's pulling?—and think to say, "Well, you shoot one of those fellas up here you don't even need a per-mit. Now you want me to tell you *my* idea? How me and you can make some quick bucks while we're waiting on the big one?"

12

HE WAS SMILING before Franny reached the porch with her sack of groceries and saw him, holding the door open.

She said, "What do you do, just hang out?"

"I'm locking up."

"This early?"

It was twenty past seven. He closed the glass door and set the lock, Franny inside now looking around the empty lobby, the last of daylight dull on the terrazzo floor that was like the floor, to LaBrava, of a government building. He turned on the cut glass chandelier and Franny looked up at it, not impressed.

"The place needs more than that, Joe."

"Color? Some paintings?"

She waited as he turned on lamps and came back. "It needs bodies, warm ones. I'm not knocking the old broads . . ."

"Bless their hearts," LaBrava said.

"Listen," Franny said, "I'm gonna be an old

broad myself someday, if I make it. But we could use a little more life around here. So far we've got you and me and the movie star and things haven't improved that much. Joe, there's a carton behind the desk with my name on it UPS dropped off. Would you mind grabbing it for me? I've got my hands full." She waited and said, "Let's see," when he brought it out and said, "Oh, shit, I was afraid of that. Another case of Bio-Energetic Breast Cream. Apply with a gentle, circular massaging motion to add bounce and resiliency." Into the elevator and up. "Do you know how much bounce and resiliency it's gonna add to the dugs around here? Contains collagen and extract of roses, but not nearly enough, I'm afraid, for South Beach bazooms. They've served their purpose, we hope. Right?" And down the hall to 204. "Maybe I can sell a couple bottles to your movie star . . . You're not talking, uh? I saw you having lunch, it looked like you were giving each other bites. When you were in there close, Joe, did you notice any little hairline scars?"

He said, "That's not nice," and was surprised he didn't feel protective or take offense. He was with Franny and they were old pals.

"But you looked, didn't you? Come on in. Don't lie to me, Joe." She went to the kitchen and he looked around the room, surprised at its lived-in appearance after only two days. It was all the color that gave the effect. The colors in the unframed canvases on the walls—bold abstract designs in shimmering gold, blues and tans—and the pillows in striking colors and shapes, on the floor and piled on the daybed she used as a sofa. Wicker chairs held stacks of books and magazines. Her voice remained with him as he looked around. "I'm jealous, if you want to know the truth." The venetian blinds were pulled up, out of the way, the evening blue in the windows faded, pale next to the paintings. "You asked me to lunch, sorta, and I see you over there with your movie star." There were cartons stenciled *SPRING SONG*, a portable television. She came out of the kitchen with white wine in stem glasses.

"Sit down and look at my Polaroids."

"You take pictures you don't fool around."

"I got about forty today. This bunch is sorta in order, starting at First Street and working up. But I don't like it around there; so I came up to Fifteenth, decided to work down, get the good stuff first." She sat next to him among pillows on the floor, their wine on a glass cocktail table. "I want consecutive views. Maybe do the whole street on a canvas about thirty feet wide. The face of South Beach."

He looked up at her paintings. "Like those?"

"That was my Jerusalem spacy period. I wanted

to get the spirit, you know, the energy of the sabras, but what stands out? The Mosque of Omar, the part that's gold. Now I'm into echo-deco, pink and green, flamingoes and palm trees, curvy corners, speed lines. I'm gonna pop my colors, get it looking so good you'll want to eat it. Hey, how about staying for dinner?"

"Maurice asked me."

"And that star of the silver screen—here she is, Jean Shaw! . . . She gonna be there? I'll get you yet, Joe."

"Will you sell me one of your new paintings?"

"I'll trade you one for that shot of Lana showing her depressing tits. That poor girl, I keep thinking about her."

LaBrava held up a Polaroid. "She lives right around the corner from here, the Chicken Shack." He began looking at storefronts and bars along the south end of Ocean Drive. The Turf Pub. The Play House, an old-time bar with photos of Jack Dempsey and Joe Louis on the walls. There were bikers outside this afternoon, in the Polaroid shots. He saw people he knew. A drunk named Wimpy. A pretty-boy Puerto Rican dealer named Guilli. He looked at figures standing, moving in suspended motion. Another one, in shadow, who seemed familiar and he studied the shot for several moments. Another figure, in the sunlit foreground, stood facing the camera with an arm raised.

"Is he waving at you?"

"Let's see. Yeah, I ran into him a couple of times."

"This the guy you were talking to, you were sitting on the wall?"

"You noticed me. I thought you'd be too busy with your movie star."

"Is it the same guy?"

"Yeah, very friendly. A little swishy maybe. He gets into a goof"—she snapped her fingers—"like that. It's hard to tell when he's serious."

"What's he do?"

"He sells real estate. What do you mean what does he *do?* He's looking for some kind of hustle, like all the rest of 'em. They deal or they break and enter."

He was looking at a hotel now on the north end of the street. "Here we are, the Elysian Fields."

He passed it to Franny and she said, "Ten million cockroaches down in the basement holding it up, straining their little backs."

He looked at several more hotels, then went back through the shots he'd already seen till he found the one he wanted, a view of the south end.

"There's a guy going in the Play House—you can only see part of him, he's right behind your friend."

"The guy in the doorway?"

"The other one. He's got on, it looks like a white silk shirt."

Franny said, "Oh, the lifeguard. Yeah, I remember him. I don't know if he's a lifeguard, but he sure is a hunk."

"Was he with your friend, the goof?"

"Gee, I don't know. Let me see those again." She went through the prints saying, "I think he's in one other one . . . Yeah, here. See the guy I was talking to? He's got his back turned, but I know it's him. Standing with the biker. That's the hunk right behind him."

"I didn't notice him in this one."

"No, the biker catches your eye. The beer gut."

"His shirt doesn't look white here. It looks silver."

"You're right. I remember now, it *is* silver. But it's not a shirt, it's a jacket, like the kind jocks wear. Yeah, I remember him now—real blond hair, the guy's a standout, Joe, you oughta shoot him."

"Not a bad idea," LaBrava said. "Where's the one you took of your friend? You were sitting on the wall."

"You don't miss a thing, do you?" Franny found it, handed it to him. "This one."

LaBrava studied the pose, the Cuban-looking guy fooling with his ear. "What's he doing?"

"I don't know—he uses his hands a lot. Let's see . . . Oh, yeah. He's playing with his earring. That's why I thought he might be gay, but you can't tell."

"What's his name?"

"I don't think he told me. He talked all the time, but really didn't say anything. Asked me where I live, if it's a nice place, would I like to have a drink with him—no, thank you—all that."

"Did he tell you, by any chance, he's Geraldo Rivera?"

Franny paused, about to raise her glass from the table. "Are you putting me on, Joe?"

"I just wondered. He looks familiar."

"You think he looks like Geraldo Rivera? He doesn't look anything like him. Joe, tell me what your game is? Are you a narc?"

Dinner at Maurice's, the picture gallery; fried sirloin and onions in candlelight with a '69 Margaux. Jean Shaw said, "If this is railroad-style it must be the Orient Express." Maurice said it was the pan, the cast-iron frying pan that was at least 100 years old he'd swiped out of a Florida East Coast caboose.

After dinner, sitting in the living room with cognac, Maurice said, "It's a fact, they go in threes. You want the latest ones? Arthur Godfrey, Meyer Lansky and Shepperd Strudwick, the actor. Jeanie, you remember him? Seventy-five when he died."

"Yeah, I read that," Jean said. "Died in New York. We did one picture together."

LaBrava knew the name, he could picture the actor and caught a glimpse of his snow-white hair, a scene in a cemetery. "Shepperd Strudwick, he was your husband in *Obituary*. Remember? We were trying to think who it was."

She looked surprised, or was trying to recall the picture. She said, "You're right, he was my husband."

"Shepperd Strudwick," LaBrava said. "You wanted to dump him. You got together with Henry Silva . . . Didn't you hire him to kill your husband?"

"Something like that."

"I know Henry Silva was the bad guy," LaBrava said. "I remember him because he was in a Western just about the same time and I saw it again in Independence. *The Tall T*, with Richard Boone and, what's his name, Randolph Scott. But I can't remember the good guy in *Obituary*."

"Arthur Godfrey's on the front page of every paper in the country," Maurice said. "Meyer Lansky gets two columns in the *New York Times*, he could a *bought* Godfrey. Arthur Godfrey gets a street named after him. What's Meyer Lansky get? A guy, I remember with the FBI, he said Meyer Lansky could a been chairman of the board of General Motors if he'd gone into legitimate business." Getting out of his La-Z-Boy, going over to a wall of photographs, Maurice said, "I'll tell you something. I bet

Meyer Lansky had a hell of a lot more fun in his life than Alfred P. Sloan or any of those GM guys."

LaBrava said to Jean, "I don't think the plan was to kill Shepperd Strudwick. It was something else. I remember he kept getting newspaper clippings that announced his death. To scare him . . ."

"Maier Suchowljansky, born in Russia," Maurice said, "that was Meyer Lansky's real name." He traced his finger over a photograph of the Miami Beach skyline.

LaBrava said, "I can't remember who played the good guy."

Jean said, "Maybe there weren't any good guys."

"Right here," Maurice said, "this is where he lived for years, the Imperial House. His wife's probably still there. That's Thelma, his second wife. She used to be a manicurist, some hotel in New York. Met Lansky, they fell in love . . ."

"Victor Mature," LaBrava said.

But Jean was watching Maurice. "Did you know Lansky?"

"Did I know him?" Maurice said, moving to another photograph. "MacFadden-Deauville . . . Lansky used to come in there. They *all* used to come in there. You know what I paid for a cabana, by the swimming pool, so I could run a horse book right there, for the guests? Woman'd send her kid over to place a bet. Forty-five grand for the season, three

months. And that doesn't count what I had to pay
S & G for the wire service, Christ."

"But you made money," Jean Shaw said.

"I did okay. Till Kefauver, the son of a bitch . . .
You know who this is? The bathing beauty. Sonja
Henie. We used to call her Sonja Heinie. Here's an-
other spot, the dog track, you used to see Meyer
Lansky once in a while. This spot here, the Play
House . . ."

LaBrava looked over.

". . . used to be big with the dog-trackers. Also
the fight fans. Fighter from I think Philly, Ice Cream
Joe Savino, he used to sell Nutty Buddies in the
park, he bought the place about twenty years ago. I
don't know what it's like now. It's all changed
down there."

"But you'd never move," Jean Shaw said, "would
you?"

"Why should I move? I own the joint—most of
it—I got the best beach in Florida . . ."

"Maury, if I'm actually harder pressed than I've
let on—"

"Harder pressed how?"

"If I get to the point I'm absolutely broke, would
you consider buying me out?"

"I told you, don't worry about money."

LaBrava listened. Watched Maurice come back
to his chair.

"Maury, you know me." She was sitting up in

the sofa now and seemed anxious. "I don't want to become dependent on anyone. I've always had my own money."

"This whole area right in here, from Sixth Street up," Maurice said, "we're in the National Register of Historic Places. That impresses buyers, Jeanie. We hold the developers off, the value can only shoot up."

"But if I *need* funds—"

"If we see values start to go down, that's different."

LaBrava listened. It didn't sound like Maurice, the old guy who loved the neighborhood and would never leave.

"Five years ago the Cardozo sold for seven hundred thousand," Maurice said. "Way they've fixed it up I bet they could sell it, double their investment. Almost double, anyway."

She was sitting back again, resigned. "What do you think the Della Robbia's worth?"

"Four and a half, five hundred, around in there. But listen," Maurice said to her, "I don't want you to ever worry about dough. You hear me?"

LaBrava listened. He heard Maurice talking like a man who had money, a lot of it.

They reached her door. She said, "How about a nightcap? Or whatever might appeal to you."

Was that from a movie?

Maybe it was the way she said it, the subtle business with the eyes. How did you tell what was real and what was from pictures?

She could surprise him, though—sitting close on the slip-covered sofa with their drinks, something to hold till they had to put them down—she could look vulnerable and come at him quietly with, "Tell me I'm pretty good for an old broad. I'll love you forever."

And his answer to that—like a knee jerk, reflecting his yes-ma'am upbringing—"Come on. What're you, about three or four years older than I am?"

She said, looking him right in the eye, "Joe, I'm forty-six years old and there's not a damn thing I can do about it."

Shoving numbers into his mind that would have made her a teen-aged bride in *Obituary* in the black dress, coming onto Henry Silva, leading him on, the two of them conspiring to sting her husband.

He pushed the numbers out of his mind by thinking: She isn't any age. She's Jean Shaw. And by looking at her face, at the little puff circles under her brown eyes that he loved to look at. If she wanted to play, what was wrong with that? Play. Maybe he could've been in the movies too if he hadn't gone to Beltsville, Maryland, learned how to shoot guns and taken an oath to protect the lives of

Presidents and important people. Bob Hope, little Sammy Davis, Jr., Fidel Castro . . .

He said, "Jean."

Within the moment her eyes became misty, smiling but a little sad. "That's the first time you've said my name. Will you say it again?"

"Jean?"

"Yes, Joe."

"You're gonna have to be very careful."

"I am?"

"I have a feeling you might be in danger."

She said, "You're serious, aren't you?"

Yes, he was serious. He was trying to be. But now even his own words were beginning to sound like lines from a movie.

He said, "Jean. Let's go to bed."

That sounded real.

She said, "I'm hard to get, Joe. All you have to do is ask me."

That didn't sound real.

13

I HAVE A FEELING you might be in danger. All the next day he would hear himself saying it.

The tone was all right, not overdone, and he believed it was true, she *was* in danger. But it didn't sound right. Because people who were into danger on an everyday basis didn't talk like that, they didn't use the word.

He remembered the guy who wholesaled funny twenties standing up in federal court hand at his throat—the judge banging his gavel—and saying, "Joe, Jesus Christ, all my life I been in shit up to here, but never, *never* would I a thought you'd be the one'd push me under."

The Miami street cop assigned to paperwork, typing memos, said, "I gotta get back out there, put it on the line with the fuckups, or I'm gonna be sniffing whiteout for my jags." A week later the Miami street cop, still doing paperwork, said, "Whatever happened to splitting heads, kicking the shit outta assholes? For the fun of it. Is the game still going on or what?"

The Dade-Metro squad-car cop, drinking Pepsi out of a paper cup, said, "The guy had the piece, he was pressing it against me—*into* me, right here, under the rib. He pulls the trigger, click. He pulls the trigger, click. He pulls the fucking trigger and I come around like this, with the elbow, hard as I can. The piece goes off—no click this time—the fucking piece goes off and smokes the guy standing at the bar next to me with his hands up. We get him for attempted, we get him for second degree, both." The Dade-Metro squad-car cop said, "Did you know you rub a plastic-coated paper cup like this on the inside of the windshield it sounds just like a cricket? Listen."

Buck Torres said, "Who is this guy? Do we know him from somewhere before?"

"That's what I want to know," LaBrava said, "if he has a before. Put him on the computer and we'll find out. But I can't believe he hasn't."

Buck Torres had been a uniformed Dade-Metro cop the time LaBrava was assigned to the Miami field office, United States Secret Service, taking pictures at work and play. Torres had showed him life on the street. They had finished off a few hundred beers together, too. Sgt. Hector Torres had transferred and was now supervisor of Crimes Against Persons, Miami Beach Police. He always wore a coat and tie—his men did too—because he would never speak to the relatives of a deceased person in shirt-sleeves.

They left the Detective Bureau—the one-story, windowless, stucco annex on the corner of First and Meridian—walked across Meridian to MBPD headquarters—the official-looking brick building with the flag—punched "Richard Nobles" into the National Crime Information Center computer and drew a blank.

"So, he's a good boy," Torres said.

"No, he isn't," LaBrava said, "he's a sneaky kind of asshole who likes to come down on people." Hearing himself falling back into police patter.

"Yeah, but he hasn't done nothing."

"I think they pulled his sheet, gave him a clean bill. He was a federal snitch. You gotta have a diseased mind or your balls in somebody's hand to do that kind of work. Check the DEA in Jacksonville when you aren't doing anything."

Torres said, "Should I care about this guy or what? What do you want me to do?"

"Nothing. I'm gonna do it."

"Let me see—then you want me to say nice things about you, you get picked up for impersonating a police officer."

"Or pick the guy up, maybe. You still have

'Strolling without a destination' on the statutes? In case he sees me and becomes irritated. See, what I'm doing, I'm trying to stay ahead of the guy, be ready for it when it comes."

"Be ready for what?"

"I don't know, but all my training and experience tells me something's gonna happen."

"Your experience—you guarded Mrs. Truman."

"That's right, and nothing happened to her, did it?"

"You're serious?"

"I'm serious."

"Then you better tell me more about the sneaky asshole," Torres said.

Paco Boza said a wheelchair was better than a bike. You could do wheelies, all this shit, also build up your arms, give you nice shoulders, the girls go for that. Also, sometimes, it was safer to be sitting in a wheelchair than to be standing up with some people. They respect you sitting in a wheelchair, yes, and some people were even afraid, like they didn't want to look at you. He loved his Eastern Airlines wheelchair.

Though it didn't seem to be doing much for his arms and shoulders. His arms became skinny cords as he collapsed the chair and strained to carry it up two steps from the sidewalk to the hotel porch. He said he wanted to leave it where it would be safe. He was going to Hialeah for a day or two.

"I do you a favor," Paco said, "you do me one. Okay?" Grinning now, being sly.

LaBrava caught on right away and grinned back at him. "You saw him, didn't you?"

"Man, you can't miss him. He's twice as big as anyone I ever see before. Has that hair . . ."

"Let's go inside," LaBrava said. He took the wheelchair and Paco followed him across the lobby to the main desk. LaBrava went around behind it, put the wheelchair down, telling Paco it would be safe here, and brought out a manila envelope sleeve from a shelf underneath.

"Hey, my pictures."

"I know why you fell in love with Lana."

"That broad, I been looking all over for *her* too." He brought three eleven-by-fourteen prints out of the envelope, laid them on the marble countertop and began to grin. "Look at her, showing herself."

"Where'd you see the guy?"

"I saw him on Collins Avenue, I saw him on Washington Avenue. You can't miss him."

"He likes to be seen," LaBrava said. "He's the Silver Kid."

"No shit, is he? . . . I like this one of me. It's cute, uh? You like it?"

"One of my favorites. You talk to anyone at the Play House?"

"Yeah. Maybe he was in there, they don't know him. But that isn't the place. The place you want to go—a guy I talk to, he say check the Paramount Hotel on Collins."

"Who was that?"

"The guy? Name is Guilli, a Puerto Rican guy. He's ascared all the time, but he's okay, you can believe him."

"I know who you mean. So you went over there?"

"Yeah, but I didn't see him."

"Where's the Paramount?"

"Is up around Twentieth. I saw him on Washington, I saw him on Collins Avenue. Two days now. Three days—man, where does the time go?"

"You doing all right?"

"Sure, I make it. You kidding? Lana is going to like this one, showing herself. I hear she went over to Hialeah, see her mother. But I don't know where her mother lives no more, I got to look for her. Man, they give you a lot of trouble."

"Dames are always pulling a switch on you," LaBrava said.

Paco said, "What?"

"Something a guy in a movie said."

"He did?"

"Listen—how about when you saw the guy, what was he doing?"

"Nothing. Walking by the street. Go in a store, come out. Go in another store, come out."

"You're not talking about drugstores."

"No, regular stores, man. Grocery store—or he go in a hotel, he come out."

"Has he bought any stuff off anybody?"

"Nobody told me he did. Guilli thinks he's a cop. But you know Guilli. Guilli thinks the other guy is a cop too, guy drives the black Pontiac Trans Am. Shit, Guilli thinks everybody he don't know is a cop."

"What other guy? Cubano?"

"Yeah—how do you know that?"

"I might've seen him. He's got a black Trans Am, uh?"

"Yeah, he stay at the La Playa Hotel. You know it? Down the end of Collins Avenue. There's a guy live there—you know a guy name David Vega?"

"I don't think so."

"David Vega told Guilli he *knows* the guy, from the boat-lift. He told him, he's not a cop, man, he's a *Marielito*. He say the guy was with some convicts they put on a boat, from a prison. He say he remember him because the guy wore a safety pin in his ear."

"That mean something?"

"Like a punk. You know, be in fashion. Now David Vega say he's got a gold one, a real one he wears."

"What's his name?"

"He don't know his name, he jus' remember him."

"Staying at the La Playa."

"Listen, the first night he come there a guy live there was ripped off. The guy come back from the pier from doing some business, he got hit on the head and somebody robbed him, took four hundred dollars."

"That happens all the time there, doesn't it?"

"Yes, of course, with guys like this guy. Tha's what I mean."

"Why does Guilli put the Cubano with the big blond guy?"

"He saw them talking, that's all, it don't mean nothing. But maybe. Who knows?"

"I'll see you in a couple days, uh?"

"Yeah, I have to go to Hialeah. Talk to Guilli or David Vega if you want to know something. Also, you want to, you can drive my wheelchair. I think you like it."

There weren't too many places had swimming pools around here. A pink and green place called the Sharon Apartment-Motel on Meridian and

Twelfth, across from Flamingo Park, had a little bitty one out front, but nobody was in it. Nice-looking pool, too, real clean, sparkling with chlorine. There hadn't been anybody in it the other time either. This was Nobles' second visit to the Sharon Apartment-Motel office, the important one.

He said to Mr. Fisk, little cigar-smoking Jew that owned the place, "Well sir, you think over my deal?"

Mr. Fisk had skinny arms and round shoulders but a big stomach and was darker than many niggers Nobles had seen in his life. Mr. Fisk said, "Go out and turn left and keep walking. What do you come to, it don't even take you ten minutes and I'm talking about on foot?"

Nobles said, "Let's see. Go out and turn left—"

"The Miami Beach Police station," Mr. Fisk said. "Look, right here I got it written down. I even got it in my head written. Six-seven-three, seven-nine-oh-oh. I pick up the phone they're here before I can say goodby even."

"Yeah, but see, by then it's already done." Nobles took out his wallet and held it open for Mr. Fisk. "What's 'at say there, under where it says Star Security?"

Mr. Fisk leaned against the counter separating them, concentrating on the open wallet. " 'Private protection means crime prevention.' Is that suppose to be clever? I got a son in the advertising game could write you a better slogan than that one, free."

"See, prevention," Nobles said, "that's what you have to think about here. See, you call the cops after something's done to you, right? Well, you call us before it happens and it don't."

Mr. Fisk said, "Wait a minute, please. Tell me what you're not gonna let happen the cops one minute away from here down the street would?"

"Well, shit, they could mess your place up all different kinds a ways."

"Who is they?"

"Well, shit, you got enough dagos living around here. You got your dagos, your dope junkies, your queers, this place's full a all kinds. But, see, five hundred dollars in advance, you don't have to worry about 'em none. It gives you protection all year, guaranteed."

"Guaranteed," Mr. Fisk said. "I always like a guarantee. But tell me what in particular could happen to my place if I don't buy your protection?"

"Well," Nobles said, "let's see . . ."

Surveillance, the way LaBrava remembered it from his Miami field-office days, was sitting across the street from a high-rise on Brickell Avenue or some place like the Mutiny or the Bamboo Lounge on South Dixie. Sitting in a car that was as close as you could come to a plain brown wrapper with wheels, so unnoticeable around those places it was hard to miss. The afternoon the wholesaler came out of the Bamboo, walked across the street to the car and said, "Joe, the lady and I're going out to Calder, catch the last couple races, then we're going up to Palm Beach, have a nice dinner at Chuck & Harold's with some friends . . ." it was time to move on, to Independence, as it turned out . . .

But not anywhere near the kind of independence he was into now—protecting his movie star— standing in some bushes on the east side of Flamingo Park, catching Richard Nobles with a long lens coming out of a motel named Sharon:

Richard Nobles walking over to the swimming pool. *Snick.* Nobles turning to say something to the little guy standing in front of the office. *Snick.* The little guy with his hands on his hips, feisty pose, extending his arm now to point at Nobles walking away. LaBrava saying, eye pressed to the Leica, "I see him." *Snick.*

The guy turned to his office, then turned back again and yelled something at Nobles. Nobles stopped. He looked as though he might go back, and the little guy ran inside the office.

LaBrava got in Maurice's car, crept along behind Nobles over Twelfth Street to Collins and parked again, got out with his camera and followed Nobles up Collins. Silver jacket and golden hair—you didn't have to worry about keeping him in sight. There he was, like he was lit up. The Silver Kid. The guy never looked around either; never even glanced over his shoulder.

From the east side of Collins, LaBrava shot him going into Eli's Star Deli. About fifteen minutes later he got him coming out. He got him going in and coming out of a dry cleaner's. Finally he got him going into the Paramount Hotel, just above Twentieth Street. LaBrava hung around about an hour. The bad part. But better than sitting in a car full of empty styrofoam cups and crunched-up paper bags. At least he could move around.

He walked to the taxi stand on the southwest corner of Collins and Twenty-first and waited nearly twenty minutes for a red Central cab to arrive with the Nigerian, Johnbull Obasanjo behind the wheel, scowling.

"What's the matter?"

"Notting is the mattah." With an accent that was both tribal and British.

"You always look pissed off."

"It is the way you see, not the way I look."

There were parallel welts across his broad face, tracks laid by a knife decades ago that Johnbull, second cousin of a Nigerian general, told were Yoruba markings of the warrior caste. Why not?

"You're disappointed."

"Ah," Johnbull said. "Perhaps what you see is disdain."

"Perhaps."

"Mon say to me, the fare, 'Did you learn your English here?' No, in Lagos, when I am a boy. 'Oh,' he say, 'and where is Lagos?'" Johnbull's twin knife scars became vivid, underlining the white-hot pissed-off expression in his eyes. "When I am a child in school, for God sake, I can draw a map of the United States. I can show you where Miami is, I can show you where Cleveland is. But nobody here, they don't know where Lagos is, where you get the second most oil from any place in the world."

"I'm looking for a guy," LaBrava said, "who doesn't know where his ass is. Big blond guy staying at the Paramount." LaBrava handed Johnbull a ten-dollar bill. "Watch for a black Pontiac Trans Am, late model. If it picks up the big blond guy, follow it. Then give me a call. I'll pay for whatever time you spend on it. If you have to leave, tell the other guys, I'll give 'em the same deal."

"I want a picture for my mother," Johnbull said. "This one smiling."

"Let's see a big one," LaBrava said. He raised his camera and shot the Nigerian framed in his window, grinning white and gold.

* * *

The woman in the office of the Sharon Apartment-Motel said, "Tell me you arrested him and you want Mr. Fisk to take a look it's the same one . . . Nuh, no such luck, uh? Oh well. Mr. Fisk is lying down he's so upset. Soon as the other police left he had to lie down. You know what he's worried you don't find him? What if he comes back?"

LaBrava waited.

Mr. Fisk came in, wary.

"You don't look like no cop to me, would wear a shirt like that. With a camera. What is this, you're on your vacation?"

LaBrava said, "We like to take a few pictures when we process a crime scene, Mr. Fisk. You by any chance speak to Sgt. Torres?"

"I don't know—they come in a car with the lights. You know how long it took them? Twenty-five minutes."

"See, they make out a U.C.R.," LaBrava said. "That's a Uniformed Crime Report. Then the Detective Bureau follows up. Did he give you his name? The big blond guy?"

"He showed me a gold star and the name of the company, something that says 'Private protection means crime prevention,' and his name printed there, typed. But I don't remember it. I should a wrote it down."

"What'd he say exactly?"

"I told the two other cops were here. I told them all that."

"In case you might've left out something important."

"Okay, he wants to sell me protection. What else is new? I tell him I don't need any, I tell him I've got the Miami Beach Police Department one minute away from here down the street. That's how dumb I am. I don't know it takes you to drive from First Street to Twelfth Street in a police squad car full speed with the siren and everything twenty-five minutes."

"How much did he ask for?"

"Five hundred. In advance, of course. He says for a year's protection guaranteed. Oh yeah? Next month he's back for another five hundred. I grow up, live forty years of my life in Crown Heights, I don't know this kind of business goes on?"

"He threaten you? Say what would happen if you didn't pay?"

"Get ready. You want me to tell you exactly what he said?"

Mrs. Fisk said, "We can't prove he said *any*thing. The policeman was here said unless the other places he did the same thing, we all speak up, then maybe."

"Tell me what he said, Mr. Fisk."

"He gives me the pitch, all this protection I'm

suppose to get for five hundred dollars. I ask him, against what? What could happen to my place? The guy says, 'Well, let's see.' He goes over to the door, looks out. He says, word for word, 'Somebody could come around and take a dump in your swimming pool every night.' Wait. Listen. Then he says, 'That wouldn't be too nice, would it?' Not, he's gonna smash all my windows, he's gonna throw a bomb in, blow the place up, like they used to do it. Or even threaten to break my legs. No, this big blond-hair son of a bitch is gonna poo poo in my swimming pool."

LaBrava shook his head. After a few moments he said, "Would you step outside here, Mr. Fisk? Thank you. Over by the pool more. Yeah, right there. Now give me kind of a pissed-off, defiant look. If you would, please."

"Then the cop comes," Mr. Fisk said, "and what does the cop do? He takes my picture. I'm telling you . . ."

LaBrava passed up dinner with Jean and Maurice to spend the evening in the darkroom, watching Nobles appear in trays of liquid, pleased with the shots because they were clear and in focus. He liked the ones where there was motion in the foreground, out of focus, the top of a car as it passed, in contrast to the clarity of Nobles' confident, all-

American boyish face. Hometown hero—the hair, the toothpick, the hint of swagger in the set of silver-clad shoulders. What an asshole.

How did they get so sure of themselves, these guys, without knowing anything? Like people who have read one book.

He hung Nobles up to dry and spent the next two and a half hours with Jean Shaw, in her apartment.

They did talk about Nobles, recapping, and he told her what Nobles had been up to and that he'd have prints in the morning, confirmation. She seemed fascinated. She sat facing him on the sofa and asked questions, probed for details, listening intently. Yes, it was fascinating—she used the word—that he could follow someone so closely, document the guy's activity, and not be detected. She asked him about the Secret Service and contin-ued to listen until—

In one of her pictures, she said, there was a sub-plot about counterfeiting and they began to talk about movies and she told him what she hated most about making pictures: the two-shot close-up face to face with an actor she often couldn't stand. Nowhere but in the movies did people stand so close when they talked—and you'd get these actors with foul morning breath or reeking of booze—the two of them on the sofa getting closer and closer and that was fine, with confident breaths, good smells, aware of nature's horny scent in there,

LaBrava ready once again to try for that over-whelming experience. He told her he wanted to see one of her pictures with her. She said she would get one; she was going home tomorrow to pick up some clothes, a few things, she'd bring the tapes. He said he would like to drive her, see her place.

She said, "Spend the night with me. Tonight."

That sounded good.

She got a wistful look and said, "I need you, Joe."

And that didn't sound so good because—there it was again—it sounded familiar, and he had to tell himself that playing was okay, they were just having some fun. Except that she made it sound serious.

She said, "Hold me."

He did, he held her tight and she felt good. Before she felt too good he sneaked a look at his watch.

LaBrava was in his own bed when Johnbull Obasanjo phoned a few minutes past 2:00 A.M.

"I have been trying to call you, you never at home."

"I'm sorry."

"You tell me you want information—"

"I apologize."

"I accept it," the Nigerian said. "Now, you want to know where they went to in the black Pontiac sportcar, I tell you. They went to a place call Cheeky's. I know a man name Chike, he is an Ibo, but not a bad man. I don't believe this place, though, is of the Ibo. I believe it is for men who have pleasure in dressing as women. So they go in there."

"You saw the driver of the Pontiac."

"Yes, a Cuban man."

"What'd he look like?"

"I told you, a Cuban man. That's what he look like."

LaBrava wondered if Nigerians told jokes and if they were funny. "Was there anything different about him?"

"My friend, you have to be different to go in there. I told you that already."

"I apologize." Maybe they had a sense of humor if you got to know them. "You didn't by any chance get the license number of the Pontiac."

Johnbull Obasanjo said, "You have a pen? You have the paper, something to write on when you ask such a question?"

LaBrava turned the light on and got out of bed. Fucking Nigerian. The guy delivered, though, didn't he?

Five and a half hours later, still in bed, the phone again lay on the pillow against his face. He raised it slightly as Buck Torres came back on with his NCIC computer report.

"Cundo Rey. That's the owner's name. You got a pencil, I'll spell it."

"Please do."

"You ready?"

"Spell the goddamn name, will you?"

Torres spelled it. "You're a bitch in the morning, aren't you?"

"What else?"

"Cuban National, came from Mariel during the boat-lift but wasn't processed. Arraigned for transporting a stolen motor vehicle, Volusia County, that's up north, no conviction. Assigned to Chatahoochee for psychiatric evaluation. He disappeared from there."

"Is there a warrant out on him?"

"Nobody wants him, figuring we got enough Cubans."

"You got his picture?"

"I can get it. Take a couple of days," Torres said. "He looks harmless to me. Refugee, fell in with some bad *hombres*."

"Get the picture," LaBrava said. "I think you're gonna need it."

14

NOBLES HAD HALF OF a Debbie Reynolds to finish and a few half-done fries left. Little Eli could make a sandwich, *damn*, but he couldn't deep-fry worth shit. Nobles said to Cundo Rey, who was playing with his coffee spoon, "You do any good last night?" and took a big bite of his Debbie.

"I don't make so much in that place as a Ladies' Night place. See, they know I don't fuck the same way they do. I mean—you know what I mean."

"That's good to hear," Nobles said. "Jesus, but that place is scary, you know it? All them queers dressed up like girls. I had to get outta there."

"I thought you might see one you like to take out and rob him. That was a good idea."

"Yeah, but I don't believe I could touch the fucker to do it. I mean they are scary. How'd you make out?"

"I made a couple hundred. Man, I need money. I have to go home and get some."

"Pretty soon." Nobles shoved the rest of the Debbie Reynolds into his mouth. "You ready?"

"What?"

Nobles chewed and chewed. "I said, you *ready?* Get the wax outta your ears."

"I was ready before you start eating."

"Go on out. I don't want Eli to see us together when I talk to him."

"He already see us together, now."

"Yeah, but he won't remember you. All you boogers look alike. Go on outside, wait in the car."

"It isn't going to work."

"Go on. Scat."

Nobles walked over to the counter, laid his check on the rubber pad next to the cash register, fished a few toothpicks out of the tray. The man that owned the place, little Eli, came over wiping his hands on his apron, sort of a worried look on his face, or sad. The Jew should shave and clean hisself up, Nobles thought, he'd feel better.

"Well, how we doing today, partner?"

Eli didn't answer him, eyes cast down. He rang up the bill, came back to the rubber pad and now had to look up, there was no money on the counter.

"Put her on account," Nobles said, "and tell me what you think of the deal I offered you."

The guy seemed afraid to move or speak.

"Hey, wake up."

What was the matter with him? He looked sickly. Refused to say a word, nod his head or blink. Nobles watched him turn to the counter behind him, move some stuff out of the way, a telephone book—the hell was he doing? The guy came back around holding up a photograph, holding it in front of his face, so that Nobles was looking at the picture and the guy's knuckles bony white pointing at him.

"Where'n the hell'd you get that?"

A shiny black and white shot of Richard Nobles coming out of Eli's Star Deli: so sharp and clear you could see the toothpick in the corner of his mouth.

The guy's shaky voice behind the shaky photograph was telling him to get out ". . . and don't ever come back again or I call the cops!"

It was getting scary. Sitting in the Trans Am with Cundo, hidden from humanity and street glare behind smoked glass, Nobles said, "You believe it?"

"I tole you it wasn't going to work."

"Guy holds it up—same kind of pitcher. That little fucker with the swimming pool, now this guy. What in the hell's going on? Somebody taking my pitcher . . . I gotta try another place. There's that dry cleaner up the street."

"I tole you," Cundo Rey said.

"You *told* me? What? You told me you saw this guy following me with a camera?"

"I tole you it wasn't going to work."

"You gonna keep saying that?"

"You want to work that kind of deal," Cundo Rey said, "you break the guy's window *first*, then you go in, sell him the protection. I tole you, it's how to do it."

"Yeah, well I want to know who's taking my pitcher."

"They hire somebody. They got more protection than you think."

"No, these people—what do you think they call 'em Jews for? They Jew you down, don't spend a dime less they have to. They ain't gonna hire a guy take pitchers."

"It couldn't be that girl," Cundo said. "No, it wouldn't be her."

"What girl?"

"She live over at the hotel where the woman is."

Nobles was half listening, staring at people going by on the sidewalk. Cundo began tapping his ring on the steering wheel and Nobles turned to him. "Cut it out."

"What am I doing?"

"I'm thinking." After a moment he said, "Oh, man, I don't know what's wrong with me. The dink I been looking for for Christ sake's a photographer. With a newspaper."

"You haven't seen him, have you?"

"I haven't seen *him*, but shit, he's seen *me*. It's got to be him."

"How could he know you down here?"

"He's *seen* us. How else you think, for Christ sake. He's seen *me*, anyway. Goddamn it."

"So, what difference does it make? Let's go see him, take his pictures away from him." Cundo paused, watching Nobles staring out the window. "What are you worried about? Take his pictures. Go in there, take the picture from the Debbie Reynolds guy. Get the picture from the swimming pool guy. Get all the pictures he has."

Nobles said, "I don't know . . ."

Cundo studied him. This Richard, most of the time you could read his face. Right now, though, it was empty, like he had been smoking some of the sky blue reefer from Santa Marta that paralyzed you, made you numb. Cundo said, "You know something? I haven' seen you hit anybody. Man, I even haven' seen you break anything. How come you not get mad?" He turned the ignition key, heard the engine come instantly awake, rumble and pop its muscle. He turned the radio on and heavy riffs filled the car, everything working now.

Cundo said, "Okay. We go see the guy."

*　　*　　*

LaBrava had taken the new issue of *Aperture* from his mail slot, opened it as he turned and got as far as the registration desk, held by a series of color photographs made by a painter, a fine artist, who shot into mirrors and got startling effects.

He had placed an envelope sleeve on the countertop. He laid the magazine over it, resting his arms on the edge, on cool marble, and wandered to the text to read that a still picture is more powerful than a motion picture, more memorable, that images from movies that stay with you are reasonably still . . . He would agree with that. Because the film pictures of Jean Shaw in his mind all seemed to be stills. Jean Shaw in black and white giving—he caught a glimpse of her giving Victor Mature the look.

Then saw her in muted color, a skirt, a top with a narrow belt, a straw bag, the real-life Jean Shaw coming off the elevator, not smiling, now trying on a faint smile as she saw him. She said, "What time did you leave?"

"It was about one-thirty. I couldn't sleep."

"Did you think about waking me up?" With almost a sly, bedroom look. But after the fact in a hotel lobby the next morning. He wondered what would have happened if he'd started in again, Jean drowsy, half awake, maybe less mechanical.

"I think the reason I couldn't sleep, I was expecting a phone call." And knew immediately it was the wrong thing to say. Giving her second billing.

She said, "Oh." Any hint of a sly look gone.

"It was important. The guy called about two."

She said, "Maurice wants to take me. You don't have to bother." Not icy, but not warm, either.

"I'd be glad to help."

"I'm just going to get a few things. Clothes, mostly. Maurice insists. I think he wants to talk." Her tone beginning to lose its stiffness. "What about the pictures?"

"Right here." He moved the magazine aside, brought the black and white eight-by-tens of Nobles out of the manila sleeve and laid them on the counter facing Jean.

She said, resigned, "Yeah, that's Richie. Are you sure he didn't see you?"

"I used a telephoto from across the street. The blur along the edge, that's a car going by. This one, I'm in a park across from the motel, the Sharon. No, I'm pretty sure he didn't see me."

Jean's eyes remained on the photos. "You're positive he's doing something illegal."

"He doesn't work for Star Security anymore," LaBrava said, "so he has nothing legal to sell. Even if he was still with them, they're not licensed in Dade County."

"But there's no way to prove he's doing something illegal, is that it?"

"Not till they catch him with a stink bomb, or

breaking windows. Then they could get him for malicious destruction. But he's fooling with extortion. That's a tough one to prove."

Jean said, "If Richie knew you had these—" She shook her head slowly and seemed almost to smile.

"How about if he thought the police had a set? Would that shake him up?"

She looked at LaBrava, brown eyes wide for a moment. "Are they after him?"

"I haven't given them the pictures yet, but I think it might be a good idea. Before somebody gets hurt." He gathered the photos together, slipped them in the envelope. "So that's your friend Richie Nobles."

"The all-American boy," Jean said. "Can I have them?" When LaBrava hesitated she said, "For my own protection. In case Richie ever comes around again." She looked over as they heard the elevator land, the door open. "Let's tell Maury about it later, okay? Or I'll never get out of here."

Maurice was taking off his nubby silk jacket as he crossed the lobby. He wore a yellow sport shirt with long collar points, the top button fastened. "You think I need a coat?"

Jean picked up the envelope with her straw bag. "If it makes you happy."

"Nah, we're not going anyplace, are we?" He folded the jacket inside out and laid it on the counter.

"Joe, lock it in the closet for me, will you? We're going up to Boca, get a few things of Jeanie's."

LaBrava said to her, "What about the tapes? You said you have a couple of your movies?"

She hesitated. "You really want to see them?"

"You kidding? With the star?"

"If you promise you won't fall asleep. We'll have to bring the VCR and plug it into Maury's TV."

Maurice said, "What? What're we talking about?"

"Jean's movies," LaBrava said and looked at her again. "What ones do you have?"

"Just the two available on tape. *Shadowland* and *Let It Ride*."

"I can hardly wait," LaBrava said, not sure if he had seen either of them. "It's been a long time."

They'd crept past the Della Robbia, past the Cardozo to park across the street from the Cavalier, on the beach side of Ocean Drive. Nobles had curled his size into an almost fetal position in the front seat, face pressed against the inside edge of the backrest so he could stare out that smoky rear window and see the Della Robbia, the bunch of old ladies sitting lined up on the porch.

Cundo Rey said, "Man, we don't have no air. How about I open it just a little?"

Nobles didn't answer him. In a moment a draft of salt air touched his face and it felt pretty good. He reached behind him and opened the window on his side a few inches. Yeah, that was better.

"I don't want to see her just yet. Till we're ready. You understand?"

Cundo said, "Sure," even though he didn't. Why ask him questions? He was acting strange.

"What I'm getting at, I walk in there I'm liable to see her. Or be seen *with* her, I mean. You follow me? Best we wait for him to come out."

They had been parked here more than a half hour. Cundo couldn't believe it, Nobles becoming cautious, not wanting to go in there and get the guy's pictures, take the guy in his hands, throw him out a window if it was high enough. He would like to have a look at this guy in the light, see him good. The guy didn't seem to scare Nobles, no, but seeing the pictures of himself had changed him; he didn't seem to know what he was doing.

Cundo said, "If the guy works, then why would he be there?" Nobles didn't answer. He didn't know anything, so why ask him?

Cundo said, "I don't like that place I'm living, La Playa. I'm going to move." The reason they were at different hotels, Nobles had said they shouldn't be seen together too much. He had asked why and Nobles had said, because. That was his answer. Because.

"I'm going to find a good place, move my things down from West Palm. What about you? You want to move your things?"

Nobles wasn't listening, he was pushing up straight against the backrest, stretching his neck, saying, "Jesus Christ, there she is."

Cundo had to press his face against the side window, his neck twisted, to see. He said, "Tha's the movie star? Man, she look pretty nice. Who's that old guy?"

"Must be the one she's staying with, one picked her up." Nobles watched them cross the street like they were going to the beach in their good clothes, but now they stopped. He watched the old man pull open a car door and get in while Jean Shaw went around to the other side. They were going someplace. Just her and the old man.

As soon as Nobles had his idea he said, "They go by, you get out. I'm own take the car, meet you later on."

"You want to take *this*?"

Nobles' head turned with the Mercedes going past them. "Okay, get out."

"Man, this is my *car*."

Nobles said, "You little booger—" Got that far.

Cundo saw the look and stepped out of the car saying, "Sure, please take it." Stood in the road saying, "Go with God," and watched until the insane creature from the Big Scrub turned left on Fifteenth Street.

Franny came out of the ocean like a commercial, body glistening in two strips of mauve material, Coppertone clean with an easy stride, letting her hips move on their own as she came up on the beach. It was empty in front of her, all the way to the park.

Where was Joe LaBrava when she needed him?

He was across the street, coming out of the Della Robbia with Paco's wheelchair, sitting in it now on the sidewalk, trying it out, talking to the old ladies leaning out of their chairs, reassuring them. By the time Franny reached the grass, he was wearing a plain, beachcomber Panama with a curvy, shapeless brim, a camera hanging from his neck, waving to the ladies as he wheeled off.

Franny yelled his name. He looked over, made an awkward turn and stroked his wheels across the street.

"How do you get up curbs?"

She helped him, came around in front of him again and he was aiming a Nikon at her. *Snick*.

"I wasn't ready."

"Yes, you were. You look good. You're the first girl in a bathing suit I've ever shot."

"None of that commercial stuff."

He gave a shrug. "Maybe there's a way to do it."

"The bathing suit in contrast to something. How about sitting on a TV set?"

He smiled and she watched him reach around to the camera bag hanging behind him, watched him bring it to his lap, the hat brim hiding his face as he snapped off the wide-angle lens, put on a long one and aimed the camera down a line of palm trees to a group of elderly people sitting on a bench.

"What're you gonna shoot, the regulars?"

"Get 'em when they aren't looking."

"Why don't you come up after . . . do me."

She was serious or she was having fun. Either way, it didn't matter.

He said, "I don't have any color."

She said, "Whatever you want to use, Joe, is fine with me."

He remembered sore feet from all that standing around steely-eyed in front of hotels and at rallies and fund-raisers, protecting important people. A numb butt from sitting in cars for days doing surveillance. Tired eyes from reading presidential pen-pal letters. Not even counting protective-detail duty in Mrs. Truman's living room, a life that sounded exciting was 80 percent boredom.

It had certainly taken a turn lately.

He cruised Lummus Park in the Eastern Airlines

wheelchair, using the Nikon with a 250-mm lens now to shoot across Ocean Drive to get porch sitters: panning a gallery of weathered faces, stopping on permanent waves, glasses flashing sunlight, false teeth grinning—peeking into their lives as he picked them off one at a time. Later on he would see their faces appear in clear liquid, in amber darkroom light, and would be alone with them again and want to ask them questions about where they'd been and what they'd seen. Raped by Cossacks, Franny said, or mugged by . . .

The Cuban-looking guy said, "What're you doing, taking pictures?"

His hair was slicked down across his forehead and he wore a gold earring. But even without it LaBrava would have known him. The way he moved, for one thing, the way his hand drifted up to touch the wavy ends of his hair.

LaBrava was happy to see him and gave him a smile and said, "Yep, that's what I'm doing, taking pictures."

"You down here on your vacation?"

"Just enjoying life," LaBrava said.

"Tha's nice, you can do that."

The guy wore a black shirt that might be silk and fit him loose. He was skinny under there, a welterweight with that high compact ass in his cream-colored slacks, the shoes white, perforated.

"Tha's a nice camera you have."

"Thanks. How about if I take a picture of you?"

"No, tha's okay."

"I like to get shots of the natives."

"Man, you think I'm a native?"

"I mean the people that live here, in Florida."

The Cuban-looking guy said, "Tha's an expensive camera, uh?" He hadn't taken his eyes from it.

"With the lens it runs about seven and a quarter."

"Seven hundred dollars?"

"The camera cost me five hundred."

"Oh, man, is a nice one, uh? You let me see it?"

"If you're careful." LaBrava had to take his hat off to lift the strap over his head.

"No, I won't drop it. Is heavy, uh?"

"Hang it around your neck."

"Yeah, tha's better."

LaBrava watched him raise the camera, almost as though he knew what he was doing, and sight toward the ocean, the breeze moving strands of the guy's raven hair.

Lowering the camera, looking at it, the guy said, "Yeah, I like it. I think I'll take it."

LaBrava watched the guy turn and walk off. Watched the easy, insolent movement of his hips.

Watched him take four, five, six strides, almost another one before he stopped—knowing the guy was going to stop, because the guy would be think-

ing by now, *Why isn't he yelling at me?* Now the
guy would be wondering whether or not he should
turn around, wondering if he had missed something he should have noticed. LaBrava saw the
guy's shoulders begin to hunch. Turn around and
look—the guy would be thinking—or take off.

But he had to look.

So he had to turn around.

LaBrava sat in the wheelchair waiting, his curvy-
brimmed Panama shading his eyes, the guy fifteen
to twenty feet away, staring at him now.

"What's the matter?"

Holding the camera like he was going to take
LaBrava's picture.

The guy said, "I have to ask you something."

"Go ahead."

"Can you walk?"

"Yeah, I can walk."

"There's nothing wrong with you?"

"You mean, you want to know if you took off
could I catch you and beat your head on the pave-
ment? There is no doubt in my mind."

"Listen—you think I was going to take this
camera?"

"Yeah, I did. You changed your mind, uh?"

"No, man, I wasn't going to take it. I was kidding you."

"You gonna give it back to me?"

"Sure. Of course."

"Well?"

The guy lifted the strap, brought it over his head. "I could leave it right here." Stepping over to the low cement wall. "How would that be?"

"I rather you hand it to me."

"Sure. Of course." Coming carefully now, extending the camera. "Yeah, is a very nice one . . . Here you are," reaching sideways to put it in LaBrava's hand and stepping back quickly, edging away.

"What's the matter?"

"Nothing is the matter. No . . ."

"I'd like to take your picture. What do you say?"

"Well, I'm busy now. We see each other again sometime."

"I mean in my studio." Motioning, thumb over his shoulder like a hitchhiker. "Up the street at the Della Robbia Hotel."

The guy's reaction was slight, but it was there, in his eyes for part of a moment, then in his casual gesture, touching the curly ends of his hair.

"Tha's where you live, uh?"

"I've got like a studio right off the lobby. When you want to come?"

He hesitated now. "Why you want to take my picture?"

"I like your style," LaBrava said, not sure how

many movies it was from. Ten? A hundred? "You ever do any acting?"

The guy was saying something. It didn't matter. LaBrava raised the Nikon and snapped his picture. *Snick*.

15

MAURICE STOOD ON THE BALCONY that ran the length of Jean Shaw's tenth-floor apartment. The Atlantic Ocean was right there. All of it, it seemed to Maurice, the whole ocean from right downstairs to as far as you could see. It was too close, like living on a ship. He said, "I sat out here at night with that surf making noise, I'd drink too. It drive you crazy."

She said from the living room, "You know that isn't my problem."

"Yeah? Well, I would a thought I drank more than you do," Maurice said, "but I never threw a glass at a cop car."

"I didn't throw the glass. I explained that, I was in a funny mood."

"They laugh? You were a guy the cops would a beat your head in, for showing disrespect. You know what your problem is? Living in a place like this. There's no atmosphere. All you got is a view." He moved to the doorway, looked into the silvery, mirrored living room. Jean stood with two hanging bags draped over a chair done in white satin. "You got to be careful not to confuse class with sterility. Clean can be classic. It can also bore the shit outta you."

She said, "Well, you built the place."

"*I* didn't build it."

"You know what I mean. You've been into more developments like this than anyone I know . . . Living on South Beach like a janitor."

"Manager's fine. Don't put me down."

"What're you into now?"

"I'm resting my money, mostly tax-free bonds. We get a Democrat in there, everything'll pick up again."

"You still giving to the Seminoles?"

"Miccosukis. Some of 'em with runaway nigger slave blood in 'em. They appealed to my imagination."

"And your pocketbook."

"I made some good friends. Buffalo Tiger, Sonny Billy, they taught me to drink corn beer. We had some laughs, I got some good shots . . . And I don't *give* money to 'em. It's a foundation—send a few Miccosukis to school every year 'stead of selling airboat rides and shooting the heads off frogs. What's wrong with that?"

"Jerry thought you were crazy," Jean said. "I

used to love to hear you argue. He couldn't believe it—all the money you were giving away."

"Yeah, well, I'm giving some to the whales, too. What would Jerry say about that, uh? I'd started a foundation for used-up lawyers he'd a loved it."

She said, "Well, Jerry wasn't the brightest guy I ever married." She sighed. "I thought he was going to be a winner, too."

Maurice said, "He stayed with the wrong guys too long, Jeanie, you and I both know that. They ate him up—used him, used his dough, he had no recourse. Who's he gonna go to, the FBI? He hadn't died of a heart attack, he'd a died a much worse kind of way, even *thinking* about pulling out. Up to Kefauver everybody's having a ball, nothing to it, you could deal with those guys. Frank Erickson, Adonis, any of 'em. After Kefauver, no way, they don't trust nobody."

She said, "Jerry was dumb. There's no other way to describe him."

"May he rest in peace."

"Yeah, wherever he is—died and gone to hell. But it doesn't help my situation."

Maurice said, "Jeanie, any woman I know would trade places with you in a minute. You got the looks, guys're attracted to you—sometimes the wrong type, I'll grant you. You got a nice life . . ."

"Go on."

"What's your problem? I know—don't tell me. But outside a money, what? You want money? I'll give you money. Tell me what you need."

She walked over to the television set, built into black formica shelves. "I don't want to forget the recorder." She picked up two tape cartridges in boxes. "Or the movies. You want to see them?"

"Of course I do. You know that."

She said, "Maury, I already owe you, what, sixty thousand."

He said, "You want to get technical we're up to seventy-two-five. But have I asked you for it?"

She said, "If I had money to invest, something working for me—"

"Jeanie. Have I asked you for it?"

"Or if you'd buy me out. Maury, I could pay you back, get out from under it."

"From under what? How many times have I said it? If you don't have it, you don't owe me. It's that simple. I buy you out, your share's worth about a hundred grand. Say a hundred and a quarter. You pay me back outta that, where are you? If I go, the hotel's yours. Don't worry about it, it's in the agreement. Until that happens—which is something I don't think about. I'm not afraid of going, it's gonna happen, but it's not something I sit down and think about. Until then, you need money, you let me know. It's that simple."

"Like an allowance."

Maurice said, "Sometimes—I don't know, Jeanie."

She put the videotapes down and seemed restless, though she didn't move. "I'm sorry, I didn't mean it that way. I'm not ungrateful, I'm frustrated. Maury, you're the best friend I've ever had. I love you, I love to be with you . . ."

"But what?"

"I feel useless, and it makes me mad."

"Then do something. Get back into acting."

"Maury, come on. I'm not going to play somebody's mother. And I'm not going to do the little-theater bit, work in a converted barn, wring my hands in *Fiddler on the Roof*. I've done all that."

"Big screen or nothing," Maurice said. "You know what I think of that particular kind of pride—from eighty-years experience, from knowing all kinds of successful people with all kinds of dough who are now dead or else in jail? I think it's a bunch of shit. Money and success've got nothing to do with making it on a day to day basis, and that's all that counts."

"I love rich old guys who say that—and don't have a worry in the world."

"Aw, Jeanie, come on"—he sounded tired—"you're smarter than that. Quit thinking, start doing something. Girl with your intelligence, your talent . . . I'm telling you, money ain't it."

"Joe thinks you're practically down and out."

"Let him think it. Either way, it wouldn't matter to him, he's an artist. He doesn't know it yet, but he is. He's gonna be a name."

She said, "Yeah, well, I wish him luck."

"Quit worrying, you get lines in your forehead."

"I always love your advice."

"Then listen to it. We ready?"

"I guess so."

"The suitcase and the two hanging bags—that's it?"

"If you'll take those," Jean said, "I'll bring the recorder. I'm going to drive, too. I want my car down there."

"For what?"

"Maury, let me feel at least a little independent."

The glare hit Nobles smack in the eyes coming up out of the Trans Am, had him squinting with a painful expression. Man, it was hot out. Walking toward the high-rise entrance he could feel the blacktop burning mushy under his cowboy boots, the heels sticking.

He had figured this deal wrong, but it was working out anyway. He believed the old man was taking Jean Shaw home, would drop her off and scat. But the old man was up there it seemed an hour— the black car ticking in the heat—then he had come out with a grip and what looked like her clothes and drove off with them.

Which meant she was going back to South Beach. Shit.

But if she wasn't home for good, least she was home now. Would she be glad to see him? He'd sure be glad to see her—thinking of words like *alone at last*. He could hardly wait.

Inside the air-conditioned elevator he pushed "10" and began to wonder what she'd say when she opened the door, what kind of look she'd have on her face.

Franny was still in the mauve string bikini.

She had a pinkish tan, freckles on her chest. She had a deep groove between her breasts, round bare hips and naked belly, like a young belly dancer on her day off—except for her round tinted glasses and that wiry hair; that hair was Franny and nobody else. She wasn't the least self-conscious. She poured wine, left the bottle on the glass table. She asked him if he was going to keep his hat on; he could if he wanted; she loved it, she thought it looked like Vincent van Gogh's a little, and didn't say much after that. She was quieter this afternoon.

He could hear the air-conditioning unit working hard. He was okay, he was just a little nervous, wanting to act as natural as this girl but knowing she had a lead on him, had not had to unlearn as many customs of propriety. He had decided she was going to fool around, make the moves on him and here he was, a guy who had gone to bed with a movie star, trying to act natural and not think of the movie star, not think at all. It wouldn't be cheating. How could it be cheating? He hardly knew the movie star. He felt he knew Franny longer, if he wanted to look at it that way. No, he was here because she'd invited him up . . . Franny wasn't sweating it. She'd probably decided it would happen or it wouldn't. No big deal. She was quieter though, at first.

Thinking about something. Rearranging the pillows, a pile of them on the daybed. She straightened and said, "Oh." Went into the bedroom and came out in less than a minute wearing a white cover, soft cotton, plain, that buttoned down the front and reached to her tan bare feet. She asked him if he wanted ice in his wine and after that began to talk. She asked how long his marriage had lasted.

"Thirty-eight months."

"You say it like that, it sounds like a long time."

"It was."

"Any kids?"

"No. How'd you know I was married?"

She said, "Maurice," and said, "What happened?"

"I don't know." He thought a moment and said, "Dames are always pulling a switch on you."

"Is that from one of your friend's movies?"

He shook his head. *"Laura."*

"Your friend's been married three times."

"How do you know that?"

"I talked to her. Showed her my wares. She uses a cream made from queen bee extract, turtle oil and seaweed."

"You talked to her?"

"She thinks it's great. I've got a book—a panel of doctors was asked their opinion of the queen bee cream and their answers were: No value, no opinion, a gimmick, quackery, and crap. She's had a tuck, Joe. Also a nose job. The nose when she was breaking into pictures."

"She told you all that?"

"Sure. Why not? She's nice, I like her."

"You do?"

"Very easy to talk to—doesn't give you any bullshit. I'd like to see one of her flicks." Franny paused. She almost smiled as she said, "Guess what I sold her?"

"You didn't . . ."

"Swear to God."

"Bio-Energetic Breast Cream."

"Listen, I showed it to her and she went ape-shit. 'Oh, for bounce and resiliency—really?' Trying to contain herself, act cool. It's about as effective as queen bee extract and turtle oil. You either have bounce, Joe, or you don't." She said, "Wait, I've got a surprise," and went into the bedroom.

In a few moments he heard soul music, a male vocal with back-up voices, a familiar melody but not a recent one. When she came out he said, "Who's that?"

Franny said, "You're putting me on. You haven't heard that a couple a hundred times?" She wasn't wearing her glasses now.

"Smokey Robinson?"

"Who else. And the Miracles. 'You've Really Got a Hold on Me.' " She came back to the daybed, her place on stage. "A big hit in Motown when you were a little kid, right?"

"I was in high school."

"See? I know all about you, LaBrava. Special Agent Joe LaBrava, United States Secret Service. I knew you were into something shady, at least at one time. So I asked Maurice. He says you're doing Murf the Surf now. I thought you were leaning more toward Iggy Pop, but you never know, do you. You quiet guys . . . Will you tell me some secrets, Joe?"

He said, "Former President Harry Truman's house has faulty wiring. You're watching a movie on TV, it goes off, comes back on, goes off, comes back on . . ."

She said, "Uh-huh, really interesting work, uh?"

"The lights would go off and on too."

She nodded, accepting this, said, "Well, you ready?" and began unbuttoning her cover, by the daybed piled with pillows, facing him.

He sat across the glass table from her in a wicker chair. There were two rolls of film on the table by the wine bottle. He raised the Nikon, made adjustments, lowered it and looked at her again.

Franny stood with her legs somewhat apart, hands on bare hips, naked beneath the cover held open behind her hands. She said, "How do you want me?"

He studied the pose.

She was playing. He hoped she was playing, giving him a line to come back to. Yeah, she was playing. Having fun. *How do you want me?* Except that her lavender eyes were serious and those big brown-tipped earth-mama breasts were serious and the belly rounding into the thickest patch of black hair he had ever seen in his life was as serious as can be. Well, you could be serious and still have fun. In fact, he believed it was the secret of a happy life, if anybody wanted to know a secret. *How do you want me?* And his line, keeping it low-key, soft, the sensitive artist:

"Just as you are."

After a moment she said, "Are you gonna take my picture?"

LaBrava said, in all honesty, feeling himself becoming more and more serious, "I doubt it."

Each time Cundo Rey thought about the guy in the wheelchair he would sooner or later see Richard driving his beautiful black car, and it was the last thing he wanted to think about.

See the guy, see Richard. Relating them, knowing he would have to do something about the guy.

Cundo sat in the lobby of the La Playa Hotel now waiting for Javier, fooling with his earring. Javier was from Cambinado. He was doing okay in his business. He had already offered to give Cundo whatever he needed.

What a place this was—the tile floor cracked and broken, pieces of it missing. He compared it in his mind to Cambinado del Este because the people who lived here reminded him of convicts. The difference, Cambinado del Este was cleaner than this place, it was still a new prison.

He compared it also to the National Hotel in Havana. The National Hotel was as dirty as this place, but instead of people who looked like convicts, there were Russians staying there, Russians smelling of garlic, talking in loud voices, complaining. They complained like children who didn't like their dinner. They didn't complain of things worth complaining about. What did they know? They didn't work on the housing brigade in Alamar twelve hours a day breathing cement dust. The Russian he had known was an engineer or a technician of some kind. In his room he had vodka, bars of chocolate, boxes of rubbers and dirty picture books he had bought in New York City. The Russian hated Cuba. Say *Cooba* with his garlic breath and spit on the floor. Cundo Rey, aching to leave, dying for the chance, defended his country because he hated the Russian and had gone back to the man's room late at night. He had almost wasted his life because of the Russian, using the Russian's own gun.

Thinking, Oh well, that was done.

Then thinking about the guy in the wheelchair again, because that wasn't done.

How many guys who lived in the Della Robbia Hotel took photographs of people from a distance, unseen, with a telephoto lens? Sure it was the same guy who had taken the photographs of Richard— oh shit, seeing Richard in his mind again . . .

And seeing a guy who was called David Vega coming into the lobby. David Vega had looked at him as though he knew him, but had never approached to speak to him. So he watched David Vega whenever he saw him.

When Javier came in David Vega was still in the

lobby, drinking a Coca-Cola from the machine. So Cundo didn't greet Javier, pretending not to notice him. Javier would see this and do the same.

Cundo waited several minutes before going up to Javier's room. He accepted a glass of rum as a formality and listened as Javier expressed his desire to move to South Miami. There was no hurry. Listening to Javier kept him from thinking about his car in the hands of Richard the swamp creature. Javier finished his rum before he brought the metal footlocker out of the closet, worked the combination and opened the lid to display his wares.

"Any pistol you want," Javier said, "wholesale price to a *Marielito*. Machine gun one-third off. MAC-10 cost you eight hundred."

"Something small," Cundo Rey said.

"You want a snubbie. This one, .38 Special, two-inch barrel. Same kind the Charlie's Angels use."

"Yeah?"

"Also Barney Miller."

"Wrap it up," Cundo Rey said.

16

NOBLES HAD HIS GRIN READY. The door opened and he said, "Well, look-it who's here, huh?"

He'd decided she would be all eyes, surprised as hell. But she wasn't. Or didn't act it. She gave him a stare like she wasn't going to move.

He said, "Sugartit, I don't want to knock you down but I been in the car it seems like all day. I gotta go pee pee so bad I'm gonna be spitting in another minute. It just come on me."

So she had to get out of his way—it was a fact, he would have picked her up and moved her—had to let him through to run down the hall to her bathroom.

Nobles loved it in here, it was full of perfume bottles, bath oils and powder in pale-colored boxes, all kinds of good-smelling stuff. He would like to look in her medicine cabinet sometime, poke around and find intimate things. It was so *clean* in here, no rust stains in the toilet or the washbasin. He looked around at all her girlish stuff relieving himself, groaning sighs and finally shuddered. Oh man.

She was still in the parlor, sitting at one end of the sofa now, her straw bag on her lap, legs crossed to show him her knee above the chrome coffee table. She seemed calm now, not drilling him with her eyes, though not with what he'd call a sweet expression, either.

He said, "You glad to see me?"

Huh-uh, she didn't look too. She said to him, "Richard, what are you doing here?" Calm and patient, like she was talking to a child.

He said, "I missed you. Did you miss anybody?"

She said, "What am I going to do with you, Richard?"

That was better. He gave her a grin. "Well, let's see . . ."

She said, "You're just a big loveable bear, aren't you?"

He had never thought of himself that way. Shit—a bear. He said, "You got anything cold to drink? Man, I'm thirsty from sitting in that car." He started for the dining room, all shiny glass and silver in there, to go through to the kitchen.

When she said, "Richie?" and he glanced over, walking past her, he saw the pictures laid out on the coffee table, his own familiar self looking up at him and he stopped, not too thirsty anymore.

He put his hands on his hips. The first thing he

thought to say was, "Man, I would like to know what's going on—this guy taking my pitcher." He squinted his eyes, looking up at Jean then. "Wait a minute. How'd you get 'em?"

Jean said, "Richard, you're priceless."

"I want to know how you got 'em."

"He gave them to me. How else?"

"What's he doing—he with a newspaper or what?"

"No, he's not with a paper. He goes out and takes pictures of people." She seemed to think about it a moment, not quite sure. Then nodded. "That's what he does."

"You don't have to get permission?" Nobles said, indignant now. "Just take pitchers of anybody you want?"

"Would you like to sue him? How about invasion of privacy?"

"Shit, it oughta be against the law."

She said, "You could go to the police . . ."

Wouldn't that be something. Get some cop he knew, like Glenn Hicks up in Boca, to come down on the scudder.

"Except they're going to find out about you anyway. He wants to give them a set of pictures."

Nobles had to squint again, trying to see this business in his head. It was a queer feeling to know somebody had been watching every move he made, like every time he stepped out of the daylight dark-

ness of that black car. He was right back where he
started, asking, "What in the hell's going on?" Asking, "Who is he, anyway?"

Jean said, "It's not so much who he is—his name
is Joe LaBrava—but what he used to be. Joe was a
Secret Service agent for nine years, Richard. He
keeps his eyes open, doesn't miss a thing."

Nobles felt just a little bit relieved and said,
"Hell, I know boys work as gover'ment agents. You
help them out, they help you out. You work a deal."

She said, "Richie, do you know what you're
talking about?"

He didn't like that bored goddamn ho-hum tone
at all and she'd better watch it. He stayed calm
though and listened. Heard her say:

"This man knows all about you. He knows
you've been bothering me. He knows I can't dis-
courage you, no matter how hard I try."

Learning amazing things from her now.

"Wait. You told him that?"

And saw her eyes catch fire.

"I *had* to, you dummy. He *saw* you. He asked me
about you."

It stung him. But he kept his mouth shut and she
seemed to settle back and it was quiet. He could
hear the ocean.

She said, "Why you came to the clinic—God, I'll
never know."

"I wanted to get you out of there."

She said, "Richard," her normal calm self again, "why do you think I got drunk? Why did I walk out of the bar? Do you know how long I had to wait for a police car? I thought I was going to have to go find one. Richard, before I left, what did I say?"

"The bar?"

"Before I walked out with the drink."

"What'd you say? You said a lot of things."

"I asked you not to drink so much."

"I was keeping up with you is all."

"I said trust me. Do you remember that?"

"Yeah, I remember."

"I wrote it on a napkin. *Trust me.* And told you to put it in your pocket. Trust me and wait, I'll call you. The police drive me to the place in Delray. I have them call Maurice and he comes immediately, anxious to take care of me."

"Yeah?"

"I stay with him. We talk. He feels even closer to me than before. He feels responsible for me. He wants to help me no matter what happens . . ."

"Yeah, but you didn't tell me any of that part—how you were gonna bring him in."

"If you trust me, Richard, I don't have to tell you anything . . . Do I?"

"Well, you could a told me *some*thing. Shit, I didn't know." He began to get tender feelings again, admiration. This little lady had put it all together, thought it up all by herself.

She said, "What did you do, the night at the clinic, start a fight? I was afraid you'd get into something."

"It was the *guy*, the one you're talking about. The scudder blindsided me while I'm talking to the girl there."

"Well, you picked the wrong guy, Richard."

"*I* didn't pick him—"

She said, "Listen to me. All right?"

She could be so calm no matter what, keeping her voice low and a little bit husky. He would look at her and get that tender feeling and not care how old she was. She was good looking, she smelled good, had nice legs—that knee looking at him, a little thigh showing . . .

"You've brought a man into it," she was telling him now, "who knows how to watch people, how to follow them. He was onto you for days and you didn't see him, did you?"

"I wasn't looking especially."

"Well, there's nothing we can do about it now. The police are going to get involved anyway, sooner or later, so maybe it doesn't make any difference. You're going to be the obvious suspect. Especially now. You've not only been bothering me, you've practically advertised—with pictures to prove it—you're into extortion, in one form or another."

"Hey, I was offering my service—"

"Richard."

"Yeah. Go on."

"They can't convict you with pictures. They've got to catch you in the act, destroying property, threatening someone. So I don't think the photographs are going to do us any harm. We have to have a suspect to make it believable and, Richard, I have to say, you're perfect."

He said, "I appreciate that."

"They might question you."

"I know it."

"They'll be convinced you're the guy."

"So?"

"It's going to be up to you, Richard, whether we succeed or not. You're the star."

"I am?"

"They could put a lot of pressure on you."

"I been in some ass-tighteners. Don't worry about it."

"And the guy who's going to help us," Jean said, "he'll have to understand a few things. At least he'll have to think he does."

"I know what you mean."

"You have someone in mind?"

"Already hired him. Cute little booger does anything I tell him. He's half queer, done hard time in Cuba—listen, you was to draw a picture of the one you got in mind, I'd turn this boy over and you'd say, that's him, don't let him get away."

"He's Cuban?"

"Pure-D. Listen, he told *me* a idea was crude, but didn't sound too bad. He's a nasty little booger. I wish you could meet him."

"I'm the victim, Richard."

"*I* know. I haven't told him any different. I'm just saying I think you'd get a kick out of him. Dances go-go when he feels like showing off. Wears a earring. Little Cundo Rey, the Cuban hot tamale. You know what they say the weather is down there? They say chili today and hot tamale."

He grinned, waiting for her to loosen up, but she was being serious about something and he could hear the ocean again.

In that quiet she said, "Why are there pictures of you and none of him?"

"I done the selling. I was gonna save Cundo for the dirty work."

"Did he like the idea?"

"Well, I wouldn't say he was real tickled. He believes you have to break the guy's window *first*, then sell him the protection. Maybe that's how they do it down in Cuba, I wouldn't know."

Jean said, "Richard, that's not unlike the way we're going to do it. Isn't that right?"

He had to think about that. "Yeah, sorta."

"Are you sure he'll do whatever you tell him?"

"No problem. The little fella's greedy."

She was staring at him now, hard.

When he'd decided she didn't intend to speak,

Nobles said, "Listen, maybe we ought to get our heads together here," coming around the coffee table to ease down next to her, "get this deal fine-tuned." But he was no sooner down, she was up.

Going over to the television set with her straw bag, telling him, "Stay there, I'll be back."

Not sounding mad or anything, just peculiar. He watched her pick up a couple of video cartridges and shove them into the straw bag, a big roomy one. She dropped the bag over on a chair, like she didn't want to forget it when she left. Then she stooped down, opened the cabinet beneath the shelves and he stared at her fanny as she brought out a third video cartridge. This one she snapped into the VCR, the movie player, and turned on the television set, telling him he could carry the recorder down to the car after.

"After what? We gonna see a movie?"

"Part of one." She stepped away from the set.

Nobles laid his arm across the sofa's backrest, waiting for her, but she stood there watching the screen as music came on over the Columbia Pictures logo. The music quit. For a moment the screen was black. Then the picture's musical score began, dirge-like, a promise of doom, as the screen turned white and the main title appeared, a single word within a black border, *OBITUARY*.

"I saw this one."

"I want you to see it again. The first part."

"That's all I ever seen, like half of it. How's it end?"

"Be quiet," Jean said.

"There you are," Nobles said, reading the titles. "Starring Victor Mature. Jean Shaw. Victor Mature—yeah, I remember this one, he's the cop. Which one's Shepperd Strudwick?"

"My husband."

"Henry Silva. Which one's he play?"

Nobles looked up. Jean was walking out of the room. He said, "Hey, get us a cold drink, okay?" He wouldn't mind something to eat, either, and raised his voice. "You know how to make a Debbie Reynolds?"

No answer.

Maybe she'd surprise him. Yeah, he remembered this one. Starts with the funeral. Jean Shaw standing there dressed all in black with her husband, old enough to be her daddy, biting his lip, man with a nervous stability, rich but afraid of dying, having to leave the cemetery in a hurry. Running off to his limousine. There, going in close to Jean Shaw watching him leave. Looking through her veil at her eyes. Something going on in her head and not sweet affection for her hubby, from the look of it.

Jean came back in the room holding something in both hands wrapped in tissue paper he hoped was a snack of some kind. She sat down next to him on the sofa, close, and Nobles said, "What a we got there, hon?" She didn't answer. She unwrapped the tissue paper and handed him—Jesus Christ—a little bluesteel automatic.

"The hell's this for?" Nobles looked at it, read on the side *Walther PPK/S Cal. 9mm* and some words in a foreign language. It was a little piece, the barrel only a couple of hairs better than three inches long.

Jean said, "I want you to show me how it works. I used to know, but I've forgotten."

"Where'd you get it?"

"It was my husband's. Be careful, I think it's loaded."

"Hey, I know how to handle guns. What do you want this peeshooter for?"

"Just in case."

"We ain't robbing a bank, sugar."

She said, "Let's watch the picture. You can show me later."

Her tone sounded encouraging, soft and husky again. She could sound pissy one minute and like she was in heat the next. He brought his arm down from the back of the sofa and she snuggled right up against him. Yeah, she seemed to be getting in the mood herself, staring at herself in the moving picture. It tickled him to see her watching herself, hardly ever blinking her eyes, her mouth open just a speck.

He bent his head to whisper to her, "My but

that's a cute-looking woman. I wouldn't mind loving her up some."

She said, "Shhhh," but laid her hand on his thigh, the red tips of her fingers touching the inside seam of his blue jeans. She began to pick at the seam as she watched herself. Pretty soon she'd begin to scratch him. He liked it when she scratched him. She was a good scratcher.

17

FRANNY SAID, "Oh man. Man oh man." She said, "I bet there's a guy somewhere right now—he's in Boston, but I forget what school it is—he's looking at a seismograph and he's going, 'Holy shit, look at this,' like he's got about a seven point five on his Richter and there's *got* to have been a major earthquake in the last five minutes or a volcano, another Mt. St. Helens, and this guy's seismograph is going crazy—a major disturbance, look, somewhere in Florida, and they narrow it down however they do it and the guy goes, 'Look, in South Beach. Ocean Drive and Thirteenth. Wait. Room two-oh-four, the Della Robbia Hotel. But what could it've been?' You know what it was? It was everything coming together—and I don't mean it that way, but that's true too, huh?—no, I mean everything, the light, the sepia tones, the room, the mood, Smokey and the Miracles, Marvin Gaye and then no sound at all, absolute silence right after. Did you notice?"

"You're saying you had a good time?"

"To feel my loins consumed by a scorching torrent of liquid fire? It wasn't bad."

"You make a lot of strange sounds."

"I know I do. I can't help it."

"You talk, too."

"Yeah, but I keep it relevant."

"You keep it basic."

"You make faces."

"Out of control."

"No, even before. But mostly you smile. You look a person right in the eye . . ."

"You want your wine?"

"Goddamn pillow. There's one that's digging into me . . . There. Next time however . . ."

"What?"

"I don't want to sound presumptuous."

"Next time in the bedroom."

"The next time you take my picture."

"I'll shoot it now if you want."

"I have to tell you something, LaBrava. I love your name—I'm gonna call you LaBrava from now on. I have to tell you, there's no guy in New York I want to send a self-portrait to. I lied."

"Women who want to be shot in the nude, they want their picture taken. It's okay with me."

"That wasn't it. I wanted to go to bed with you. You know why?"

"Tell me."

"Because I knew it would work. I mean I knew it

would be the complete, ultimate act, every part of it first rate."

"First rate—"

"Certain types, when you see the person you just *know*. You know what I mean? Also I like older guys. You're not that old, but you're still older. You've been to bed with the movie star, haven't you?"

"You can't ask a question like that."

"I know, but the reason I did—well, I'm sure you have, otherwise you'd have said no, you haven't. I think. But the reason I mention it—"

"This's gonna be good."

"If it was just for fun and not serious—I mean if you're not in love with her, and I don't think you are or you wouldn't be here. Some guys, it wouldn't matter, but not you. Anyway, if it was just for fun with the movie star, you weren't exactly disappointed, but it wasn't the big thrill you thought it was gonna be either. How do I know that? Because you like it sorta wacky, goof around and have a good time. I knew that just from talking to you. But she's too much into herself for that. I don't mean because she's especially proper or ladylike. I can tell she gets right down to business and it's more like jogging with somebody than making love. You know what I mean? Of course you do."

"You're sure of that."

"Oh shit—now you're mad at me."

"What'm I supposed to say?"

"What're you doing now, pouting? Christ—"

"I'm not doing anything."

"I'm sorry. I thought we were pals."

There was a silence.

"We're pals. Here's your wine."

"Thanks."

"You said you thought she was nice."

"I do, I like her."

"But you think she's too much into herself."

"I get the feeling she's always on stage."

"Not altogether honest?"

"No, I don't mean she's devious. It's just that she's never right out in front. Movie stars, they either seem to fade away or James Dean out, but Jean—maybe she's played so many different parts she doesn't know who she is anymore."

"She always played the same one."

"Well, there you are. What do I know."

"But you like her."

"Sometimes, that quiet way you have of sneaking up—you know what you sound like?"

"A cop?"

"You sound like a cop."

Nobles told her sometime he'd like to see how it ended, it was just getting good. She asked if he thought the beginning slow. He said no, he meant it was getting even better. It was a real good movie. It was fun to watch her put on that sexy look and work her scheme.

He said, "Just tell me, do they catch you or not?"

Jean said, "No, but something happens I never expected."

They had talked, going over the plan in detail. Now Jean had him sitting at her desk in what she called her study. It was full of books and framed pictures of guys Jean told him were famous movie producers and directors. Nobles did not know any of them or was able to read the names they signed. One guy, Harry Cohn, she said he'd owned a movie studio but acted more like a gangster than any real gangster she had ever known. She had told Nobles about some of the S & G Syndicate people her husband worked for and they hadn't sounded very tough to him. They sounded like any dagos that dressed up in suits and snap-brimmed hats and showed off by spending money. That wasn't being tough. Being tough was doing brutish work as a boy, getting into fights on Saturday night and drinking till you foundered. Being tough was going into dark places with a .357 and a sap and praying to Jesus some nigger would try to jump you. Being tough—shit, it was not poking your fingers at a typewriter that looked like a little toy one.

He'd told her he didn't know how to work it. She said he showed her how to use the gun, she'd show him how to use the typewriter. He was suppose to put what she dictated to him into his own words.

Like Jean said, very slowly, "You know what will happen to you now. You will die. If you don't—"

He said, "Wait, hold it." He kept forgetting to press down the key on the left side, hold it down, to make a capital letter. She told him to type the capital letter over the small letter. It would be all right if it was messy. Nobles said, "Neatness don't count in a deal like this, huh?"

"If you don't leave the money—" She stopped and said, "No, start over. In all capital letters— push the one right above it down and it locks. Here." She did it for him, leaning over him, giving him her nice perfume smell. "Now, the first line, all in caps, your life is worth six hundred thousand dollars. Go ahead."

He typed, *YOUR LIFE IS WORTH $—)),)))*

He said, "Shit, I can't type."

She didn't get mad. She pulled the sheet out and rolled in a clean one, regular tablet paper with lines, telling him not to touch it, and he decided schemers had to be patient so as not to seriously fuck up. She bent over the side of the desk and began writing in the tablet, printing the words faster than he had ever seen anybody write. She said, "There," when she'd finished, "that's what the note should say. But you have to put it in your own words."

He read what she had written and said, "This here looks fine to me."

She said, "Listen to yourself. That's what I want it to sound like."

It didn't make any sense to him that writing would sound like a person. Writing was writing, it wasn't like talking. But he did as he was told, fought that dinky typewriter and finished the note.

Jean said, "All right, read it to me."

" 'Your life is worth six hunnert thousand dollars,' " Nobles began, rolling the sheet up out of the typewriter, remembering not to touch it. " 'You have three days to get the money. It must be *used* money with nothing smaller than a twenty and nothing bigger than a hunnert dollar bill and don't say you can't get it. You are worth a sight more than that.' " Nobles looked up. "I added that part."

"Fine," Jean said. "Go on."

"Let see. 'Get four thousand hunnerts, three thousand fifties and twenty-five hunnert twenties.' " Nobles paused. "How you know the bag'll hold it?"

"It will," Jean said. "Go on."

" 'You are to put the money in a Hefty thirty-gallon, two-ply trash bag. Put this one in another Hefty trash bag of the same size and tie it closed with some type of wire. Hay-baling wire is good. You will be told where to take the money. If you do not do as you are told you will *die*.' I like that part.

' . . . you will *die*.' Underlined. 'If you try any tricks you will *die*. If you tell the police or anybody you will *die*. Look at your car. You know this is not just a threat. You have two days to get the money and your car fixed. *I am watching you*.' Underlined. I said baling wire there, so it won't come undone. Is that okay?"

"Good idea," Jean said. She leaned close to him to look at the note. "You misspelled *baling*, as in *hay-baling wire*."

"Shit," Nobles said.

"That's all right, leave it," Jean said. "But if the police question you they might get tricky and pick up on that word, ask you how to spell it."

"Yeah?"

"There's no *e* in it. It's b-a-l-i-n-g."

"That's *balling*," Nobles said and started to grin and said, "Hey, puss . . ."

"Richard, we have a lot of work to do and I have to get back."

He hunched in to look at the note with her. "Hey, what should we sign it?"

"Well, *Cordially*, would be nice," Jean said. "No, that's fine the way it is. Now we'll write what you're going to say when you call, so you'll have it word for word. You'll tell me to go to a phone booth, you'll call me there at a certain time." Nobles was shaking his head. She said, "What's the matter?"

LaBRAVA

"Nuh-uh, they're gonna have traps on the phone. Shit, I know that much. I seen the feds do it when I was on the Opa-locka Police, setting up drug busts. They can't prove what I write, but they can sure as hell get my voice print on a phone. You have to tell 'em where you're suppose to go, don't you? Make it look real?"

"Yeah, you're right."

"By the time you get to Boca they got a trap on the phone booth. It tells 'em right away what number I'm calling from. See, it's different from a movie. They got equipment now, shit, you don't have a chance of doing something like that. You might as well give 'em your phone number."

Jean said, "All right, we'll do it with notes. Instead of a call I receive a note at the hotel, telling me where to go . . ."

"Find it on the porch, say."

"I'll go to the phone booth in Boca, find another one—"

"Hold it there. I'm being watched how'm I gonna put the note in the phone booth?"

"I'll have it with me," Jean said. "Make it look as though I found it. Hello—what's this?"

"That'd work."

"The note tells me to go to my apartment." She gave him a wink. "Got it?"

"Gotcha."

"I find another note, slipped under the door."

"You have *it* with you too."

"Or we write it now and leave it here."

"Yeah?" Nobles was thinking. "You know where you go next?"

"Of course."

"Got the whole deal worked out, haven't you?"

"Every step. The only change, notes instead of phone calls. I like it even better—they'll be playing with all their electronics for nothing."

"They love it, the feds, all that technical shit. Where's my little Cuban come in at?"

"The next stop."

"You're still gonna have a tail on you, you know that."

Jean nodded, smoking a cigarette, blowing the smoke out in a slow stream. Boy she was calm.

"All I'll need is to be out of their sight for about twenty seconds."

"You got the place?"

"I've got the place. I'm pretty sure. But I'm going to look at it again when I leave here."

"Cundo's gonna take it from you by force."

"There's no other way," Jean said. "But I'll cooperate, you can be sure of that. Does he have a gun?"

"Doesn't like guns or rough stuff. Talks big but being half queer he's girlish."

Jean said, "Okay, we'll write the notes. We'll need three . . ." She paused. "You'll have to take the typewriter with you when we're finished here."

"Yeah, I guess I better."

"Drop it in the Intracoastal. That area just before you come to the Hillsboro Inlet, there're a lot of trees."

"It's a shame, it's a nice typewriter."

"Richard?"

"Don't worry, I'll get rid of it. Or I could sell it."

She said, "Oh, Christ."

"Just kidding. Don't you worry, it's good as done."

She was thinking or worrying about something though. This little schemer—boy, she was a sketch.

She said, "Does your friend Cundo know where you live?"

"You mean up here or down there?"

"In Lake Worth."

"Nobody does, 'cept you."

"You can't go there while you're being watched."

"I know it."

"Promise?"

Nobles said, "Hey, you think I'm stupid or something?"

She thought of handkerchiefs and how simply it was done in the movies: Henry Silva making phone calls with a handkerchief over the mouthpiece, in a time before electronic surveillance; the movie cop using a handkerchief to pick up the murder weapon. Henry Silva had used a second-hand typewriter and dropped it off the side of his boat on their good-luck cruise to Catalina, their last time together before her husband would receive the letter—*$150,000 or you're dead*. Impressive enough as a pre-inflation demand; today it would hardly be worth the risk. She remembered her line: "You can't come near the boat as long as the cops are tailing you." (Beat) "Promise?" And Henry Silva's line: "Do I look stupid?"

Some of it was different, some of it almost exactly the same. One thing she was certain of, it wouldn't end the way the movie did.

18

THE OLD MAN SAID it was Joe Stella up in Lantana had given him this address, so he had come on down in his pickup truck. There it was across the street. It had dust-settle on top of that salt stickiness and he hadn't had no place to wash it, being too busy looking for his sister's boy, Richard Nobles. The old man said his name was Miney Combs.

His pickup was parked behind Jean Shaw's clean white Eldorado.

LaBrava told Miney yes, he had heard his name from Joe Stella.

The old man looked like he had lived outdoors all his life, the kind of man who knows where to fish and dig wells, how to fix pumps and tune his truck. He was heavyset with a belly; wore a John Deere hat, suspenders over his gray work clothes, long-sleeved underwear beneath, and carried about him the sour smell of aged sweat.

They sat on the porch of the Della Robbia talking, in the front corner section next to Thirteenth

Street. The old ladies would bend forward to look over because the old man was using a snuff stick and they had never seen one before. LaBrava hadn't either.

It was like the man was brushing his teeth. The twig was about the size of a toothbrush, frayed soft on the end and stained the color of brown shoe polish from sticking it into his Copenhagen and then massaging his gums with it, sometimes leaving it in his mouth like a cigar. LaBrava went over to the Cardozo and brought back four bottles of cold beer. The old man sighed and his metal chair groaned as he settled in, resting his work shoes on the rail.

Miney said, "There's parts of that swamp you'd think nobody but Jesus would dare walk it. Richard, he'd go in there be right at home. Preferred it to his own home I believe account of the way my brother-in-law raised him. See, he believed you whupped boys you made 'em humble. Twist you a half-dozen lengths of hay-baling wire and whup 'em regular. See, my sister, what she did she run a grits mill. Had a old tractor engine tied onto the mill and would grind up was nothing but mule corn, hard as gravel, but it made pretty fair grits and she sold it, fresh grits. See, Richard worked there till finally he left to peck it out on his own, sport around in the swamp and hire out to take folks for canoe rides, so they could watch birds. You imagine? I said to Miz Combs, watch 'em do what? I heard it I wondered if they'd pay to watch me plow a field. First I heard of Mr. John after him was when he killed the eagle. Why did he kill it. Knowing Richard it was to see it die. All right, then here was these two boys working a still I heard from cane skimmings. But that couldn't a been, 'cause the first time they was brought up I knew the judge said it ought to be against the law to arrest anybody could make whiskey good as theirs. Then the second time, with our Richard testifying, swearing in court, they got sent to Ohio. Same as my boy and in the same court. My boy had done his time once. Yes, he bought weed from the shrimpers and sold it to college boys, but he never smoked it once. Now Richard come along and tells on him and some others to Mr. John—only the Lord Jesus knows why—and my boy is doing thirty-five years in a gover'ment lockup."

LaBrava said, "What do you want to do to Richard?"

Miney said, "What do I *want* to do? I want to put a thirty-ought-six in him, right here." Miney touched the bridge of his nose with a finger that looked hard as bark. "But what I am *going* to do is put him in the back of my truck rolled in a dirty tarp and take him on home. We'll decide fair. Maybe lock him in a root cellar for up to thirty-five years—how's that sound? Let him out when Buster gets his release."

That didn't sound too bad.

LaBrava said, "You think you can handle him?"

"He's big as a two-hole shithouse and I'm blocky," Miney said, "but once I lay my ax handle across his head I don't expect trouble."

"He's over at the Paramount Hotel on Collins Avenue," LaBrava said.

Nobles walked into the lobby, his head aching with images of things to come, little details he had to remember. Like—Jesus, *the typewriter!* Already he'd forgot one. He was suppose to have taken care of that on the way down. He saw himself in darkness dropping it off the MacArthur Causeway . . .

And saw his Uncle Miney in that same moment—Miney sitting asleep with a snuff stick in his mouth, right there in the Paramount Hotel lobby. Nobles felt himself yanked out of that future time and back into a Jacksonville courtroom past, Miney extending his arm, his finger, pointing the Last Judgment at him . . . He got out of that lobby. Ran up to Wolfie's on the corner of Twenty-first to phone Cundo.

But the little booger wasn't in his room.

Nobles didn't want to go over there. He didn't like the feel of the place, all the foreigners hanging around. So in the next couple of hours he killed time having snacks, corned beef sandwiches, and checking the lobby, each time seeing Miney sitting in the same goddamn chair like he would let moss grow on him if he had to.

Finally, when it was dark he drove over to the La Playa Hotel, checked to see if Cundo had returned—not yet—and sat outside in the car to wait, listening to the jabber of dagos passing on the street. Little fuckers, ought to be sent back where they came from.

Send Cundo back too when they were through with him.

He heard Cundo's voice before he saw him—like a dago prayer shouted to heaven. The next thing, Cundo was feeling his car, running his hands over it in the streetlight, asking had he hit anything, had he stripped the gears, had he got bugs on it. Try to get a word in about something important. Nobles had to wait and found it was worth it. For once Cundo saw his car was okay the little fucker was so grateful he nodded yes, right away, and kept nodding yes to everything Nobles told him.

Go see Uncle Miney and give him a story. Yes. Tell him Richard's moved and nobody knows where. "Convince him or he'll ruin this deal we got. You understand?" Yes, of course. "Send him on his way or he'll mess us up good." Don't worry. Still looking now and again at his black Pontiac.

"The woman's car's over there at the ho-tel. El-dorado parked on the street." Yes? "Smash the windows with something. Windshield, headlights, 'specially the window on the driver side." Yes, okay. "Later on tonight I'll tell you the rest, what you're gonna do, then we don't see each other for a while. You understand?" Yes. "You gonna miss me?" Of course.

"Something else. Shit, I almost forgot. There's a typewriter in your trunk I want you to throw in the ocean, in Biscayne Bay. You hear me? Not in a garbage can or out in some alley, it's got to be sunk for good."

Yes, of course. Not even asking why—the little booger was so grateful to see his car again.

Sitting in the middle of the sofa LaBrava would lose himself for a time, watching Jean Shaw on the tele-vision screen and feeling her next to him. He could turn his head and see her, right there, the same face in profile. In the darkness of the room the two Jean Shaws were nearly identical, pale black and white. But he would not lose himself for long, because Franny Kaufman sat close on his other side and he was aware of her too. He would hear her, soft sounds in response to what she was watching, and feel her leg and sometimes her hand. She was here because Jean Shaw had invited her. Maurice, in his La-Z-Boy, paid no attention to Jean's whispers to be quiet. If he felt like making comments he made them.

"I'm gonna tell you something. Guys that ran dice games never looked like Dick Powell."

"Shhhh."

"I never knew a good-looking guy ran a dice game. I tell you about a guy named Peanuts?"

"Maury—"

"Edmund O'Brien was starting to get fat even then, you notice?"

At one point Franny's voice in the darkness said, "Hey, Jean?" a tone of mild surprise. "I've seen you before . . . I can't think of the name of the picture."

LaBrava was aware of the silence until Maurice said, "Jeanie, you still know how to deal cards like that?"

Cundo Rey said to the old man he understood from the guy over at the desk, the hotel guy, that he was looking for Richard. Cundo watched this Uncle Miney take the stick out of his mouth, almost gagging as he saw the dirty brown end of it.

"You a friend of Richard?"

Like he was accusing him. From the sound and the look of the man, another strange creature from the swamp, Cundo didn't believe he should tell him yes. He said he *knew* Richard, he had seen him around here.

The old man said, "Where?" He said, "Take me where I might find the son of a bitch."

They got in the old man's pickup truck and the old man began talking about Richard Nobles, saying he had "fell from grace once he got his ass up against hard work." Saying he had become nothing but a mean rascal who would sell his friends and blood kin to save his own hide, or maybe just for fun—Cundo understanding only some of what the old man said, but getting enough to hold his interest and want to keep the old man talking. Miney saying there was a time he himself was "wilder'n a buck and went looking for women and to do some drinking," but a man had to reach a point where he left that behind him. Richard's appetite was such he must be "holler to his heels." The old man said Richard—maybe what was wrong with him—had never looked up to nobody. He said to Cundo, "Who's you all's hero? People like you."

Cundo had to think. Fidel? No. Well, yes and no. Tony Perez? Of course. Roberto Ramos, if he was still playing in the big leagues. But he didn't know if the old man had ever heard of Tony Perez or Roberto Ramos, so he said, "The President of the United States."

Miney said, "Shit, that scudder—they's people

eating nothing better'n swamp cabbage, he don't give a shit."

Cundo asked him what he wanted Richard for and Miney said, "You shake him out of the tree and I'll take care of the rest." Yes, as Nobles had said, it sounded like this old guy could make trouble for them. Cundo gave him directions. Take a left. Take another left. They were on Ocean Drive now coming up on the Della Robbia from the south.

Cundo touched the old man's arm. "You see that white Cadillac there? That's Richard's car."

Jean got up to turn the lights on. It was her show, she had insisted on turning them off. Maurice, trapped in his recliner, extended his empty glass, and LaBrava got up to make drinks, remembering a Bogart line to the question, "How do you like your brandy?" Bogart, as Sam Spade: "In a glass." In that frame of mind after seeing Jean's picture. Hearing Franny say, "Well. I loved it. I loved your part especially. Lila. She was neat. Wonderful situation, if she wins the money she loses the guy, but she has to go for it. Say the line again."

Jean: Let it ride?

Franny: Yeah. Like you did in the movie.

Jean: Let it ride.

Franny: Perfect. I love it.

LaBrava poured drinks with his back to the room, listening to movie voices.

Franny: I wasn't sure, but I had the feeling Lila was getting a little psycho.

Jean: No, not at all. It's more an obsession. She's in a hopelessly corrupt situation, she's disillusioned, but you know she has to play the game.

Franny: It's the lighting and composition—

Jean: That's part of it, the ominous *mise en scène*.

Franny: I mean if she's not psychotic then it's the look of the picture, the expressionistic realism that gives that feeling.

Maurice: You two know what you're talking about?

Jean: You do see a change. She's essentially content in the beginning, an ordinary young woman . . .

Franny: I don't know. I think subconsciously she's looking for action. Like in that other picture I saw of yours . . .

Jean (pause): Which one?

Franny: I only saw like the last half, but the character was a lot like Lila. Your husband's gonna die, he knows it and also knows about this shifty business you have going with the private eye—

Jean: Oh, that one.

Franny: So he kills himself, commits suicide— shoots himself and makes it look like you did it. I mean, what a guy. He was a lot older than you.

LaBrava turned with Franny's and Maurice's drinks. In almost the same moment, with the sound of glass shattering outside, he was moving toward the nearest of the front windows.

Cundo Rey used the blunt side of the ax head, smashed the windshield of the Eldorado first, hitting it three times thinking the whole thing would shatter, fly apart, but it didn't; the ax punched holes and the windshield looked like it had frost on it, ice. He smashed the headlights, one swing for each, and remembered Richard saying the driver side window too, 'specially for some reason. He swung the ax like he was hitting a line drive and that window did shatter, fly all apart.

"Let's go, man. Come *on*."

He had to shove the old man, still looking out the back window of the truck, to get him to drive off. "Left. This street, *left*. Keep going . . . Go past Collins Avenue. Go on, keep going." The old man didn't know what was happening.

"Somebody's gonna call the police."

Listen to him. "That's why we want to get away from here."

"That was Richard's car?"

"Yeah, see, now you know he isn' going to leave. He has to get it fix."

"But where's he at?"

"I'm going take you where I think he is."

"Why's he leave his car there?"

"He has a girlfriend, you know, live by there."

"Well, if his car's setting there—"

"No, he leave it on the street there." Jesus Christ. "See, is more safe for the car there than where he live. Yeah, he leave it there all the time."

"We going back to the ho-tel?"

"We going to another place where I think he is." Jesus, this old guy with his questions. "You know, where he like to go sometime. We maybe have to look for him different places."

The old man turned the snuff stick in his mouth as he drove. They went over Thirteenth Street to Alton Road, on the bay side of South Beach, turned left and drove in silence until Cundo told him to go slow, to turn right on Sixth Street and then left on West Avenue. "Right here. Stop," Cundo said. "The Biscaya Hotel. Yes, this is good."

The old man was looking up at the building enclosed behind a chainlink fence. "I don't see no lights on in there."

"Is nobody live there anymore," Cundo said. "Is all a wreck. People go in there and wreck it. One time the Biscaya Hotel, now is nothing."

They got out and Cundo led the way through an open gate in the fence, in close darkness through rubble—just like buildings he had seen in Cuba in the revolution—through overgrown bushes and weeds choking the walk that had once led through a garden along the side of the hotel. There were rusted beer cans and maybe rats. As they reached the open ground behind the hotel, Cundo watched the headlights on the MacArthur Causeway off to the left, not far, the cars coming out of darkness from the distant Miami skyline. The old man was missing it. His head was bent back to look up at all those dark windows—hotel this big and not one light showing. He should go inside and see the destruction, like it was in a war.

"How come nobody stays here?"

"It's all wrecked."

"Well, how come it closed up?"

Cundo said he didn't know, maybe the service was no good. He said, "Come on, we take a look. Be careful where you walk, you don't hurt yourself," leading the old man through weeds, out beyond the empty building that seemed to have eyes, following a walk now that led down to the seawall—the old man turning to look up at the nine stories of pale stone, black windows, staring, like he couldn't believe a place this size could be empty, not used for anything.

"Some bums stay there," Cundo said, "sometime."

"What's Richard do around here?"

"I tole you, didn't I? He has a boat," Cundo said. "See, he like to go out in his boat at night, be at peace. When he come back he come here. See? Tie it there by the dock."

"Richard drives a boat?"

"Yeah, a nice boat. Look out there in the water. You see a light moving?"

"They's about five, six of 'em."

"Those are boats. One of them I think is Richard."

"How you tell?"

"Well, he isn't no place we look and his boat isn't at the dock over there. Tha's how you can tell. Yeah, I think one of them is Richard. Watch those lights, see if one it comes here. He would be coming pretty soon."

Cundo pulled his silk shirt out of his pants, reached around to the small of his back and felt the grip of the snubbie, the pistol Javier had sold him for one hundred and fifty dollars. Man, that gun kept pressing into his spine, killing him.

Miney said, "That's Miami right there, is it?"

"Tha's a island right in front of you," Cundo said. "Way off over there, that's the famous city of Miami, Florida. Yes, where you see all those lights."

"There's an airplane," Miney said. "Look at it up there."

"Take you far away," Cundo said. He raised the .38 Special and from less than a foot away shot Miney in the back of the head. Man, that snubbie was loud. He didn't think it would be that loud. It caused him to hesitate and he had time to shoot Miney in the head only once more as he pitched forward into Biscayne Bay.

There was something he was supposed to throw in there, Richard had told him. He was right here looking at the water, but he couldn't think of what it was.

19

BUCK TORRES SAID TO THE MAN who had waited in Mrs. Truman's living room for the mailman and in unmarked cars among empty paper containers, waited in Mrs. Truman's piano parlor watching movies and in more unmarked cars, "Wait while I talk to the Major."

So LaBrava waited. Holding the phone. Staring at a photograph of an elephant named Rosie pulling a cement roller over a Miami Beach polo field sometime in the 1920s.

Jean Shaw and Maurice waited, seated at Maurice's dining room table where the note waited, open, out of its envelope but creased twice so that it did not lie flat.

Buck Torres was talking to his superior, the major in charge of the Detective Bureau, Miami Beach Police. When Torres came back on he said, "It wasn't mailed, right? She found it in her car."

"This morning," LaBrava said. "The windows

were broken last night at ten past ten, that's the exact time. But the note wasn't found till this morning."

"You went out to the car last night . . ."

"We heard it, glass breaking. We went out, but didn't see the note. It was on the front seat. The car was locked, the guy had to break the side window to drop the note inside. This morning, when the lady went out to her car, she found the note."

"Nothing came in the mail."

"I just told you," LaBrava said, "it was in the car."

"This's the first one."

"Right."

"Nothing in the mail, no out-of-state phone calls."

"Look, it's yours," LaBrava said. "You want to bring the FBI in that's up to you."

"The Major isn't sure."

LaBrava shifted his weight from one foot to the other, looking at the elephant named Rosie pulling the cement roller. There were small figures, men wearing blazers and white trousers in the background of the photograph. He said, "Well, it wouldn't be a bad idea if somebody looked at the note. You know what I mean? Got off their ass"—getting an edge in his tone—"since it's a murder threat if the money isn't paid." He had to take it easy, stay calm, but it was hard. He knew what Torres was up against.

Buck Torres said, "How much was it?"

"I told you, six hundred thousand."

"I thought you said six thousand," Buck Torres said, calm, and was silent.

"You gonna choke?" LaBrava said. "If you're gonna choke then get some help."

"Take it easy," Torres said. "I'll be over in a few minutes." He paused and said, "Joe, don't let anybody touch the note."

"I'm glad you mentioned that," LaBrava said and hung up. He was on edge, out of practice. Or on edge because he felt involved in this, a personal matter. But he shouldn't have said that about choking, or any of the dumb things he said. He said to Jean and Maurice, looking at Jean, "They don't know if they should call in the FBI."

Jean straightened. She said, "Well, *I* do."

"Or if they should come here or you should go there," LaBrava said, approaching the dining room table. "This's a big one and it caught them by surprise. I can understand that, they have to stop and think for a minute. But Hector Torres, I know him, he's very good; he's their star, he's closed homicides over a year old. He'll look it over and then decide about the Bureau, whether they should bring in the feds or not. But technically it's not their case—at least not yet. I think, the way Torres sees it, it would be better if he came here—and I mean without any show, no police cars—than if we went down to the station. In case the hotel's being watched."

Jean said, "Well, it's fairly obvious who to look for. It can't be anyone else."

"Last night," Maurice said, "I thought it was some kids got high on something. You see in the paper this morning, Beirut, they blew up a Mercedes this time with a car bomb. A white one. You wonder why they didn't use a Ford or a Chevy." He looked at LaBrava. "You didn't see anybody?"

"It was too dark."

"It's Richard Nobles," Jean said. "As soon as I read the note—I can hear him, the way he talks."

"The hay-baling wire," LaBrava said. "His uncle, Miney Combs, when I was talking to him yesterday he mentioned hay-baling wire. He said Richard's dad used to twist a few lengths of it together and beat him with it when he was a boy, to teach him humility."

"It didn't work," Jean said.

"I looked at the note, that word jumped right out at me," LaBrava said. "He doesn't know how to spell it though."

He leaned over the back of a chair to look down at the typewritten message, a man who had experienced a great deal of waiting, a man who had read several thousand threatening letters at a desk in the Protective Research Section, Washington, D.C. This one was typed single-spaced on ruled steno notebook paper, a vertical red line down the center of the sheet, the top serrated where it had been torn from a spiral binding. The type was elite in a common serif-ed face. There were typos, capital letters struck over lowercase letters, as in the words *Hefty* and *Hay*. Only the one word, *baleing*, was misspelled. The type was clear, without filled-in or broken letters, or irregularities; though the touch of whoever had typed the note was not consistent, there were dark letters and several very faint ones. The I.D. technicians would photograph the note, print blow-ups, then check for latents with an iodine solution that would stiffen the paper and turn it a tie-dyed purple.

LaBrava pictured Nobles hunched over a portable typewriter pecking the note out slowly, painfully, with two fingers. The message read:

YOUR LIFE IS WORTH $600,000

You have three days to get the money. It must be <u>used</u> money with nothing smaller than a 20 or bigger than a $100 bill and don't say you can't get it. You are worth a sight more than that. Get 4000 100s, 3000 50s and 2500 20s. You are to put the money in a Hefty 30 gallon 2-ply trash bag. Put this one into another Hefty trash bag of the same size and tie it closed with some type of wire. Hay baleing

wire is good. You will be told where to take
the money. If you do not do as you are told
you will <u>die</u>. If you try any tricks you will <u>die</u>.
Look at your car. You know this is not just a
threat. You have 2 DAYS to get the money and
your car fixed. <u>I am watching you</u>.

Buck Torres came with an I.D. technician, both
of them in shirt sleeves, without ties, Torres with a
jacket over his arm. The I.D. technician, young and
respectful, brought their holstered revolvers out of
a black athletic bag and they hooked them on—
both at the point of the right hip—before approaching the note lying on the dining-room table,
moving toward it almost cautiously.

LaBrava, waiting a few feet away, watched
them read the note, neither of them touching it.
Jean and Maurice watched from the living room.
Torres—white Latin male, forty-three, with hard-
boned, tough-guy features that made him almost
handsome—appeared older today. Immobile, lit by
the hanging dining-room fixture, his face was a
wood carving for several minutes, a man looking
into a casket. He brought a notebook out of his hip
pocket, sat down at the table and copied the typed
message word for word. Then said something to
the I.D. technician who used the eraser end of a
pencil to slide the note and envelope into a file
folder. The I.D. technician opened his black leather

bag and Torres said to Jean, "Miss Shaw, we have to fingerprint you, if you don't mind, for elimination prints." He said, "You understand, if you're the only person who's touched the note."

Jean said, "Joe made sure of that."

Torres looked at LaBrava, waiting. "I'm glad you were here."

LaBrava was glad too, about some things. He was glad he had felt this coming and had got the shots of Nobles and the boat-lifter. He was glad Torres was handling it; but he knew what was going to happen now and he wasn't glad about the waiting.

There was no way to hurry it. There was no way yet to pull Richard Nobles out of a hotel room and throw him into a police car. LaBrava thought only of Nobles at this point. He believed once they had Richard they would also have the boat-lifter, the *Marielito*.

The I.D. technician left. They waited for Jean to wash her hands, then waited again while she made coffee in Maurice's kitchen, LaBrava knowing he would keep his mouth shut through the next part and listen to things he already knew about.

For the good part of an hour then, Jean told Buck Torres about Richard Nobles, Torres waiting for long pauses before he asked questions, always quietly, never interrupting, taking only a few notes. She had the photographs of Nobles ready, the ones

LaBrava had given her. Torres studied them and looked at LaBrava.

"The same guy?"

"He's at the Paramount Hotel on Collins," LaBrava said. "Or was."

While Torres was making a phone call LaBrava went downstairs to the darkroom. He came back with a black and white eight-by-ten of Cundo Rey standing on the beachfront sidewalk, one hand going up to his face, almost to his chin, his eyes alive, a startled expression, as he looked directly into the camera held by the guy in the curvy straw hat sitting in the wheelchair.

"He's at the La Playa on Collins," LaBrava said. "Or was. I almost made him last night busting windows, but I wouldn't tell it in court. You don't want him for busting windows anyway. I'll give you the negatives, both guys."

Buck Torres made another phone call. He came back and asked Jean about Cundo Rey. Jean shook her head. She stared at the photograph a long time but still shook her head. Finally Torres asked the question LaBrava had been waiting to hear:

"Why six hundred thousand?"

Jean didn't answer right away.

Maurice said, "What difference does it make? It's a nice round number with a lot of oughts."

Torres said, "So is five hundred thousand. So is a million."

Jean said, "I've been wondering about that. The only reason I can think of, my condominium is worth about six hundred." She paused, looked at Maurice as though for help, then back to Torres and said, "I hate to admit it, but I did tell him one time my apartment was paid for. Richard has a very . . . sort of homespun way about him."

He does? LaBrava thought.

"A country-boy charm."

He remembered her saying that, in this room, telling about Nobles that first time.

"He gives you the feeling you can confide in him, trust him," Jean said. "I think I told him the apartment was really the only thing I had, making a point that appearances can be misleading, that a lot of wealth down here is like a Hollywood set, a facade." She said, "Now that I think of it . . . I remember one day in the parking lot I ran into him. He mentioned a couple in the building had their condominium up for sale and were asking four hundred and fifty thousand. I told him they ran from about four to six hundred, as you go up. He knows, of course, I live on the top floor, oceanfront."

LaBrava listened to her quiet delivery, Jean Shaw being contrite, owning up. He wondered if it was hard for her to tell it.

"Obviously I misjudged him. As I told Maury, and Joe, you were there"—looking at him for a moment—"Richard comes on as a friendly, honest guy; so I was nice to him, I didn't treat him like one of the help."

"But he intimidated you," Maurice said. "Kind a guy, you give him a hand he grabs it, he wants more. What'd I tell you you first mentioned the guy? I said he's out for something, he's gonna take you for all he can get."

"You did," Jean said, "I know."

"I told you, guys like that, they been working Miami Beach since the day they built the bridge. Now they hop on the freeway, go up to Boca, Palm Beach."

Torres said, "Did he ever come right out and ask for anything?"

Jean said no. "But he seemed to take for granted he could stop by whenever he felt like it. After a while he became—the only word I can think of is possessive."

LaBrava remembered her saying, that first night, when she had told them about Nobles, *The way he walks around the apartment, looks at my things.*

But she didn't say it this time.

Torres said, "Have you seen him since you've been staying here at the hotel?"

"No."

"But he knows you're here."

She said, "That's fairly obvious, isn't it?"

Torres was thoughtful, arranging information in

his mind and coming down to: "Six hundred thousand, it's a lot of money."

And LaBrava remembered her saying that first night, *Then there's nothing to worry about, because I don't have any*.

But this time she didn't mention that either.

In the afternoon LaBrava took Maurice's car and drove past the Paramount Hotel and the La Playa. The Miami Beach detectives were hard to spot using confiscated cars rather than the plain unmarked Dodge and Plymouth models they drove on duty. He made one cop doing surveillance in a red Chevy cab, No. 208, knowing that official Central Cab numbers were in the 1100s or higher. When he returned to the Della Robbia a Southern Bell truck was parked in front.

Torres was going according to the handbook: he'd got State Attorney OK for a wire tap on Maurice's line and was letting the telephone company do the installation. They would put a second phone in Maurice's apartment along with the tap. If a call came for Jean Shaw Maurice would use the second phone to call Southern Bell security and they'd trap Maurice's line to get the source of the incoming call. At the telephone switching office they would install Pen Registers on the lines of both the Paramount and La Playa hotels to record the numbers of all out-going calls; no court approval required. A police command post, with phones and a recorder, was located in an area that used to be part of the Della Robbia kitchen, next to the darkroom. LaBrava believed the taps and traps would prove to be a waste of time.

Torres knocked on his door a few minutes past six. Torres said they had the Eldorado towed to a Cadillac dealership, dusted it for prints and left it to have the glass replaced. For a while then they sat with cans of beer, Torres quiet, tired; LaBrava patient, still in his waiting period. He had resolved, as a civilian, not to ask questions or offer opinions unless asked. But when Torres said, "Well, all we can do now is wait."

LaBrava said, "For how long?"

"There you are," Torres said. "Do it right I need almost half the Detective Bureau, pull three shifts a day at three locations. They're sitting in cars, hotel lobbies—all the bad guys hanging out would love to hear about it. See, if it goes down soon, right away—get the money in two days, deliver on the third—we're all set. Otherwise I have to bring in the *federales*."

"He's not gonna call," LaBrava said.

"You don't think so."

"He was a cop. He knows about traps and voice prints."

"Yeah, but he's strange," Torres said. "You ever hear of one like this? The guy wants a garbage bag full of money. He says, use hay-baling wire, it's good. Guy's right off the farm. Look how he tried to intimidate, use that old protection shit. Like he was trying to get caught."

"You know where he is?"

"Sure, he's at his hotel. He walks up to Wolfie's, walks back. Only place he's gone."

"You got a tap on his room phone?"

"His Honor the judge said no. So all we got is the Pen Register. He calls her we'll know it."

"What about the boat-lifter?"

"He hasn't been home."

"He check out?"

"No, he just hasn't been around. We had a guy owes us one go in and ask for him."

"Why don't you take a look in his room?"

"His Honor the judge said no."

"What about the boat-lifter's car?"

"Nowhere around. You can't miss that kind of car, but it's no place we've heard, Dade, Broward or Palm Beach."

"What bothers you the most?"

"About what?"

"The whole thing. How it looks."

"Is the guy this dumb? That's what I keep asking," Torres said. "You say he was a cop, he was a gypsy. Then a rent-a-cop, four bucks an hour. He's got a license for a three-fifty-seven, that's pretty interesting. But does he know how to work extortion or is he dreaming?"

"What else?"

"I don't believe he knows what he's doing."

"Thank you, Jesus—you hope and pray. Please let him fuck up, quick. What if nothing happens?"

"The Major says after three days we bring in the Bureau. Let the college boys run it. Send the letter to Washington, they analyze it sideways, upside down and tell us it's a Smith-Corona on steno notebook paper, done with a black ribbon. Oh, is that right? Hey, thanks. Let's go, boys, get out there and find that fucking Smith-Corona. The guy moves, Joe, or he's full of shit and he doesn't."

"Maybe waits till some other time."

"I got three days, that's all."

"He contacts her again. Then what?"

"She makes the delivery, we go with her."

"With the six hundred thousand?"

"There's no other way."

"You can cut up paper."

"What did the note say, Joe? *You try any tricks you will die.* We have to believe that. If we say, 'Oh, he's full of shit, don't believe it,' and it turns out the guy's crazy and he whacks her? We don't look so good. The woman, she looks terrible. Maybe the way it has to be, the way it turns out, he has to see the money before we can touch him. It has to look real. You know that. Long as we don't let the movie star or the money out of our sight. Then it's up to him, how good he is. But nobody's that good and can sound so fucking dumb."

"You ever see one of her movies?"

"I probably did, I don't remember. I know her name and she looks kind a familiar, that's all. Was she a big star?"

"No, but she was good. I mean she was good."

"I like to see her sometime."

"What about the money? Where's she getting it? Six hundred thousand in cash?"

"You kidding? Miami banks, they got that lying around in boxes. Same ones the dope guys used."

LaBrava didn't say anything for a moment. "She tell you she could get the money?"

"I asked her, I said I don't want to get personal, but are you able to put up that much? She said yes. She said since we know who it is she doesn't consider it much of a risk. Also, considering the fact the guy's a dummy."

"She said that?"

"Words, you know, like that. She seems pretty sure Richard's going to fuck up."

"But first she has to come up with the money," LaBrava said.

"Where she gets it," Torres said, "she could have it under her bed, it's none of my business."

"You're gonna copy the serial numbers."

"Photograph the bills. I assume at the bank, I don't know yet. But if the guy gets away with them, they're gone."

LaBrava was silent. He sipped his beer, looked out the window at the sky over the ocean, all that space in fading light; it was pure out there, nothing going on. Dirty ideas came about indoors. Now Torres looked out the window. He saw no answers there and turned back to LaBrava.

"What bothers you the most?"

"Same thing you're wondering. Is he that dumb?"

"I have to believe it."

"Or does he want you to think he's dumb?"

"He doesn't have to try very hard."

"But what if he's not the guy in charge?"

Torres had to think about that one. He said, "Who, the boat-lifter?"

"Cundo's been around a few days looking things over," LaBrava said. "The note's delivered, he drops out of sight. He gives you Richard to watch. Maybe to keep you busy while he operates."

"I wish we could check him out, see what he did in Cuba."

"He did time. According to David Vega by way of Guilli and Paco Boza."

"You got more informants than I do."

"I don't bust them."

"Maybe you can find out some more about the boat-lifter, what he did."

"Maybe all you have to do," LaBrava said, "is pick up Richard. Are you smarter than he is?"

"Jesus, I hope so."

"Put on a show, like you got hard evidence. Then tell him you'll trade off for the boat-lifter. Richard loves to make deals with policemen. Pick up the boat-lifter and put 'em in a room together. The one that comes out alive gets ten to twenty-five."

"Yeah, or they both walk."

"It's an idea."

Torres said, "You know what I get, listen to you say something like that? What I feel?"

"Tell me."

"You don't seem too worried about the movie star, her best interest."

LaBrava didn't say anything.

"I don't want those guys for 'Attempted,' I want them with the garbage bag in their hand. So what I have to do, I have to keep my eyes on her and on the garbage bag. Never let them out of my sight. That's the only thing I have to worry about. I don't want her to lose her life on account of me and I don't want to look bad," Torres said. "In that order."

20

IT WAS LIKE *one of her movies.*

It came into his mind at different times now because of what Buck Torres had said. "You don't seem too worried about the movie star."

He had to think about that, see if it was true. If it was true then it was because he was getting the two Jean Shaws mixed up. The real one and the one on the screen. He had never worried about the one on the screen because she could take care of herself, or because she wasn't a person who deserved a lot of sympathy. She was often the perpetrator, never the victim. But now she was in something that was like one of her movies and she *was* the victim in this one and not playing the part of the spider woman or the other woman or the girl with the greedy eyes. This time she was the good girl. Except that good girls were usually blond, wonderfully wide-eyed, fairly chaste, and ended up with Robert Mitchum, Dick Powell . . .

Victor Mature.

He could see her, a glimpse of her with Victor Mature in a room with barred windows. Blowing cigarette smoke in his face. (Good girls didn't blow smoke of any kind.) The bars casting striped shadows in the bare room. And Victor Mature making his jaw muscle jump but not blinking at the smoke. Not pissed off as much as disappointed. Near the end of the picture . . . She blows the smoke at him, walks into a courtroom and is sentenced to life in prison. For murder.

She screams at the judge, "I didn't do it! I swear I didn't!" And they lead her off as the newspaper guys are running out putting on their hats and Victor Mature is standing with the good girl now, the professional virgin, in the back of the courtroom, Victor clenching his jaw but with a wistful look in his eyes.

And he remembered Franny Kaufman saying to Jean, after they had seen *Let It Ride* and Franny was trying to identify another Jean Shaw picture, "Your husband commits suicide . . . what a guy . . . and makes it look like you did it." And Jean said . . .

Jean said, "Oh, that one."

And he had turned from Maurice's bar with a drink in each hand and heard Jean's car windows being smashed.

Like one of her movies?

The movie audience didn't worry about the girl who played Lila in *Let It Ride*. Poisoned her husband in *Nightshade*. Had her lover thrown off the Golden Gate Bridge in *Deadfall*. They could worry about the good girl if they wanted to, but the good girl always won out in the end. The good guy saying to her, "You crazy kid, don't you know it was you all the time? How could I ever fall for a dame like that?" And the dame, out of the picture, is saying, "Swell."

So he had to remind himself: she's the good girl in this one. But this one isn't a movie and doesn't have to end the way movies end. Okay. Except that when he thought of the real Jean Shaw he saw the same confidence, the same quiet awareness that he saw in the screen Jean Shaw. He had to somehow separate the two images in order to be able to worry about her. If there were background-music scores in real life it would be easier to identify her.

There she was in his mind again with Victor Mature. Blowing smoke at him. Bits of the picture coming back. He believed it was the same Jean Shaw picture Franny had seen and mentioned the other night.

Now it was the morning of the day after the note was delivered. He had not yet seen Jean or Maurice. He knocked on Franny's door, waited, went down to the lobby and there she was surrounded by Della Robbia ladies. At first he thought she was giving them a skin-cream demonstration, using one of the old ladies, Mrs. Heffel, who sat rigidly in front of her.

But she wasn't. Franny was sketching the woman in pastels. She looked up at him and said, "Well, say it, Joe."

He was surprised. "I thought you did hotels."

"Sit down, I'll tell you about it."

At this point he saw the cop across the lobby motion to him: a young, clean-cut guy in plainclothes standing by the alcove that led to the darkroom and the command post in the hotel kitchen. Walking away he heard Franny say, "Hey, Joe, what's going on?"

The young cop glanced around before saying, "Sergeant Torres, I'm suppose to tell you, wants you to meet him at the M.E.'s office, Jackson Memorial."

"For what?"

"They got a floater he wants you to identify."

"Why me?"

The young cop didn't know.

The body of Miney Combs lay naked, autopsied and closed, on a metal tray-table inside a refrigerated semitrailer.

The Dade County Morgue, Jackson Memorial Hospital, had become overbooked since Miami's jump in population, the 120,000 who rode in on the Mariel boat-lift. Some of them were now killing each other. So the Medical Examiner had rented the refrigerated semitrailer to accommodate the overflow. It stood behind the morgue and at one time had displayed the name *Burger King* on the side panels. But the words had finally been painted over and it was no longer something to write about in the paper.

LaBrava stared at the man's face, bloated, mutilated, no longer a face he would recognize, as Buck Torres told him about gunshot entrance wounds in the back of the head, one through and through, one hollow-nose .38 caliber slug deflected—hard-headed old guy—lodged within the frontal lobe of the brain. The old man's body had been picked up by the Coast Guard on its way out Government Cut on the tide. He had been in the water close to twenty-four hours. LaBrava was called because his name and address were found in Miney Combs' wallet, written in ballpoint pen on a five-by-seven memo sheet imprinted with the name *STAR SECURITY, Private Protection Means Crime Prevention*. The dead man's pickup truck had been found in front of the abandoned Biscaya Hotel.

His gray work clothes, work shoes, keys, a can of Copenhagen, wallet containing a driver's license and thirty-eight dollars, were in a paper bag wedged between legs that resembled marble tubes about to burst. A white tag was attached to the big toe of his right foot. Torres said no, they didn't find a snuff stick. What was a snuff stick?

LaBrava stared at the bulge of the old man's body, the crude incision from breastbone to navel, and again at the mutilated face.

LaBrava said, "He's Richard Nobles' uncle." He said, "I sent him over there, to Richard's hotel." After several moments he said, "Well, you have a reason to pick him up now, don't you?"

He could hear himself, his voice, amazed that he sounded as calm as he did. He was not calm inside his body. He felt his waiting period coming to an end.

He went home. Jean's car stood on the street, whole again. He wanted to see her, but he went to the darkroom instead and printed a set of Richard Nobles eight-by-tens. Then sat alone in his living room looking at the former rent-a-cop Franny thought was a hunk. A hunk of what? He wanted to say to Franny, "Look at him closely. Watch him move. Listen to him talk."

Could you lean on a guy like Richard? Scare him? Make him run?

Torres called in the late afternoon and said to stop by.

LaBrava walked down Collins. Was the guy

dumb or not? When he reached the La Playa Hotel he hesitated. Was the boat-lifter running it or had he pulled out? LaBrava continued on to the MBPD Detective Bureau, the windowless stucco building built like a blockhouse on the corner of First and Meridian.

The squad room inside was like all the squad rooms he had ever seen in older police buildings: different types of desks and tables bunched in rows to conserve space, a few men at desks who might have been athletes at one time, solidly built, or had the look of career noncoms in civilian clothes. No one wore a shoulder holster anymore; they packed Smiths on their hipbones, short-barreled mags with big grips. In a corner of the room was the holding cell—and this was different than all the others he had ever seen—made of wrought-iron bars, the kind of ornamental grillwork you might find on a Spanish patio.

Buck Torres' desk was in the opposite corner, next to the door that led to the lavatory, the coffeemaker and the four-and-a-half by five-and-a-half interrogation room. LaBrava sat down and Torres pushed Richard Nobles' *Advice of Rights* toward him, the Miranda sheet.

"We interviewed Richie."

LaBrava saw Richard's initials after each statement on the sheet—the Buck Torres method of avoiding surprises in court. Interviewees read their rights aloud, initialed each one as they went along and signed just below the *Waiver of Rights* statement. The signature read *Richie Nobles*.

"You show him Miney Combs?"

"First, before we brought him here. Driving over to Miami he says, 'You guys are making a big mistake. You maybe think you have something'—called me *partner*—'but you can't touch me for nothing.'"

LaBrava listened to each word.

"We take him inside the truck over there. I'm going to tell you something," Torres said. "It was a shock to him. He wasn't acting, it was a shock."

"Is he dumb?" LaBrava said.

Torres hesitated. "He's not smart enough to fake it."

"You have to be smart to be an actor?"

"Joe, he wasn't faking it. He sees the old guy, he couldn't believe it."

"He identified him?"

"Sure. His Uncle Miney. Surprised. 'What is Uncle Miney doing here?'"

"So you sat down with him in the little room, the closet, and got intimate."

"He says he had no idea the old man was down here. Swears he didn't see him. The desk clerk at Richie's hotel puts the old man in the lobby a couple hours or more the evening of the day before yesterday. But he can't put Richie with him. He can put a little Latin dude with him . . ."

"Like a boat-lifter?"

"Like maybe a boat-lifter, guy with wavy hair and an earring. But he can't put Richie with him."

"You ask Richie if anybody he knows saw the old man?"

"Sure. He says no. Let's say the Latin dude is the boat-lifter. Okay, I can put him with the old man, but I can't put him with Richie. I want to, man, but I can't."

"You know Johnbull, drives for Central?"

"Guy, he's always pissed off about something?"

"That one. He can put Richie with the boat-lifter. Find out if Johnbull saw the boat-lifter's Trans Am at the hotel the same time the desk clerk saw the Latin dude and if they left together in the car."

"No, they must've left in the old man's truck, because it was sitting at the Biscaya and the old man had the keys. We got latents, all over that truck. Okay now, if it's the boat-lifter, this guy Cundo Rey, we got to get his prints from Volusia County, where they had him on possession of a stolen motor vehicle. That would be pretty nice if we can put him in the truck. Richie swears he never saw it."

"Maybe," LaBrava said, "but he knew the old

man was looking for him. Talk to the guy, Joe
Stella, at Star Security, Lantana, where Richie used
to work. There's no way he can be clean. You're
gonna find out he sent the boat-lifter to get rid of
him. What do you think?"

"To kill him?"

"That's one way."

"Richie was shocked, Joe. I'm not kidding."

"How many floaters has he seen, gunshot? You
can know a person's dead, but when you see him
like that . . . You know what I mean."

"Joe, the guy let us look in his room."

LaBrava was aware of voices in the squad room
for the first time, a telephone ringing.

"It was clean," Torres said. "Like he had the
maid come in every hour."

"He show you his gun?"

"And his license. He hands me the piece, says,
'Here, you want to check it?' "

"Looking you right in the eye."

"He didn't do the old man, Joe."

There was a silence again, until LaBrava said,
"You mind if I suggest something?"

"What?"

"Pick up a guy at the La Playa Hotel named
David Vega, he's a *Marielito*, and ask him about the
boat-lifter. See if you can find out if Cundo's got a
gun and happened to buy any hollow-nose, steel-

jacket thirty-eights. There's a guy at the hotel sells guns and ammo, anything you want."

"How do you know that?"

"I took his picture. Holding a sawed-off shotgun."

"Jesus Christ," Torres said.

"I asked him, 'You don't care who sees your picture?' He's stoned most of the time. He said, no, it would be good for his business."

"Jesus Christ," Torres said.

"David Vega's the guy you want. If he gives you the gun seller, do whatever you feel like, but ask him about Cundo first. If you can't find David Vega look for a guy named Guilli, he deals out on the Pier."

Torres said, "How do you know all these guys?"

"They like to have their picture taken. But let's get back to Richie. Was he nervous anytime?"

"Once we got here he was cool. Or he acted surprised at everything."

"Acted," LaBrava said.

"Eyes open real wide. Who, me? They all do that. But I think he was waiting to see if I'm going to mention a note or the six hundred thousand or if he knows a movie star."

"You didn't though."

"I can play dumb too. But he knows we know. Last night and this morning he's walking around

Collins Avenue, Lincoln Mall, he goes in a place, comes out the back, or all of a sudden he crosses the street against the light. Bullshit stuff. He follows girls a lot, makes the moves, then looks around, wants to make sure he has an audience. He does everything but wave at my guys. I'm finished talking to him about the old man, he says, 'There anything else you want to ask me about?' You see what I mean? He knows. He's telling us he knows."

"You turn him loose?"

"What have I got? Man, if I brought in every suspect fits something like this I'd have to pick up half the neighborhood. I told him to stay close by."

"It didn't bother him?"

"He gives me some you-all shit, he be obliged we get the scudder 'at done it."

"Is he dumb?" LaBrava said.

"Guy's a showoff."

"But is he dumb?"

"I think it could be what you said before. The boat-lifter's running it and Richie's the beard."

"Put a clown suit on him," LaBrava said, thoughtful, wondering. "Got him in the trick bag and he doesn't know it. You think?"

"Could be."

"If he's dumb enough," LaBrava said. "It keeps coming back to that."

"And if the boat-lifter is smarter than he is."

"Or if there's somebody else smarter than both of them," LaBrava said. "Have you thought of that?"

"Maybe I should talk to the movie star again," Torres said. "See who else's been in her life since she became a widow."

"It wouldn't hurt," LaBrava said.

21

PACO BOZA CAME FOR HIS WHEELCHAIR, a happy guy. Lana was back with him. She hated Hialeah, it was like in the country and she was a big-city girl. She loved her photograph. She wanted LaBrava to send it someplace, some magazine, be a centerfold girl. It was early evening and they were out on the sidewalk, the street quiet, Paco wearing his straw hat cocked, about to take off in his wheelchair.

LaBrava said, "You know the big blond guy."

"The Silver Kid," Paco said, "of course."

"I want somebody to deliver a note to him, at his hotel."

"Sure."

"And write it."

"What does it say?"

"I want him to come to the park tonight, 1:00 A.M., across from the Play House Bar."

"Sign your name?"

"No, sign it C.R."

"Just C.R."

"That's the *Marielito*, the one with the earring."

"Oh," Paco said, "yes, I remember."

"But I have to make sure the big blond guy gets the message and not the police."

Paco said, "Man, you got something going on."

"If I can, I'd like to get hold of a baseball bat," LaBrava said. "But I think the stores are closed."

"You and this guy going to play ball? In the dark? Never mind, don't tell me," Paco said. "I got one for softball, you can use."

"I'll take good care of it," LaBrava said.

Nobles wished he had a car; he'd take the cops on a tour of Dade County, see if they were any good at tailing. Man, he would love to get them up in the Big Scrub, lose their ass in two minutes. This walking the streets, stopping at bars, was getting to be a bunch of shit. One more day he could take off. Tomorrow night sometime.

When he got back to the hotel, about ten, the desk clerk waved and held out a plain white envelope with his name printed on it in pencil. It was not only sealed, there was a hunk of pink chewing gum stuck to the flap. The desk clerk worked his eyebrows up and down as he said a girl delivered it, a little Latin mama. Nobles said, a girl uh? He took the envelope across the lobby, looking at his name that some kid or halfwit might've printed.

The message inside, on plain white paper, printed in pencil, said for him to come to the park tonight . . . and *Do not bring police* and *Do not phone*. Signed, *C.R.*

It didn't make sense. Cundo was supposed to be long gone, hiding somewhere until it was his turn again. Unless something had happened to him or they were watching him.

But the cops didn't know anything about Cundo. How could they?

Maybe the little booger was sick.

What Nobles finally decided, he'd slip out of the hotel and go have a look. It would be like a dry run, disappear in the night. Then do it the same way tomorrow when he'd take off for good. He wondered if he should pay his hotel bill before he left. Shit, he needed money. The idea came to him then: long as he was out, going over to the park anyway, he could mug a queer and pick up some change. Queers—he couldn't imagine why—always had jobs that paid good money. Slip out like old Zorro used to do it with his mask and sword. Zip, zip, zip, mark a big fucking Z on the wall. Soldiers come busting in, old Zorro he's back sitting by the fire, pretending *he's* queer. There were enough real ones out there, hanging around the south end of the park, he ought to be able to cut a straggler. He wondered why he hadn't thought of it before. Man, he needed something to *do*.

*   *   *

At 1:05 A.M. Buck Torres got a call at home from one of his guys on the Paramount Hotel surveillance detail. Nobles had temporarily disappeared. Torres, lying in bed in the dark, said, "Temporarily. Oh, that means he told you he was coming back?" No, it meant he didn't have anything with him, any luggage. Torres said, "Oh, did he check in with luggage?" Then said, "Forget it, tell me what happened." Resigned himself and listened to the flat, boring tone of the guy's story: how Richard had walked out of the hotel at 12:32 giving them the same old shit, looking back every once in a while, walked south on Collins to Sixteenth, over Sixteenth to the St. Moritz, walked through the hotel to the beach and that was the last they saw of him. There was no way two guys could keep a subject under surveillance out on that beach, a beach that big, at night. You would have to stay within twenty feet of the subject and even then it would be almost impossible with just two guys. There was a moon but also clouds; it was supposed to rain tomorrow, intermittent showers until sometime in the afternoon. Torres listened to the weather report, his guy trying to give him at least some predictable information. Torres suggested they go back to the Paramount and wait. He called the Della Robbia command post and told them to keep their eyes open, Richard was loose.

*   *   *

Hell, he just waited till there was cloud cover,
ducked over that hump of sand that was like a low
hogback down the length of the beach near the water, kept to the smooth hardpack where the surf
was washing in and headed south. Nothing to it.
Around Tenth Street he came up, crossed the beach
to Lummus Park and had it made. From here down
there was more vegetation—lot of screw pine and
what looked like pitchapple, but was probably sea-
grape trimmed back; kind of dark, creepy place he
was used to. Hardly any people. Pairs here and
there on benches he'd pass and leave be. First rule
of fairy-hawking, pick a stray. Let the sweet boy
have the first word. *H'ar you tonight?* Just fine,
h'ar you? *Beautiful night, ain't it?* Ain't it though.
*Are you tired? Would you like me to give you a
back rub?* No, but you can do old Hank the shank
if you've a mind. Let the boy get down there and
gobble, then as you feel the juice commence to flow,
club that sucker with a right hook to put him away.
Pick him clean as he whimpers and moans. Then
walk, don't run. Only thing queers don't blow is a
whistle.

There was one.

Sweet boy sitting on the wall with his hands
folded.

But he'd better check on Cundo first. So Nobles

walked out to the street. The Play House Bar was almost right across the way. There didn't seem to be any little Cubans hanging around anyplace. Well, it wasn't one o'clock yet. He'd make a quick score and then look for him. So he cut back through the trees to where that boy was waiting, sitting on the low cement wall, waiting for a lover. Shit, guy like that, anybody'd do.

Sucker had designs—like big flowers, Nobles saw as he got closer—all over his shirt. No, they weren't flowers, they were palm trees and sailboats. Guy had trees and boats for Christ sake all over his sport shirt.

The guy looked up at him, just a few feet away, and said, "Richie, how you doing?"

Nobles had to take a moment. He said, "Je-sus Christ, look-it who's here. I been wondering what in the hell ever become of you, you know it? It's something, meeting like this again, ain't it?" Nobles glanced around, both ways. It was nice and quiet here.

He had time. He couldn't think of the guy's name now. Joe something, like a dago name. He sure did not look like any government agent Nobles had ever seen. It was in his mind to make a remark about that when he remembered just in time, shit no, he wasn't suppose to know anything about the guy or even he was the guy'd been taking his picture and was a friend of the cops. He had to realize all that at once now, try to play dumb and not make any mistakes.

What shook him was, thinking that, right *as* he was thinking that, the guy saying, "Are you dumb, Richard?"

He didn't know how to answer. The guy wasn't calling him dumb, he was asking him if he was, like he wanted to know. Then the guy was confusing him some more, saying, "Hay-baling wire is good."

Je-sus Christ.

"Your Uncle Miney said your dad used to whip you with it. Teach you humility."

Nobles stared at him.

"But that isn't something you need for extortion, is it? And if you're any good and get the six hundred grand, the last thing you're gonna be is humble, huh?"

"Oh my," Nobles said, "we sure think we're clever, don't we?"

"You're not supposed to know what I'm talking about."

Nobles said, "Mister, I'm gonna run my hands over you. I feel a wire, me and you are gonna say nighty-night. I don't, well, we can see where it goes. Stand up and turn around."

LaBrava got up slowly, raising his arms straight out to the sides as he turned, and Nobles moved in close to run his hands up to LaBrava's shoulders, took hold of the muscles close to his neck and began to pinch hard. LaBrava tried to hunch and twist free and Nobles grabbed him by the hair with one hand and punched him in the back of the neck with the other, jabbed him hard with the knuckles you use to knock on a door.

"So you're the blindsider," Nobles said, and rabbit-punched him again. "Huh, is that right?" Pulled up on his hair and drove those knuckles in again. "You the blindsider?" Rabbit-punched him again. Then punched him with shoulder behind it, letting go of the hair. LaBrava fell forward to hit the low wall made of cement and coral and had to catch himself, hold on with his thighs to keep from going over. He hung there, moving his head carefully from side to side, feeling pain, throbs of it up through his skull, and seeing black objects crawling around the edges of his vision. Nobles, behind him, kept at it. "Yeah, blindsider, they like to sneak up on you, hit you when you're not looking." LaBrava was looking down at sand on the beach side of the wall, close to his face, hoping for his head to clear. High overhead clouds moved and moonlight edged toward the wall—Nobles saying yeah, goddamn blindsider, I love to get me a blindsider—and now LaBrava was looking at the softball bat lying in the sand, the bat the same color as sand. His hands, hanging over the wall, went to the handle right-over-left to bat right-handed. He was about ready.

* * *

When he came up with it he pushed off the wall with his knees, came around from the left and saw Nobles doing a quick backstep jig, right hand going into his silver jacket—LaBrava seeing it and believing in that moment he should be hitting from the other side tonight. But it was all right. Nobles brought up his left arm for protection, instinct jerking it up, and LaBrava found it between wrist and elbow with a bone-cracking, line-drive swing that brought a gasp from the big guy, and his right hand out of the silver jacket empty to grab hold of the broken arm. LaBrava came back for good measure with a left-side, cross-hand swing to pound shoulder and muscle, getting a grunt this time, Nobles covering his head with his good arm. So LaBrava hit him across the shins and that brought him down to the grass with a scream, trying to curl up, cover himself. LaBrava was finished with the bat. He dropped it as he straddled the big guy, yanked the .357 Smith out of his belt and worked the blunt bluesteel tip, once again, into Nobles' mouth.

LaBrava said, feeling he should tell him, "I think you're in the wrong line of work. You've got size and you look mean enough, but I believe you lack desire. Open your eyes."

Nobles had them squeezed closed and seemed in

pain. LaBrava slipped the gun out of his mouth, barely out, laying the sight under the lower lip, and Nobles said, "Jesus Christ, I'm hurt. My goddamn arm is broke." He turned his head to look at it, outstretched on the grass.

LaBrava said, "I hope it is. But let me tell you what's more important, to your welfare as well as your health. You like to deal. I think you ought to make one, give the cops the boat-lifter."

"The what?"

"Cundo Rey, your little buddy."

Nobles stared at him, maybe thinking faster than he had ever thought in his life, but thinking within his limitations. He did appear dumb, the vacant look giving him away.

"Let the cops have Cundo . . . and whoever else you got. They'll make you a nice deal."

Look at him thinking. Now trying to show some pain, going for sympathy.

"The cops have you made, Richard. You know that. They can put Cundo with your uncle and you with Cundo."

"I never *saw* Uncle Miney. I told 'em that."

"Doesn't matter," LaBrava said. "You don't give 'em Cundo Rey they'll pick the little Cuban up— guy like him, he's hard to miss—they'll offer him the same kind of deal and he'll give 'em Mr. Richard Nobles. He'd be dumb if he didn't."

Nobles was listening closely to this.

"He gets something like five to twenty up at Raiford, you move up there for life. He'll do three out of the five, and if you don't get him in the yard, he walks."

Nobles said, "Wait a second. What one are we talking about?"

"Take your pick. Murder first degree or the threat of it, for money. Either one'll put you away." LaBrava paused, looking down at him. Big dumb blond-haired clown. He did look mean. But deep down where it counted, all he could claim to be was a snitch. "Go make your deal and let the state attorney get you a lawyer. You'll come out all right."

He was so quiet now, staring up, moonlight catching his eyes.

"First thing in the morning," LaBrava said. "You don't want to spend the night locked up." Keeping his tone mild, almost soothing. What a nice guy. "You want, I'll tell the lady never mind about getting the money, and the trash bag. Say you changed your mind."

Those eyes staring up at him.

"You want me to tell her that?"

Those dumb eyes in moonlight began to change, trying for a different look, creasing, getting a crafty gleam.

Nobles said, "I know who you are. You and all them other copsuckers, you're about to get the surprise of your life." That greasy tone sliding out and his mouth barely moving. "Now get offa me or I'm gonna have your ass up on charges."

See? Try to be reasonable what happens? He'd be talking about his rights next. Waving a Xeroxed copy of his Miranda sheet.

LaBrava cocked the Smith, for effect, for the sound of it, stuck the tip of the barrel into Nobles' mouth, hooking the front sight in behind his upper teeth and saw him gag as the gleam went out of his eyes.

He said, "Richard, are you trying to fuck with me?" Getting that flat, effortless cop sound. He believed in this moment he would have been a good one.

He said, "Richard, I got the gun. You don't have it, I do. But you threaten me. I don't understand that. What'd you think I was gonna do?" He drew the barrel out enough to lay it on Nobles' lower lip. "Tell me."

Nobles said, "You don't have no right—"

See? LaBrava shoved the barrel back into his mouth. It was that goddamn Miranda thing. They packed, swaggered, picked on and scared the shit out of civilians, then ran and got behind Miranda.

He said, "Richard," wanting to make it clear but no big deal. "If I got the gun, asshole, I got the right." The way a Metro cop would say it. The one doing paperwork sniffing whiteout wanting to get back on the street so bad. He knew something the Metro cop knew. He could sit on Nobles' belly and feel him breathing in and out beneath him, feel the man's life between his own thighs, and be detached and deal with the man on a mutual basis of understanding. It was a strange feeling, but natural; like discovering something about yourself you never knew before. He felt that he could kill Nobles; in this moment he could. Pull the trigger. But he didn't know what he would feel the moment after, with the sound fading and hearing the surf again. Something was happening to him. The cop in him coming out. After all that waiting. Nine years or more of official waiting, hanging back steely-eyed and looking smart. He had heard Buck Torres say one time to a witness, pleading for information, "I give you my word as a man." Not as a policeman, a man. He would never forget that. It was what it came down to here, in this situation. Man to man he said to Nobles, "Bullshit time's over. Are you dumb?"

He eased the barrel out and watched that all-American face, pale in moonlight, move from side to side.

"I can't hear you."

"No, I ain't dumb. Jesus."

"How do you know who I am?"

"I don't."

"You said, a minute ago, 'I know who you are.' "

Look at him thinking, trying to be careful. LaBrava moved the barrel along the curve of Nobles' chin. "They wire your mouth shut for a broken jaw. Talk while you can."

"You already broke my goddamn arm!"

"See what I mean? . . . How do you know who I am?"

"I heard, around."

"Where?"

"On the street. I heard you live at that ho-tel."

LaBrava drew the barrel down the bridge of his nose. Look at those eyes, trying to be sincere.

"I heard you was a secret agent of some kind with the gover'ment. Listen, I know some of those boys. Maybe're friends of yours. Up in Jacksonville."

"Who told you?"

"Nobody, I just heard. Was some guy, you know, in a bar."

"What's the surprise?"

"What?"

"You said, 'You're about to get the surprise of your life.' What's the surprise?"

"I was just, you know, talking. Jesus, my goddamn arm hurts something terrible."

"What's the surprise, Richard?"

"Nothing. I was talking is all."

See? It reached the point every time where you had to deliver or let the guy up. Tell him one time

what you're going to do. Tell him twice, he knows
you're full of shit. Once you started to lose it it was
over. LaBrava leaned in closer, eye to eye, the gun
barrel beneath Nobles' chin, raising it slightly.

"The surprise is how six hundred thousand dollars disappear. Look at me, Richard. The surprise—
you see all the cops standing around scratching
their head. You're undoing the baling wire, opening the garbage bag, taking out all that money.
Look at me, Richard."

He did. Nobles met his eyes and said, "I ain't
done nothing."

"What else do you see, Richard?"

"I ain't done nothing."

He was losing it.

"What movie did she show you?"

"What?"

"She said she showed you a movie."

He was getting it back. Maybe.

Nobles was thinking again. "She told you that?"

"What was the name of it?"

"I don't know, I forget."

"Who was in it?"

"You kidding me? Shit, I don't know."

"Where's your partner?"

"I don't know—I don't have no partner."

"The little Cuban."

"I met the booger one time, 'at's all."

"You came to meet him tonight."

"Shit, it was you. God*damn*, we're clever."

He felt tired knowing he was losing it. It was hard to keep it up unless you were honestly detached enough to go all the way and break the guy's jaw looking into his eyes. He could sit on the guy all night and threaten and never deliver and finally the guy would get tired of it. So who was full of shit?

He tried again, though, one more time. Said, "Richard, call it off."

Heard himself and knew it was over.

Nobles said, "Or what?"

See?

Nobles said, "I gotta go the hospital."

See?

"So get the fuck offa me."

Man, lost and gone forever. He would give anything to be able to bust the guy's jaw. He couldn't do it. So he reached out and hacked the gun barrel across that forearm—already broken—a gesture, for Uncle Miney if not his own peace of mind—and had to roll for his life as Nobles screamed and erupted beneath him, came up in a crouch holding his arm tight to his body, ran hunched into tree shadow a dozen yards away and must have felt protected. He took time to yell at LaBrava, back there on his knees, "You're crazy! You know it? You're fucking crazy!"

22

BUCK TORRES THOUGHT he was crazy, too. He didn't say he was crazy, he said, "You broke the guy's arm?" and asked if he was crazy; it was the same thing. He came at 7:30 in the morning to say Nobles had left his hotel during the night and never returned.

Once LaBrava told him to check Sinai and Jackson Memorial Out-Patient and look for a guy walking around with his left arm in a cast, he had to tell it all. He wondered if Torres was going to comment. He was silent for so long after, staring at him in the kitchenette pouring coffee for them. Finally, that was when Torres said it.

"Are you crazy?"

"I don't think so."

"What's the matter with you?"

"Maybe I'm a little crazy. But maybe you have to be crazy to make something happen or make it hard for them," LaBrava said. "Look at it. A note comes asking for money. Jean goes to the bank, picks it up. Another note comes, it'll tell her to take the money to a certain place and she'll do it." LaBrava paused and said, "Is it that easy?"

"We're with her every step, Joe."

"They know you're gonna be with her."

"We have to wait and see." Torres sounded helpless. "What else can we do?"

"You ever had one like this or heard of one?"

"Only dope, dopers trying to score off each other. The Major called the Bureau and they never had one like this either. They said, what is this? Your suspect is practically wearing a sign."

"The Bureau's in it now?"

"Miami office. They're busy on some Castro spy stuff they didn't care to discuss, but they took the note for analysis. They give us their R.A. in West Palm, the resident agent, and some words of wisdom. 'Don't lose the woman or the money or it'll fuck up your day.' "

Jean Shaw came into LaBrava's mind in black and white and then in color and then in black and white again. He brought the color picture back, saw her eyes looking at him and wanted to be with her, talk to her. He saw Richard Nobles' face now, in moonlight, and said, "The guy can't wait for it to happen. He tells us we're about to get the surprise of our life."

"He had to say something like that," Torres said,

"you're sitting on him. It's like what a kid would say."

"The whole thing is like a bunch of kids made it up," LaBrava said. "Gimme the money or I'll kill you. Are you gonna play with them? You say you have to. All you've got is this six-foot-three-and-a-half blond asshole in a silver jacket waving at you, trying to get your attention."

"Not anymore we don't."

"He could've left anytime. He stayed around long enough so you notice him. Jean says, 'This guy's been bothering me,' and there he is, right there. That one. What does that tell you?"

"If he's running it," Torres said, "he has to be pretty fucking dumb."

LaBrava smiled, because he could feel they were looking into the center of it. He blew on his coffee and took a sip.

"Or somebody else is running it and using Richard," LaBrava said, "I like to think because he *is* pretty fucking dumb."

"Using him—who, the boat-lifter?"

"The boat-lifter and somebody we don't know about who's smarter than both of them." LaBrava paused and said, "What about the old man's pickup?"

Torres shook his head. "No boat-lifter prints; I couldn't believe it. We found any the Bureau was ready to put out a fugitive warrant. But . . . the way it goes."

LaBrava said, "Think about the boat-lifter and somebody else we don't know about who's using Richard. If they're gonna stand him out in the open and hang a sign on him . . . what does that tell you?"

Torres said, "They make it they're not gonna cut him in. They'd be dumb as him if they did."

"That's right," LaBrava said, "Richard's a celebrity now. The first twenty he breaks he's in jail. If he does it around here, and I don't think he could wait. So if they don't give him a cut . . ."

"They have to dump him," Torres said.

"There you are," LaBrava said, and sipped his coffee. "Richard's a throw-away and doesn't know it."

"You tell him that?"

"I hadn't thought of it yet."

"You still have his gun?"

"He can get another one. I think he better."

"Joe, come on . . ."

"Don't ask, you won't have to worry about it."

"You don't carry a gun anymore, Joe, you're a civilian now. You and I can talk, I appreciate it; but you got to stay out of it when the time comes. You understand? It's not anything personal, it's the way it is."

"I know that."

"You don't want to get mad, do something dumb."

"I'm not mad at anybody."

"Yeah? How come you broke the guy's arm?"

"I didn't mean to. He raised it to protect his head."

Torres said, "Oh, Joe. Man, come on . . . You're kidding me, aren't you?"

LaBrava said, "Yeah, I'm kidding."

For a while last night he had become detached, able to respond impersonally rather than in a role with conditions. He felt this detachment again and liked the feeling, content to be a watcher, though not for too long.

Mrs. Heffel, the Della Robbia lady who picked up the envelope from the floor and placed it on the marble counter, said it was not so long ago that she found it. She put it there at once. She said she didn't open it and read it so don't accuse me. Maurice said, no one is accusing you; these gentlemen want to know what time it was and if you saw anybody in the lobby might have left it. Mrs. Heffel said, I put it over there, I minded my own business, so please don't accuse me, you don't know what you're talking about.

It was close to four o'clock by the time Jean and then Buck Torres read the note lying open on the

marble counter. It was typed on the same kind of
steno paper as the first one and said:

Here we go. Put the Hefty bag with the money
in it in the front seat of your car and no place
else. You are to drive ALONE north on I-95 to
Atlantic Blvd, Pompano Beach. Go over to
AIA and drive up to the market on the corner
of Spring St. where you see the Coppertone
sign (almost to the Hillsboro Inlet) and you
will find 4 outside telephone booths. Wait at
the second phone from the left as you face the
street. Be there at exactly 6 PM ALONE. No
cops. No tricks. Or you will be sorry. I am
watching you.

LaBrava read the note and became an observer
they let hang around.

He saw the plainclothes cops, Jean, Maurice,
everyone in a hurry to do what was expected, hurrying to follow instructions. He wanted to talk to
Jean, but it wasn't possible now. After he read the
note, he went into the area of the hotel kitchen
where the police had set up their telephones and
recording equipment. A detective was talking to the
resident FBI man in West Palm, requesting traps on
the Hillsboro phones. Jean Shaw was unbuttoning
her blouse. He watched Jean, he watched Torres,
solemn, impassive, tape a GE body pack to her rib

cage, close beneath the white bra cup covering her right breast. The pack was smaller than a package of cigarettes and contained microphone, battery and transmitter in one. She would be wired without wires. He saw her eyes gazing at him, solemn—everyone solemn—over Buck Torres' dark head bent close to her body, as though he might be listening to her heartbeat. She didn't say anything to him. She raised her eyebrows a little, resigned, that was all. She buttoned her blouse. Maurice came in with a detective carrying the Hefty trash bag that bulged out in a smooth round shape about half full; not heavy, the detective carrying it easily with one hand, holding it by the neck that was secured with a twist of baling wire. An I.D. technician came in and gave Jean and Torres each a handwritten copy of the second note. Jean went upstairs to get her purse. Torres spoke to the West Palm R.A. on the phone, giving him a description of Jean's Cadillac and the three surveillance cars they would be using. Another detective was talking to the Broward County sheriff's office. All of them serious, playing the game almost deadpan. The only evidence of emotion before they left: Torres wanted to get in the back seat of Jean's car, lie on the floor. She refused. He tried to insist and she said, then she wasn't going. She said, "It's my life, not yours." Torres gave in.

*   *   *

Maurice said, "Thank the Lord it's cocktail time," sounding more relieved than worried. He poured Scotch over ice at his credenza, brought one to LaBrava looking at a photograph on a wall of the living-room gallery, and climbed into his La-Z-Boy.

The photograph, a half century old, showed a bearded man in a dark business suit standing in sunlight at the brushy edge of a stream.

"Guy claims that's the site of the original Garden of Eden," Maurice said. "On the east bank of the Apalachicola River between Bristol and Chatahoochee, and you know the kind live up at Chatahoochee. Guy also said Noah built his ark right there, in Bristol. When the flood came he floated around about five months, landed on Mount Ararat and thought he was in West Tennessee. Kind a mistake people make all the time."

"Did you give her the money?"

"I loaned it to her. That would be ridiculous have to mortgage her condo. This guy, he don't know what he's doing, they'll pick him up. Guy's a clown."

LaBrava came over and sat down. "You went to your bank and drew six hundred thousand, just like that."

"Signed some bonds over to her. You want to know how much money I got? Don't worry about it."

"Can you afford to lose it?"

"Joe, I ran a horse book. Don't try and tell me anything about risk, what the odds are in a deal like this. It's a lot of money, but at the same time it's only money. I know what I'm doing."

"The cops think it's Jean's."

"They're suppose to. Jeanie doesn't want it to get out I'm the bank, give anybody ideas. So don't say anything, even to your pal."

"Jean's idea."

"We agreed it's the way to do it. I never went in for publicity like some guys. I don't say anything that ever gets on the financial page. I could, Joe. I could tell the experts a few things, where to put your dough while the government's fucking up the economy; but nobody asks me and that's fine."

"You don't seem too worried about her."

"Yeah, is that right? You know what I'm thinking?"

"She doesn't seem too worried either. Everybody's just sort a going along with it."

"Your experience, Secret Agent X-9, what would you do?"

"No—what I'm saying, it can't be this simple. There's gotta be a surprise . . ." LaBrava stopped and looked at Maurice. "You put real money in the bag?"

"You think we cut up paper? You gotta assume the guy's gonna look at it, whether he does or not."

"And he could take her along, couldn't he?"

"I worry the guy might be psycho, yeah, do something crazy," Maurice said. "I'll tell you, Jeanie gets into some situations. She's very bright, except she's not too good a judge a character—some of the bums she gets mixed up with, guys on the make. But she's a tough lady, she always comes out okay. Sees what she has to do . . ." Maurice looked over at the wall of photographs. "Like Noah . . . Guy says he built the ark out of Florida gopher wood and if you don't believe him look it up."

LaBrava had never heard of gopher wood. He said, "Has this ever happened to her before?"

"What?"

"Extortion. Somebody threatens her."

"Oh no, nothing like this. Couple of times she got in the hole gambling—she was in that movie she thinks she knows how. They threatened her, yeah, but they didn't have to. She paid. Another time she paid off a guy's wife was gonna drag her into a divorce action. She gets into these situations, she seems to have a knack for it."

"I thought she was smarter than that."

"She's smart. But like I've said, Joe, you gotta remember she was a movie star. Movie stars are different than you and I."

23

SHE HAD WRITTEN a script once, walked into Harry Cohn's office at Columbia and handed it to him. In a bright red cover. He threw it on the desk, said, "Tell me what it's about in three sentences, and no cheating." She told him: smart, attractive girl is offered anything she wants by rich playboy who's nuts about her, furs, jewels, you name it. Harry Cohn said, "Yeah?" Girl turns him down because getting it that way is unsatisfying, too easy. Harry Cohn said, "She nuts? I never met a fucking broad yet'd turn down anything." Jean said, wait. The girl cons the playboy out of a lot of money and is happy because *she* did it, she earned it herself. Harry Cohn said, "You mean the broad wins?" She said, "You bet." He told her the idea stunk.

The pay phones, four in a row, were in Plexiglas shells mounted on metal posts. Jean stood by the second phone, waiting, giving it another minute. It was 6:12. Two of the police surveillance cars were across A1A at the Sunoco station; she didn't see the third one, or signs of any local police. Her purse rested on the metal ledge beneath the phone, open toward her. She might as well do it now. Sgt. Torres, his nose practically in her bra, had told her to speak normally, they'd pick up her voice. She straightened, getting ready, and could feel the tape pull against her skin.

Jean said, as though talking to herself, "If he doesn't call, what do I do? This has to be the right place." She waited a few moments, then took the folded sheet of steno paper from her purse.

Ready? With curiosity, then surprise:

"There's something . . . It looks like . . . My God, it's a piece of note paper just like the ones . . . It's sticking out of the phone book." She unfolded the sheet and looked at the note she had dictated to Richard. "It says . . . 'Go directly to your apartment. Now. Bring the money with you. Now. I am watching you.' "

She looked up, looked around for effect. She could see them, inside the cars at the Sunoco station. They started their engines. She said, "I'll leave the note here."

Victim eager to cooperate. Don't think. Play the part.

*　　*　　*

Seventeen minutes later, in the guest parking area of Jean Shaw's condominium on Ocean Drive, Boca Raton:

Torres sat in the communications surveillance car, a black Mercedes sedan that had once transported heroin, and watched Jean Shaw walk into the building, her upper body slightly twisted, using both hands to hold the trash bag bouncing against her leg.

Her voice said, "I don't see anyone." The sound thin, coming from a tunnel or from across the ocean. "Isn't someone supposed to be here? . . . I'm going to pick up my mail."

He had told her police would be in the building, never more than a few seconds away from her. The FBI's West Palm resident agent and people from the Palm Beach County Sheriff's. The West Palm R.A. would be up on her floor.

"I'm entering the elevator now."

Nearly thirty seconds passed.

"I'm at my apartment . . . I think there's someone . . . I heard the fire exit close, at the end of the hall. If it isn't one of ours you'd better get up here."

He liked her voice. No strain. Being transmitted from beneath those softly scented breasts. The tape had stuck to his fingers and he'd had a time trying to act natural, putting the body pack on her. She had a mole beneath her left breast, about an inch down.

Her voice said, "I'm in my apartment. Should I wait for a call? I don't see a note anywhere."

Torres picked up his Walkie and said to the West Palm R.A., a guy named Jim McCormick he had met for the first time at the Sunoco station, "Jim, she's in there. The door should be open. See how she's doing."

Almost a minute passed. Her voice said, "Do you think he'll call?" Torres could hear sounds, another voice. A couple of minutes passed.

The West Palm R.A.'s voice came on the Walkie. "Sergeant, we got another note. It was in with the mail."

Torres, feeling a degree of relief, said, "Then it's your case, man."

The West Palm R.A. said, "It wasn't mailed, it was stuck in the box, hand delivered."

Torres said, "Oh."

The West Palm R.A. said, "This guy thinks he's a joker. Now we go back. Ms. Shaw is to proceed to Fort Lauderdale, take I-95 to Sunrise. Proceed east to Northeast Twenty-fourth and turn right past Burdine's in the Galleria Mall. Turn left on Ninth Street and proceed to the end. You got it?"

"It's not clear," Torres said.

"Then write it down," the West Palm R.A. said.

"I did write it down. What else does it say?"

" 'I am watching you.' "

She liked the idea of leading a procession of law-enforcement officers—city, county, federal, losing some, picking up others as she left Palm Beach County and entered Broward—and not a soul through miles of freeway traffic knew it . . . all these people poking along, heading for their little stucco ranch homes and an evening of real-life nothing. She liked the idea of reaching Sunrise with the sun poetically down, to drive east toward a darkening sky, still in traffic, taking her time, wanting the light down fairly low for the last act.

She wasn't sure, at first, if she liked having the West Palm FBI guy along. Then decided she liked it, because he added a little class without being much more than an observer. She liked him for the same reason she liked Torres—good casting, big-city cop type with ethnic color—and liked having Joe LaBrava involved. Though she was just as glad he wasn't in the procession, noticing every detail; he could be scary. She liked them because working with professionals brought out the best in you; you could count on them for cues, sometimes inspiration. Whereas amateurs could ruin your concentration and timing, make you look awkward. She guessed she liked Joe LaBrava for a lot of reasons. He was imaginative. He acted without acting. Played a street character with marvelous restraint, a natural innocence. He was agreeable, understanding, sensitive. He liked Maurice a lot, a big plus. Seemed to have an open mind. A fairly keen one. He certainly had a sense of the dramatic; look at his pictures. Finally, and it could be worth putting at the top of the list, he was a fan.

True fans understood and were willing to make excuses. If they had to. Joe was a fan for the right reason, he recognized her as an actress.

But, my God, he didn't miss a thing. Had even identified and photographed Richard's little helper—whom she was about to meet for the first time and had better get mentally prepared. She hoped he would have something heavy enough to break the glass. She hoped he would be reasonably calm but quick and, please, wouldn't have a gun.

The shopping center was coming up on the right. She had to assume there would be Lauderdale or Broward Sheriff's cops around somewhere. There was Burdine's, the name against the rising wall of the store. Just beyond were Neiman-Marcus and Saks. She approached the light at Northwest Twenty-fourth.

The instructions were intentionally vague from here, Twenty-fourth to Ninth Street to the end, because she wasn't going that far.

She would turn right onto Twenty-fourth, follow the street-level underpass to the rear of the mall and be out of sight of the surveillance cars for about fifteen seconds. No more than that.

The light was green. She turned, passed beneath the drive-through to Ninth and turned left. She was now approaching the only weak sequence in the script. Later, she would have to explain in detail why she suddenly left Ninth and turned into the parking structure instead of proceeding to the end of the street, according to instructions.

For the time being, she said to the mike beneath her breast, "There's someone waving!" Got some urgency in her tone, then doubt, fear, saying, "Is he one of ours?" and let it go at that.

They heard it in the Mercedes approaching Twenty-fourth. Torres said, "Go—" and the detective driving mashed the accelerator, then had to brake hard to make the turn. "Where are you?" Torres said, as they came out of the underpass and did not see the Eldorado. "Say something." But there would be nothing for the next minute or so, until they heard the sound of breaking glass.

Cundo Rey watched the Cadillac come out of the underpass, dull white car way down there. Yes, the same one, the windows fixed now. He turned and moved down the nearly empty aisle to the ramp, where cars turned off at this level, and stood against the column with a brick in his left hand, a red brick with some mortar stuck to it. He wore white work gloves, new ones. He could hear the Cadillac, inside now, somewhere below him.

Richard said he didn't need to have a gun, she would be so scared she would let him have the money and not give him any trouble. He had the gun anyway, under his shirt hanging out. He didn't know this woman; what if *she* had a gun? He knew what he was going to do. Step out, raise his right hand . . .

Richard said don't say anything because the woman would have a wire on her. Richard, the creature, knew a few things, but not too many.

The car sounded like it was in a hurry, tires squealing in the turns. It reached the third level. Now it was coming, he saw the front end, coming up the ramp. The car got louder. He stepped out, extending his right hand, stopping the car like Superman, the fender coming to touch his hand gently, without a sound. There she was looking at him. He took the brick in his right hand, saw her turn away, bringing up her arm, as he smashed the brick through the passenger-side window, unlocked the door, opened it. Yes, she was a beautiful woman and very calm, her eyes looking at him. Taking the trash bag by the neck he had to say something to her, so he said, "Thank you very much, lady—" and ran for the exit sign above the door to the stairway.

He would go to the ground level and walk behind the stores to come out on Twenty-sixth Avenue where the new Buick Skylark, stolen this afternoon, waited on the street. Nothing to it. He wished he could take off in the Skylark, go to Georgia right now; but he had to go back to Miami Beach to get his car. Sure, he could buy a new one. But he loved that car too much. He felt good in that car. He said, "Yeah? Well, how does it feel to be rich?" He said, "You kidding me?"

She couldn't afford to wait too long—twenty seconds from the time the Exit door closed. She concentrated a moment, worked up a feeling of agitated fear, careful to keep it just short of hysteria, and shouted, "He's got it! He broke the window!" She paused, opened her door and heard tires squealing, more than one car, and pulled the door closed. "Will you please hurry? He's getting away!" Without telling them the direction he'd taken. A lapse she would attribute later to fear, anxiety, so much happening at once—wring hands and look helpless. The black Mercedes was coming off the third level, up the ramp now, followed closely by another car, then another. She could hear sirens outside. Torres was in her rearview mirror, running toward her with a radio in his hand.

She'd push the door open, come out with her big brown eyes glistening, pleading, and maybe even throw herself in his arms.

24

IT WAS LATE NOW. Joe LaBrava sat alone on the porch of the Cardozo Hotel thinking about a zebra he had seen a few hours before. A zebra run to the ground by wild dogs, a dog with the zebra's upper lip clamped in its jaw, a dog hanging to its tail, dogs frisking, dying to join the dogs tearing open the zebra's loins from underneath, pulling out entrails. The voice of the narrator—an actor who played heavies but had hired on for this film as an animal behaviorist—said the zebra was in a state of deep shock and felt no pain. And LaBrava had thought, Oh, is that right? Look at the zebra's eyes and tell us what it's like to stand there and get your ass eaten out fucking alive.

He couldn't stop thinking about the zebra and the actor who knew so much about zebra anxieties and pain thresholds. What was the zebra thinking through all that? Torres came over from the Della Robbia, sat down at the table in the edge of street-light and popped open one of the six cans of beer the waiter had left saying goodnight. Torres placed a tape recorder on the table, said, "This is at Hillsboro," and turned it on.

LaBrava listened to Jean Shaw's voice over the pictures he saw of her. He could see her very clearly, most of the pictures, new to him, composed in his mind in black and white.

"This is at her apartment."

LaBrava listened, seeing pictures of the zebra again among pictures of the movie actress, wondering what they were both thinking.

"This is the West Palm R.A., McCormick."

LaBrava listened.

"This is at Galleria Mall."

LaBrava listened, and when it ended he sat in silence looking at palm-tree silhouettes beyond the streetlights, stars over the ocean, the zebra gone. He picked up the recorder, pressed buttons and listened again to the last part, waiting for:

"Will you please hurry? He's getting away!"

Rewound, stopped and played it again.

"Will you please hurry? He's getting away!"

He could see her. Except that she wasn't in a white Cadillac in a parking structure. He saw an old picture of her in a black car, some kind of expensive long black car, at night. She looked scared as she called out, "He's getting away!" Then sat back and didn't look scared.

He rewound to the middle part, searched, found

what he wanted and heard her say, "Isn't someone supposed to be here? . . . I'm going to pick up my mail." There was a pause. He heard her say, "I'm entering the elevator—" and shut it off. McCormick was coming up on the porch. McCormick said, "One of those have my name on it? Christ, I hope so." Sturdy, compact, in Brooks Brothers khakis, blue button-down shirt, beige necktie, the West Palm R.A.

"That is a very attractive, very intelligent lady," McCormick said. "I found out in about five minutes I wasn't gonna learn shit I didn't know or suspect going in, but I talked to her an hour and a half anyway. She is a sharp lady."

Torres said, "You're the first Bureau guy—you actually admit you didn't learn anything?"

"For two reasons," McCormick said. "One, it isn't my case, you poor bastard. Two, I'm gonna retire the end of the month and become a stockbroker, so either way I don't give a shit. It's all yours, man, and it's getting away from you by the minute. You've got nothing firm. No positive I.D. of the guy who grabbed the bag or the guy who waved to her to come in the garage. Never seen them before. I showed her the pictures of the two guys you like, Mutt and Jeff; wasn't either of them. I asked her why she went in there. She says she thought the guy who waved at her was a police officer, but even if he wasn't we were supposed to be right behind her.

Where in the hell were we? . . . Outside of that there's only one part that bothers me." Mc-Cormick paused and then said to Torres, "You know what it is?"

Torres thought about it, looking off at the ocean.

McCormick poured a beer, began to drink.

LaBrava said, "Why did she stop to pick up her mail?" If he didn't say it, McCormick would. Or he wanted to hear himself admit what he was beginning to feel.

McCormick put his glass down. "You want a job? Uncle Sam can use you."

"He already did," LaBrava said. "You ask her?"

"She said habit. She comes in, she always checks the mail. I said even when you're carrying six hundred grand in a garbage bag?"

Torres said, "Wait a minute—"

"It probably doesn't mean shit," McCormick said. "It's like a reflex, she comes in, she checks the mail. Okay, she goes up to her apartment, she's in there a few minutes before I come from down the hall. She says to me, 'You think he'll call?' and starts looking through the mail. But what if she hadn't picked it up? The whole schmear falls apart. The other thing is the few minutes she's in there alone . . ."

Torres said, "You're making her a suspect. She's the victim, for Christ sake."

McCormick said, "At this point everybody's a

suspect, I don't give a shit. I don't know for sure where she got the six hundred gees, do you? She said she cashed some bonds. Maybe she did. On the other hand maybe she borrowed it and she's gonna stiff the guy. I don't know this broad, but I'll tell you what you better do, to be safe. Tomorrow morning—in fact I'll do it for you, it's out of your jurisdiction. I'll go up to her apartment and take a casual look around for different items, trash bags, a typewriter . . . It happens all the time, you don't know shit till you open some drawers, feel under the undies, you can find things you didn't even know you were looking for." He glanced at LaBrava. "Am I right? I forgot there for a minute you used to be with Treasury."

"Cover your ass at all times," LaBrava said.

"Cover it first," McCormick said, "then worry about what people think of you, if you worry about such things. Next, get the Lauderdale cops to canvas the mall, see if they can get a lead on the two guys. They'll give you a lot of shit, but at least you tried. After that . . . what've you got? Nothing. I don't see the big blond guy in the picture anywhere."

"Richard—" Torres began to say.

"If those two guys have the balls to grab the bag, what do they want to cut Richard in for? What's he, their typist?"

"Listen, Richard—I didn't tell you," Torres said

to LaBrava, "we found out was treated early this morning at Bethesda Memorial, compound fracture. The nurse said a cop brought him in."

LaBrava was wondering why he'd gone all the way up to Boynton Beach, fifty miles, as McCormick said, "Cop from where?"

"She didn't know where the cop was from," Torres said, looking at LaBrava again. " 'But a real one,' she said, not a rent-a-cop. We called every town from West Palm down. Nobody's got him or has a record of him."

"He has a friend who's a cop," LaBrava said, and could see Richard Nobles in the Delray Crisis Center flashing his badge and the slim girl standing up to him, Jill Wilkinson, and Richard saying he had a friend . . . either with the Delray or Boca police . . . the other girl, Pam, saying yes, she knew him. "I'll see if I can get his name for you."

He wondered if the slim girl was back from Key West.

McCormick said, "Let me take a look in her apartment tomorrow, maybe give you a better idea what you have to do next."

LaBrava said, "You gonna get her permission?"

"I could do that," McCormick said. "Or I could take a peek first. See, then if it looks interesting, get a warrant. Why bother the lady?"

"Get her permission," LaBrava said.

McCormick stared, smiled a little. "Well, now, what have we here?"

"Get her permission," LaBrava said.

"You don't," Torres said, "I bet you could open the door and get your arm broke."

Nobles could see without even trying there was no way he could get a uniform shirt on. The goddamn cast came all the way bent-arm to his shoulder. He ended up he had to cut the left arm out of his good silver jacket; put on uniform pants and the goddamn police hat to make him look at least semi-official. No sense wearing the holster, empty.

It was too late to get another gun. It was too late to get anything to eat and he was hungry for a Big Mac and some fries. He thought about the snake eating the bat—the lesson there, be patient. He thought about—the idea he liked best—walking up behind that blindsider and tapping him on the shoulder. " 'Scuse me." And as the blindsider comes around hit him in the face with the goddamn cast. Then say to him laying there on the ground . . .

He'd have to think of something good.

Going on 3:00 A.M. he hiked the two and a half miles from his dumpy place out Township, cut across the county airport past a lot of rich guys' planes, then over Lantana to Star Security, across from the state hospital. It was not luck he had kept a set of patrol car keys, it was using the old bean.

Going on 4:00 A.M. Nobles was down on Ocean Drive, Boca Raton, slow-cruising the beach condos like a regular security service car, except now he was looking for the law instead of boogers. He did not expect any sign of them. Why would there be with the horse out of the barn? He rode up to the top floor in that goddamn pokey elevator, went into her place with the key she'd given him and right away could smell her. Taking a leak he began to feel horny. She had yelled at him one time, "Close the door, you sound like a horse." And he had yelled back, "Puss? Come in here and help me hold this hog, would you, please?" They'd had some times. In her bedroom he was tempted to poke through her drawers, but knew he'd best take it and get.

It was in the walk-in closet. Lord have mercy, it actually was. Round fat garbage bag of money he and her had agreed to split two to one in her favor, which he believed was fair. Shit, $200,000 he could buy any goddamn thing he wanted, starting with a pair of lizard wingtip cowboy boots he'd seen on Burt Reynolds one time up in Jupiter. Buy the boots, buy a 'Vette, buy some guns, have 'em in glass cabinets in his knotty-pine den . . .

He had to drive back to his place first, which had two rooms and not any kind of den, to store the loot. He had to drive back on over to Star Security and leave the car, shit, then hike the two and a half miles back home. It wasn't so bad though. He started out thinking of what he would say to the blindsider laying there on the ground.

"You mess with me, boy—"

"You fuck with me, boy—"

"You fuck with the bull, boy—"

He liked "bull" but he didn't like "bull, boy."

How about, "Boy, you fuck with the bull . . . you see what you get."

"You see what can befall you."

Be*fall* you? He sounded like a preacher.

Saw the blindsider being struck by a bolt of lightning.

Saw him through a car windshield as he ran over the son of a bitch.

Then saw Cundo Rey, Lord have mercy, and felt tears come into his eyes it was so funny to imagine. The little booger opening that other Hefty bag. Sure, he would, set to skip with the whole load. The dink might even skip and *then* open the bag. Get to some motel up around Valdosta, open her up . . . The poor little fucker. He'd blame it on the law doing him a tricky turn, and there wouldn't be a goddamn thing he could do about it.

Cundo Rey woke up the next morning, 6:00 A.M., he didn't sleep so good, he opened his eyes he had a headache. Ouuuuu, he had a good one. He believed it was from not using his anger.

Anger was good if you could use it right away, let it pick you up and carry you. But if you didn't use it, then it passed and it left your brain sore. Like balls became sore if you were ready to make love but for some reason didn't do it. Like you had to get out of her house quick. Man, they ached. It was the same thing with the brain. He took aspirin and Pepsi-Cola. Pretty soon he was able to think. In time he began to wonder why he had got angry.

The creature had told him to get a good place close by to hide. He had found a perfect place, Bonita Drive, a one-block curve of apartments, cheap, between Seventy-first Street and Indian Creek Drive. Ten minutes from the action down on South Beach. One minute from the North Bay Causeway, shoot over to Miami, you're on the freeway. He rented the first floor of a two-story place for a month; it even had a garage to hide the car in.

He had given the address to the creature and the creature said good, here's what I do and here's what you do, and told him all the things he eventually did. Take the bag from the woman, who would follow a note to the car-park building. Run home and hide the bag. Get rid of the stolen car . . . Then after a week or so, when it was cool, the creature said he would come and pick up his half of the money and they would never see each other again.

But the creature never told where *he* was going to be hiding. The creature never called him a name and said, don't try to take the money for yourself or I'll find you and kill you. That should have opened his eyes. But his own greed, thinking how easy it would be to take it all, had perhaps blinded him.

So last night, 8:30, he came back from getting rid of the Skylark, a nice car; he opened the Hefty bag upside down, and for a long time he sat looking at the pile of cut-up newspaper on the floor, the *Miami Herald* and one called the *Post*.

What made him angry was thinking the cops did this to him. The cops not caring if it endangered the woman. The dirty cops, like all cops, full of cop tricks. He drank a pint of rum and a liter of Pepsi-Cola to become tranquil, but it didn't do any good.

This morning, a beautiful day outside, he looked at the pieces of newspaper he had kicked all over the living room, at the pieces of broken glass and dishes on the floor, and began to wonder different things.

Why the creature hadn't tried to frighten him: take the money, you die.

How the creature himself was able to put the note in the woman's car and in that hotel if the cops were watching. How he could do it, a man who always wished to be seen, and *not* be seen.

Why there were no cops in the car-park building

if the note told her to go there. He had been very careful entering, looked in cars, all over.

Why, if the note *didn't* say to go there, she did.

It was getting good.

Why she seemed to be stopping the car—there was no sound of her car's tires—before he came out from behind the post.

Why she looked at him so calm and did not appear frightened. Like she expected him to be there.

He sat staring at the pieces of newspaper, thinking again of the notes the creature said he had written, wondering again how he could have given them to the woman, beginning to see the fucking creature was a liar—as a thought related to this lifted him out of the chair.

He went through the kitchen to the garage that was part of the building, and looked in the trunk of his car. There it was in a case—which he opened to make sure—the typewriter he had forgot to drop into Biscayne Bay. He touched the typewriter and the carriage slid out to one side and locked there; he couldn't get it back. So he left the case and took the typewriter into the apartment.

That typewriter got him thinking some more and he sat without moving, letting thoughts of Richard and the woman slide through his mind, seeing the two of them friends, good friends. Seeing the woman, again and again, stopping her car as though she knew exactly where he would be, almost smiling at him, so calm, knowing he wasn't going to hurt her, knowing he was taking pieces of paper.

He sat without moving and thought, Richard isn't coming. Of course not. It was Richard and the woman. He didn't know how. He didn't know why she would be stealing from herself, except that Richard was a liar and maybe she wasn't rich and it wasn't her money they were stealing. Richard was a liar and it was Richard and the woman.

Cundo sat without moving for so long that finally when he moved he knew he would keep moving and get out of here. What was he hiding for? He didn't do nothing. What did he steal, some pieces of newspaper? He didn't have to stay here, he could go any place he wanted . . .

Because if it was Richard and the woman they wouldn't want him to be caught and talk to the police. So she wouldn't look at pictures and identify him. Afraid he might tell the police about Richard. He would, too.

Uh-oh. It made him think of something else he had forgot about just as he had forgot about the typewriter.

What if it wasn't the woman and the creature stealing the money but the woman and the picture-taker?

He had forgot about that fucking picture-taker.

If he'd had the snubbie when the picture-taker sat in the wheelchair and took his picture . . . But he had bought the snubbie *after*, to use on the picture-taker, and then had become too busy preparing to steal a bag of newspapers cut in pieces. Oh, man . . . crazy.

And thought of the time he walked in the crazy-place in Delray naked, to get information. He had to smile. There was always a way to find out what you need to know.

Sure, call up the woman. Don't worry about the picture-taker, if he's in this or not. What difference does it make?

Call up the woman and ask her she wants to buy a typewriter, cheap. Only six hundred thousand dollars.

See what she says.

25

MCCORMICK SAID HE DIDN'T WANT to bother her, he could get the manager, with her OK, to let them in. This was Bureau check-list routine, go over any area known to the suspect. Jean said no, it wasn't a bother—immediately establishing an attitude—she'd be glad to drive up and meet them; not asking, which suspect? In the car she tried on several attitudes from wide-eyed innocence to cold resentment, cutting remarks, but decided she'd been instinctively right on the phone: victim with a passive respect for authority was still the way to play it.

They were waiting downstairs when she arrived, Mr. McCormick and two officers from the Palm Beach County Sheriff's Department with their evidence kits; McCormick explaining they would like to pull a good set of Nobles' prints if they could, also look around in case he might've left something; Jean nodding, following every word, showing how fascinated she was; Mc-

Cormick saying clues turned up in unexpected places; Jean saying yes, she imagined so; thinking, You sneaky FBI son of a bitch. Both sides buttoned up with respect.

Jean had to play it with a knot in her stomach at first—until McCormick came out of her closet; then, for a while, with mild apprehension. She could have overlooked something. A crumpled sheet of steno paper behind the desk, a scrap of newspaper in the closet. She had gone over the apartment thoroughly once the plan was set. There were no Hefty bags around. No Walther automatic to find unexpectedly. All old Miami and Palm Beach papers had been thrown out . . .

As apprehension eased, left her, McCormick became fun to watch. Neat but beefy in his seersucker suit, blue Oxford cloth button-down, beige and blue rep tie—he dressed like so many guys she used to know—glancing at his reflections in silver and glass, trying to remain offhand, polite. But losing it as he looked in or behind every closet, cabinet, piece of furniture and found nothing. He did come up with a pair of sunglasses she'd misplaced and her gratitude, at this time and somewhat overstated, apparently rubbed him. With suspicion in his eyes, quiet awareness in hers, he seemed bound to pull out something, if even remotely incriminating.

McCormick said, "I understand this place was bought for you."

Jean said, "That's right." Nothing to hide.

"But not by your husband."

"He died," Jean said. "A friend bought me the place."

"A boyfriend?"

"A benefactor." She loved the word, the prim sound of it. "You know what he paid? Less than a hundred thousand, back when real estate was relatively sane."

"I understand," McCormick said, voice flat, eyes watchful, about to ambush her, "he was a member of organized crime."

"A *mem*ber," Jean said, smiling. "As opposed to what, an independent contractor?" Turning the smile then gradually from shy to off. "That was so long ago." Getting a little sigh in her tone. "It was an exciting time and I'm afraid I was, well, impressionable, to say the least. If you will accept that, Mr. McCormick . . ."

"Jim—"

Wanting to add, Then you'll accept anything.

"But I'm positive this doesn't involve anyone I used to know, Jim . . . From out of the past." Starring Bob Mitchum; she'd really wanted the Jane Greer part. Giving him her aware brown eyes straight on. "Aside from Mr. Zola, of course. He's advised me all through this, suggested I cash in bonds rather than re-mortgage the apartment. I'm not left with much." Chin up, resolute, but eyes beginning to mist. "I'll make it though. I can always sell the place, move back to the Coast." Wistful hint of a smile. "I know, this is a coast too. But once you've been in film, Jim"—tough line—"there's really only one Coast."

"I understand," Jim said.

"I think you should put all your effort into finding Richard Nobles," Jean said, "though he's probably far away from here by now." Looking off, coming back suddenly then to hold his gaze. "He did mention once he'd love to go out to the Coast, try the movies. Like several hundred others who look just like him try every year, and maybe a couple of them make it in television, wrecking cars. The only thing I can suggest"—sigh, tired but still willing to help—"alert your office on the Coast, send them Richard's picture . . . and if I should think of anything else in the meantime, Jim . . ."

Jim told her that once Richard was established as a fugitive the entire Bureau would be on him from Seat of Government through every field office in the country, the case tagged a major.

"I'm flattered," Jean said.

"Maybe we can have a drink sometime," Jim said.

"I'd like that," Jean said. Pause. "I'd like that very much."

Not a memorable performance, but not bad. About average. Not nearly as difficult to make convincing as the love scene in *Treasure of the Aztecs*. God—telling Audie Murphy that neither the sacrificial dagger of Montezuma nor the conquering sword of Cortes could stop her heart, her *pagan* heart, from throbbing with desire, "my golden Lord." And Audie in his jerkin and codpiece squirming, eating it up. She wondered if she could update it and run it past LaBrava, just for fun.

She felt like performing . . . She could get on the freeway and be at Richard's house in about fifteen minutes; she'd memorized the directions. They had planned to wait at least a week, give the police time to relax. But she was so close and her mood was perfect.

She could hear the elevator door close across the hall, the elevator begin to descend with McCormick and the two Palm Beach officers.

It might be the best time of all. Richard would be surprised. Just in case he had ideas . . .

Coming away from the door Jean paused, looking at herself in the wall of glass behind the sofa. She smiled. Too much. Staring at herself she saw a worried expression now, with a smile trying to break through. "Richard, is everything all right?"

Make it a little more personal. "Richard, are you all right?" Maybe even, "Richard, I couldn't wait to see you." Well—disarm him, but don't overdo it.

LaBrava stood by his window with the phone. He could see Franny in the park across the street, sitting at an easel in shade, painting one of the Della Robbia women who sat facing the ocean. When the slim girl, Jill Wilkinson, came on he said, "How was Key West?"

She said, "I love it. It's the only place I know you can rest and not get hit on all the time. I mean a girl. Wait a minute." She was gone several minutes. When she came back she said, "I'm sorry. We've got a guy took one of the panels out of the ceiling and crawled up into the overhead. He won't come down because he says the office is full of alligators. Keeps saying 'They's gators down there.' He's right, but we're not supposed to let on." He asked her the name of the cop Richard Nobles had mentioned that night, the one Pam said she knew. Jill said, "Hold on." He heard her call to Pam and ask her. Jill came back on and said, "Glenn Hicks, he's Boca P.D. But tell me about Richard. What's that subhuman piece of shit up to now?"

Franny looked naked at her easel; and her hair made her look like a little girl. The Della Robbia woman was getting up, walking around behind

Franny to look at the painting. Watching them
LaBrava phoned Torres and gave him the name of
Richard's friend. Glenn Hicks.

He crossed the street from the Cardozo to Lummus
Park, two ice-cold cans of beer in each of his hands.
Boy, did she look good: the mauve bikini top with
cutoff jeans, artist at work under a palm tree, very
nice if you can get away with it, if you're any good.
Artist concentrating, showing the tip of her tongue,
touching up, canvas chair where the subject had
been sitting, empty. Her weird hair moved, she was
looking at him, waiting.

"Well, how're you doing?"

She said, "How am I doing. I went home for a
wedding three days ago, you didn't even know I
was gone."

"You got married? Here I've been looking all
over for you."

"Why, were you horny?"

"Reasonably."

"You don't get reasonably horny, Joe, you are or
you aren't."

"I was more than horny, I missed you." He
handed her a can of beer, then paused as he was
about to sink into the canvas chair, looking at the
easel. "That's very good. You know it?"

"Who is it?"

"It's Mrs. Heffel. Don't you know who you're painting?" He was pretty sure it was Mrs. Heffel.

"*I* know. I didn't think you did."

"Even without the nose shield. You know how I know her? I took her picture. She's got a little girl inside her that shows every once in a while, when she doesn't think people are accusing her of something. You caught the little girl. A glimpse of her." He sat down and popped a beer.

"You think so?"

He handed her the opened beer, took the one Franny was holding and popped it. "I think so. What happened to your hotels?"

"I like hotels okay, but hotels are things. I've decided my interests lie more in people. That's your influence, LaBrava. I look at your work, I want to see what you see."

"You do, you see things."

"I don't know. I see a certain thing in your work because you caught it, there it is. But I don't know if I'd see the same thing before. I don't know if I have the eye."

"You got Mrs. Heffel."

"I've been watching her for a week."

"You've got the eye. The secret is, don't look at everything at once, concentrate on one part at a time."

She said, "Maybe I'm doing it, I'll find out." She sipped her beer and said, "So what've you been up to while I was in New York having the time of my life with my relatives?"

He said, "Not too much. I've been trying to think of a movie I saw a long time ago."

"Don't tell me, starring Jean Shaw. You still have the hots for her? She's too old for you."

"As a matter of fact it *was* a Jean Shaw movie. You saw it too, because you mentioned it that night we saw *Let It Ride*."

"What's the name of it?"

"*Obituary.*"

"The one, her husband knows he's gonna die of an incurable illness so he kills himself, then makes it look like she did it because she and her boyfriend took him for a lot of money?"

"That one."

"I didn't see it."

"How much of it do you remember?"

"I think I saw like the last half."

"She go to jail?"

"Yes, there's a trial, and she's found guilty, not for what she did but for killing her husband, which she didn't do. Heavy irony."

"Who was the guy, the hero?"

"I don't know. He had sort of a chiseled face and the muscle in his jaw kept jumping. He had sorta wet lips too. The other girl, the good one, is the daughter of Jean Shaw's husband by his first wife. The daughter, when her dad starts getting his own death notices clipped from out-of-town papers, the daughter right away thinks Jean's doing it, but nobody believes her, including the cop."

"Victor Mature."

"Yeah, that's who it is. I forgot his name."

"The husband's afraid of death anyway—"

"It petrifies him. Anybody mentions death, he looks like he's gonna throw up. Until near the end of the picture, when he finds out he's got this incurable illness and he really *is* gonna die, then he accepts it. His daughter gives him a talk about dying being part of living and he buys it. It's really dumb."

"So they send the death notices to scare hell out of him, set him up . . ."

"Yeah, and then the death *threat*, pay up or you're dead. Jean, the wife, is not only in on it, it's her idea from the beginning."

"She delivers the payoff?"

"Yeah, but not really. Let me think . . . They get a phone call to deliver the money to a motel somewhere, a certain room. She goes there, gets another phone call to go someplace else. But first she switches the suitcase full of money with a suitcase full of newspapers or something that's already in the motel room. You understand?"

"Yeah, go on."

"So then she makes the drop. Along comes some guy her boyfriend hired, a weirdo with big eyes—"

"Elisha Cook."

"He swings with what he thinks is a suitcase full of money. He opens it, goes berserk when he sees newspapers and falls out of his hotel-room window."

"He didn't know the wife was in on it."

"He didn't know shit, he's just sorta in the picture."

"Then what? The boyfriend . . ."

"The boyfriend goes to the motel and picks up the real stuff. He takes it to a cabin up in the mountains, opens the suitcase . . . You think Jean is jobbing this guy too, but it's all there."

"Henry Silva."

"Right, the same guy that played Mother in *A Hatful of Rain*. I just saw that one too."

"So after a while Jean arrives at the cabin . . ."

"She comes in with her own suitcase, an empty one."

"And what happens?"

"You're going west on Lantana, okay, you take a right just past the county airport and go on up," Richard had told her, "till almost you come to like a subdivision and you take a left onto Township, it's a dirt road, and you go on out till you see a whole bunch of scrub pine and this house setting by itself, cute little place used to be painted white."

No telephone, but it had propane gas and running water, inside toilet, stove, fridge, hundred a month, shit. Kind of place you think it'd been left to weather, no reason to go near it. Perfect spot, Richard said.

Poor Richard, peeking out the front door.

Jean parked in tree shade, left the key in the ignition and released the trunk. She did not look at the house now, knowing Richard was watching her open the trunk, lift out the tan leather suitcase. There was the sound of a light plane circling the county airport, the sound persisting, fading, coming back. There was dusty summer heat in the air, a depressed rural feel to the location; not anything like the cabin up near Big Bear. It had been cool, she'd worn a trenchcoat and a black beret. She had the line ready. "Richard, I couldn't wait."

But when he appeared in the doorway Jean revised it without thinking and said, "What happened to you?"

"I got my goddamn arm broke."

"I can see that. How did you do it?"

He was squinting at the road, in the direction of the airport. "You sure nobody followed you?"

"I'm sure."

"I wasn't expecting you for least a week."

"I couldn't wait, Richard." There, getting back to the script. But then forced away from it again with, "What happened to your arm?" Moving past him into the house, dim with shades drawn, depressing, a musty smell to the place.

"You want me to tell you? It was that goddamn friend of yours, that blindsider, same guy 'at hit me the time up in Delray, that place they took you."

They were way off the script and might not return for some time; but she had to sit down, stare at him and hear every word of this, Richard's version of what happened in the park: how he was struck from behind, arm broken before he even saw the guy, hit in the legs, the head; man was like he was crazy.

Jean said, "He brought you there . . ."

"He tricked me."

"To ask you questions?"

"I didn't tell him nothing."

She said, "Richard, how do you know you didn't?"

"I know what I told him. He didn't have no wire on him, I checked. Listen, with one hand 'fore we were through there I punched the sucker out and I told him, 'You got a surprise coming, asshole,' just that much, without telling him nothing. Shit, I wasn't gonna let the scudder get off."

Jean said, "Oh, Richard," her tone soft, almost loving. She sat in a wornout easy chair, her head back against the cushion, feeling the bristly mohair of the arms beneath her hands, damp with perspiration. Her straw bag was on her lap. She reached into it, found a pack of cigarettes and lighted one, inhaled, blew the smoke out slowly.

She said, "Well, it doesn't matter."

Nobles said, "Shit, no. We done it, didn't we? You haven't asked did I get the sack or not. You ready to have a look, divvy up?"

"I guess I'm ready," Jean said.

Nobles walked into the bedroom and got down on the floor. She could see the bed from where she sat, blanket folded on a soiled mattress. He would try to get her in there, with sticky words, mouth curled. She watched him pull the Hefty bag from under the bed—each move separate, deliberate— rising to his knees, to one foot, standing, turning to come out . . . He sat on a straight chair facing her, the bag between his legs. Jean watched the fingers of one hand working to unwind the baling wire. She said, "Richard, how did you get here?"

"I didn't know how I was gonna make it to the hospital, see. So I called this boy Glenn Hicks I know. I told you, he's with the Boca Police?"

"Yes?"

"He drove me to Bethesda, the one in Boynton 'cause he didn't know any others without going clear to Palm Beach."

"Then how did you get here?"

"Yeah, Glenn drove me."

She said it again, "Oh, Richard," with that same weariness.

"Glenn's a good boy, does what I tell him. Don't you worry 'bout old Glenn." He held the Hefty bag open. "Here, look-it in here. I want to see your eyes pop out."

"Did you count it?"

"Did I count it?" He grinned at her. "I been counting it since I drug the sack in. It's fun, you know it, count money?" He frowned then, reaching into the bag. "What I couldn't figure out, what you put this in there for?" His hand came out holding the Walther PPK, the little bluesteel automatic.

Jean raised her hand from the arm of the chair and Nobles hesitated, then shrugged, reached over, and laid the grip in her upturned palm. "She's on safety. That's a cute little piece, but be careful now."

Jean brought the gun up, looking at it. "I didn't want to leave it at home, risk someone finding it. And with all those cops I didn't want to carry it, have someone pick up my bag, feel the weight."

Nobles sat hunched over the Hefty bag between his legs. "Lady carries around a suitcase full a money, she needs a gun. Keep the boogers off her."

"That's it," Jean said. He was so close, hunched over, his cast resting on his knees. "Aren't you going to offer me a drink?"

That got him up. "Well, sure. You want a cold beer or a warm one?"

"Cold, please."

Nobles went into the kitchen and was out of view. She heard the refrigerator door, heard the popping sound as he opened the cans. Henry Silva had poured Scotch, no ice, turned with a tall glass in each hand . . . She raised the Walther in her right hand, six rounds in the clip, one in the chamber, extended it toward the doorway to the kitchen and waited for Nobles to appear.

Both cans of beer were in his right hand; his left arm, in the cast, covered his stomach. So she aimed just above the cast. When he looked up, one stride out of the doorway, he paused, seemed to smile, trying to at least, and said, "Hey, puss, be careful now—"

She shot him where she aimed, shot him again and shot him again, quickly, the sound so overpowering she missed details. Already he seemed in shock, pressed against the door frame, eyes glazed, the cast painted with blood. So much blood. Where were the beer cans? She had only a moment to notice effects. Henry Silva had touched the neat wound in his chest, looked at his hand with disbelief, looked up . . . She shot Henry Silva again and he did a slow movie die, reflecting betrayal right to the end. She shot Nobles again and he might have already been dead, sliding down the door frame to the floor.

LaBrava said to Franny, sitting in Lummus Park among palm trees, sipping cold beer, "Then what happens?"

Franny said, "Well, nothing happens after that the way it's supposed to."

26

HE SAW ONLY HER EYES, her bland expression, and wondered who she was at this moment and if she was going to say anything, and after another moment if she was ever going to say anything. He watched her turn from the door without a word, hands coming away from the front of her robe, the robe falling open as she entered the bedroom.

So LaBrava went to the kitchen where an open bottle of Scotch and tray of melting ice cubes stood on the sink, decided, as he poured himself a good one, to let her lead; he'd catch on soon enough. He picked up the ice tray to put it in the refrigerator and hesitated—why should he?—then had to make another decision and did put the tray in the refrigerator and crossed to the bedroom with his drink.

Jean sat at the vanity in a halfslip doing her eyes, classic nose in the air, eyes indifferent, bare breasts indifferent, pale shoulders rounded in a slouch that described her attitude. He saw her drink waiting among cosmetics. She took time now to pick it up, her breasts rising as her eyes raised, two sets of brown eyes in the mirror watching him. He believed he could outwait them but would have to sit down. Tell Maurice they would be late for dinner, bring the bottle in here and then sit down. He had never played this game before. She was putting on eyeliner now. Then surprised him.

"Have you spoken to your friend McCormick?"

"About what?"

"I can believe he didn't report to you, since there was nothing to report. But you must've been curious enough to call him."

She sounded like his former wife, tone full of dry innocence, delivered deadpan. Taking the long way around.

He said, "Let's see. McCormick searched your place . . ."

"As you suggested."

He almost smiled. "He told you that?"

"Your words, according to Jim, 'Why don't you get her permission to have a look around?' I'd call that a suggestion."

"I'm surprised," LaBrava said.

"At what?"

"McCormick does care what people think. Wants you to like him." He watched her move to the other eye. "But he didn't find anything, uh?"

"Did you think he would?"

One way or another they were going to reach

this point. It wasn't something he had to think about anymore. It would be good to get it out in the open. It was time.

He said, "Probably not, but there was always the possibility."

She paused, holding the eyeliner away from her, looking at him in the mirror. "You mean something Richard might have left behind? Fingerprints?"

"Something," LaBrava said, "either of you might have overlooked."

There was a silence. He expected it and waited, leaning in the doorway. It wouldn't be her style to let go, throw a jar of cold cream at him. She would adjust, making her own decision now, staring at him in the mirror, eyes telling nothing, eyes lowering then as her hand went to the vanity table. She picked up a pearl earring, cocked her head as her eyes raised to look at him again and a new Jean Shaw appeared, a playful expression in her eyes now, a glow of anticipation.

He said, "How do you do that?"

"How do I do what, Joe?" Her tone different, relaxed, ready to be amused. "How do I manage to . . . get by, survive? It ain't easy, kid. Learn to adapt, use whatever is at hand. I was just getting to like it here and now it's time to go home, or somewhere. I may go abroad . . . if anyone wonders where I am."

"If you think you can afford it."

Jean smiled, or seemed to. Her head turned slowly as she picked up the other earring, still looking at him. "Tell me what's bothering you, Joe."

"How you can do this to Maurice. That bothers me more than anything else."

"What am I doing?"

"It's *his* money."

Her hands came away from her face and she straightened, looking at him directly. "Maury and I have known each other forever. You have to understand that first."

"Yeah?"

"He happens to love me."

LaBrava kept quiet.

"And knows I wouldn't hurt him for the world."

"How about for six hundred thousand?"

Jean got up from the vanity, moved to the bed where she picked up a white cotton shift, brought it carefully over her head, down past her hips. Standing erect, hands flat on her thighs, she said, "Do you think I need a bra?"

"You look fine."

"Not too flat? I've never had the nerve to go without one until lately."

"It couldn't have been lack of nerve."

"Modesty, then." She got her drink from the vanity, held his eyes as she came over. He didn't move. She turned to edge past him through the doorway, her body, her breast, brushing his arm, still looking at him and said, "You have to be very careful or people get the wrong idea, they think you're immodest."

"You haven't answered my question."

"So why ask?"

She took his glass and he followed her to the kitchen, wondering if he should put her flat on the floor, sit on her holding her arms, face to face, close. *You give?* And not let her up until she did.

She brought the ice tray out of the refrigerator saying, "I have a question. *Did* you tell Mc-Cormick to search my apartment?"

"What difference does it make?"

"My opinion of you, Joe. That's important to me."

"Look, one way or another, even if he had to get a federal warrant, McCormick was gonna search your place. I told him to ask you first."

"Why?"

"So you'd understand what you're into. You'd see these guys are serious, they're the pros and they've got you down as a suspect."

"Not anymore."

"Jean? . . . Listen to me."

She poured Scotch in their glasses before raising her eyes, mildly interested, patient.

"This isn't the movies," LaBrava said, "an hour and a half it's over." Using a quiet, confiding tone, one she might appreciate and believe. "This one doesn't end. Once they make it their case they'll take it all the way and sooner or later they bring in this guy, that guy, and your name comes up and they say, 'Oh, yeah, Jean Shaw, the movie star, what do you suppose she was thinking, dream up a scheme like that? Swindle six hundred grand from a nice old guy's supposed to be her friend.' And there's no way, I give you my word, it's not gonna happen."

In the silence she took time to sip her drink. She said, "What makes you think I did it?" with little more than mild curiosity in her tone.

"I *know*," LaBrava said, still quietly. "It doesn't matter how or whether I can prove it or not. I *know*. And if I know then they're gonna find out. What you have to do is get the money. Now, as soon as you can. Give it back to Maurice before you do anything else—and you know what I'm talking about. If it's not too late I'll help you every way I can, see if we can cover it up and hope no one asks too many questions."

She said, "Would you do that for me, Joe?" Got sad stars in her eyes and said, "What a guy."

LaBrava had to take a moment. He wasn't sure if the line was familiar but it was her kind of line and her delivery. He paused to remember where he was, to bring Jean Shaw back into perspective and detach himself from reality. She knew what she was doing. Performing, but she still knew what she was doing.

With that easy delivery, looking at her drink now, she said, "It sounds like a wonderful part. Innocent woman unjustly accused, a wall of evidence against her. I'd love to play it."

"You did," LaBrava said, "in *Obituary*."

She looked up at him abruptly.

"Don't you remember? I do. I can tell you the whole picture, beginning to end, and I saw it when I was twelve years old."

She said, "*Obituary*, yes, you're right," but sounded unsure, vague. "I wasn't only accused of something I didn't do, I was found guilty." Her tone picked up a little. "I had a wonderful courtroom scene. I lost my voice screaming—there must have been fifteen takes. But it was worth it."

He said, "Jean, where's Richard?"

She continued to look at him but seemed lost now. Her gleam had faded and he wondered if it might be gone forever, there was so little hope in her eyes.

She said, "Joe, were you really only twelve years old?"

He had to take another moment. She was serious now and he had to adjust. He said, "Jean, you're so good you could act your way out of a safe deposit box."

She seemed to smile. "Who was it said that?"

"I think it was James Garner doing Philip Marlowe. But it's true. You're even better now than you used to be, and you were my favorite as far back as I can remember."

She said, "Were you only twelve, Joe?"

"That's all. But I was horny as a grown man, if that'll make you feel better."

Maurice opened the door, a dish towel over his shoulder, a cooking spoon in his hand. He said to Jean, "Go pick up the phone, there's a call for you."

She walked past him, not asking who it was. LaBrava closed the door as Maurice said, after her, "Guy tried to get you earlier, I told him to call back around eight." He turned to LaBrava, extending the spoon. "Smell. We're having gumbo. Make the drinks while I go stir it."

Jean was at the desk in the living room, pulling off her earring as she raised the phone.

LaBrava said to Maurice, "Who is it, Torres?"

"Some guy with an accent. I don't know."

"You ask him his name?"

"Hey, go make the drinks, will you?"

He tried to read her expression. She stood holding the phone in both hands, listening. He heard her say, "What?" a sharp sound. She was about fifteen feet away from him. He could make her a drink and take it over. She said something else but he didn't hear it because Maurice was telling him to be careful if he opened the freezer, there was half a peck of okra in there he didn't want all over the floor. Maurice saying, "Come here and taste this," as he watched Jean speaking into the phone, a few words. He started toward her and Maurice was next to him with the big spoon, offering it, putting it in his face. "Taste it, authentic Creole gumbo, recipe I got from a lady brought it here from Gretna, Louisiana. Little broad, her name was Toddy, she wore those pinch-nose glasses, weighed about eighty-two pounds, and made the best gumbo you ever tasted in your life. I would a married her, I mean just for her gumbo . . . Hey, Jean? Where you going?"

She stood holding the door open. Then closed it as they watched her.

"What's the matter? . . . Who was that on the phone?"

"Nothing important. Somebody with the police."

"It wasn't Torres. I know Torres' voice."

"No, one of the other ones. He was just checking, see if I'm okay."

"Yeah? Are you? You look funny. You feel okay?"

"Well"—she hesitated—"I do feel a little . . . strange. I think I'll go get some air."

"All you been through," Maurice said, "I can understand it. Stick your head out the window."

"No, I think I'll go outside."

"I'll go with you," LaBrava said.

"No, please, stay here. I'll be all right. Maury, do you mind? I'm just not hungry at the moment."

"You sure you're all right? You want any kind of pills? Alka-Seltzer?"

"No, I'm fine. Really."

They sat eating. Maurice said, "Ordinarily I put crabs in it, with the shrimp, but I didn't see any I liked at the market. So I put in some oysters. It's good with oysters. Or you can put chicken in it. The secret is in the preparation of the okra. When you sauté it you have to keep stirring it, fast. Also you have to stir the hell out of your roux when you're browning it, have to stir it and stir it. You know what I'm talking about?"

LaBrava said, "Maury, who's crazy, you or me?"

"How do I know?" Maurice said. "Maybe both of us. Don't ask me any hard ones."

When the phone rang Maurice took his time, waving LaBrava off as he started to get up. Maurice went over, answered the phone and laid the receiver on the desk.

"I should a let you. It's your friend Torres."

* * *

He said to her, "You might as well tell me."

They sat on the Della Robbia porch. He would look at her as she stared at the view that was every picture ever taken of a moonlit sandy beach through palm trees, ocean in background. The view did nothing for either of them.

He said, "All right, let me see if I can tell it. The guy in the movie who picked up the bag went out a hotel-room window, but this one didn't. He found out, somehow, you've got the money and he wants his cut instead of a bunch of old newspapers, and if you don't pay him he'll turn you in." LaBrava waited. "It isn't fun anymore, is it?" He waited again and said, "Just say it, you'll feel better. You don't say it, I won't be able to help you."

A car passed on Ocean Drive, shined in the streetlight for a moment and their view returned.

She said, "What would you do?" her voice clear but subdued.

"Get him off your back."

"How?"

"I don't know yet. I'll have to talk to him first."

"You know who it is?"

"The boat-lifter. Cundo Rey."

She turned her head to stare at him. "How do you know that?"

"I showed you his picture, didn't I? You use somebody you never saw before. That was your first mistake. No, it would be your second mistake. Richard was your first."

She was silent again.

"How much does he want?"

After a moment she said, "All of it."

"Or what?"

"He didn't say."

"Tell me what he did say."

"He asked me if I wanted to buy a typewriter."

There was a silence.

"Your typewriter?"

"Yes."

"It can be traced to you?"

"I think so. There's a little sticker on the back—the name of the place where I have it serviced. I forgot about that."

They all forget something. "How'd the boat-lifter get it? You didn't give it to him, did you?"

"No, someone else."

"You gave it to a world-class fuckup to get rid of and he gave it to the boat-lifter who probably sold it and then had to get it back, once he figured everything out . . . What else did he say?"

"He wants me to meet him, so we can talk."

"Where?"

"A bar on LeJeune, Skippy's Lounge."

"Skippy's Lounge. Jesus. Are you supposed to bring the money?"

"No, that's what we're going to talk about. Where we make the exchange."

"Where is it, the money?"

She paused. "In my apartment."

"You think the place is safe now because they tossed it?"

She said, "Joe, if you'll help me . . ."

He waited and she seemed to start over. She said, "You have to understand something. I love Maury in a very special way. I know him better than you or anyone else ever will, and he knows me, he understands me." She said, "Joe, I promise you, I would never do anything in the world to hurt him."

Something she had said before, but in real life, not in a movie that he remembered. He said, "That's nice but we're past that. Torres called. They found Richard."

She stared straight ahead.

"It wasn't a cabin up in the mountains. It wasn't even that far from other houses . . ." He gave her a moment, but she said nothing. "I told Torres to have a talk with Richard's pal, Glenn Hicks." She turned again to stare at him and he said, "You get the feeling I know more about it than you do?"

After a moment she looked at the view again and

said, "Joe, you have to believe how I feel about Maury . . ."

"I thought we were on Richard now."

She said, quietly, "There is no way anyone can prove I killed him."

"I didn't even say he was dead. But I'm not gonna tell on you. You're grown up enough to do it yourself."

She said, "Does he really matter?"

"Not to me, no. But the state attorney, you hear him you're gonna think Richard was his kid brother. See, you shoot and kill somebody you have to have a better reason than for money."

She said, "You broke his arm. What if you had hit him in the head?"

"I had a chance to and I didn't. That's the difference. Richard could've brought me up if he wanted to, I accepted that possibility. You're trying, as they say, to get away with murder." He realized he was at ease because he was in control and it didn't matter what role she tried on him. The poor lady didn't know who to be, so she was playing a straight part for a change and not coming off anything like a star. She was beginning to look older to him.

The view was the same. It didn't change.

She started to get up and he said, "Where you going?"

"To buy a typewriter."

Good line. He liked the way she said it; it gave him a feeling for her again.

He said, "Put your bra on and relax. I'll go talk to him, see if he wants to turn himself in."

"Why would he?"

"It's better than getting shot . . . I'll need the key to your apartment, to pick up the money."

"Swell," Jean said.

"Save that one," LaBrava said. "It's not over yet."

27

IT WAS LADIES' NIGHT at Skippy's Lounge. *Ladies Only. Drinks two for one till 9 P.M.*

So LaBrava hung a Leica and a camera bag on him and told the manager he was doing a photo story for the *Herald's* Sunday magazine, "Tropic," and the manager said to be his guest—but don't shoot any housewives supposed to be at K-mart shopping and a movie after unless you get a release. There were about a hundred of them, all ages, crowded around the circular stage watching the all-male go-go show. LaBrava said, "Let me get one of you while we're standing here, Skip." The manager said, "I look like a Skip to you? Those assholes up there with the razor cuts and the baby oil all over 'em are the Skips."

Five of them plus Cundo Rey doing their show opener.

The five Debonaires wore wing collars with little black bow ties, cuffs with sparkly cuff links and black bikinis. Cundo Rey wore a leopard jock and cat whiskers painted on his face, streaked out from his nose to his ears. He was the one and only Cat Prince, extra added attraction, who hung back in the opening number and did not new-wave-it the way the serious all-white Debonaires did. It was their set, repetitious, robotic, each Debonaire dancing with his own ego, three of the five in front of the beat, stepping all over it; they ducked and hopped to *I Do* coming out of the sound system and set J. Geils back ten years.

Cundo Rey came on for his solo with his raven hair, his earring, his painted-on whiskers, with West African riffs out of a Havana whorehouse, and Cundo was the show, man turned on with flake and blood into the cat-stud prince come to set the ladies free; his body glistened, his moves purred with promise, said stuff a five into my polyester leopard-skin, ladies, and we'll all be richer for it.

Many of them did and Cundo followed the waitress to LaBrava's table counting his sweaty wet take. He eyed LaBrava, smiled at the camera, blinked in the flash.

"So, the picture-taker."

LaBrava lowered the camera. "The boat-lifter."

Cundo ordered a sugar-free soft drink from the waitress, slipped into a chair still glistening, smelling of cologne, cat whiskers waved by his smile. "So, you and the woman. Is all the same to me. I sell you the typewriter, a nice one. I think you have to give me the camera, too. Is it the same one?"

"A better one," LaBrava said. "Older but more expensive."

"That's okay, I'll take it."

"Why didn't you try to take the other one?"

"I didn't know it would be so easy like this."

LaBrava said, "Is it?" He pushed the camera bag toward Cundo, who leaned over the table to look inside. As he looked up, LaBrava pulled the bag back, closer to him.

"Tha's Richard's gun?"

LaBrava nodded.

"What happen to him?"

"He got shot."

"I believe it," Cundo Rey said. "Guy like him, he would get shot. Did it kill him?"

LaBrava nodded.

"That guy, he don't know what he was doing. I don't know what he was doing either. Or you, or the woman. But I know what I'm doing, man, I'm going to sell you a typewriter or that woman is going to jail. Maybe you going too."

LaBrava said, "What would you think—you give me the typewriter, then give yourself up?"

Cundo said, "Give myself to the police?" He sat back as the waitress, with dollar bills folded through her fingers, placed a glass in front of him and filled it from a can of Tab. She walked away and Cundo leaned in, frowning. "I look crazy to you?"

"I don't know you," LaBrava said. "You could be some broke dick going from failure to failure, never gonna make it. See, if you're like that maybe you ought to turn yourself in, they'll take off a few years. You go up to Raiford and do your go-go number they'll make you Homecoming Queen."

"Man, I don't steal nothing. Why do I want to go to jail?"

"For killing that old man, Richard's Uncle Miney."

"Man, what is this? Some shit you telling me. What we have to talk about—you like to see that woman go to jail?"

"No, I wouldn't," LaBrava said, "and I'll tell you why. I don't trust her. I think just for a kick she could put the stuff on us. I mean the whole thing with her is for fun. She doesn't need the money, it's for thrills."

"For thrills . . ."

"You understand what I mean? She's a very emotional person."

"Yes, I understand."

"She borrows the money from the old guy that owns the hotel . . ."

"Yes?"

"Then steals it from him."

"She's some woman."

"Very determined. You know, hardheaded. She says she doesn't want to buy the typewriter."

"She doesn't? Why?"

"Because of her honor. She won't be forced to do it. She doesn't think you'd give the typewriter to the police."

"No?"

"No, because if you turn her in—she said for me to tell you—she'll give them your name. They already have your picture, your fingerprints . . . Is that true?"

"Yes, is true."

"So if she goes to jail, you go to jail."

"What about you, yourself?"

"What did I do?"

"You kill Richard?"

"I never said that. But I see what you mean. You got a point."

"I do?"

"Yeah, she could lay Richard off on me. Try to."

"So why don't you kill her? You want me to?"

"I don't think we have to go that far. But I don't think you should try and sell her the typewriter, either."

"No?"

"See, if the cops even suspect her, they search her place and find it?"

"Yes?"

"She could be pissed off enough she'd finger both of us."

"Yes, so what do we do?"

"You give me the typewriter. I'll take care of it."

"Give it to you . . . What do I get?"

"Half the money."

Cundo had to bite on his lip and think about it. "Three hundred thousand dollars?"

"That's right."

"How would you do it?"

"No problem. She already gave me the money, to hide. See, in case they search her place. So I give half to you and you give me the typewriter."

"What does she do then? Her money's gone."

"Who gives a shit? The typewriter's gone, too; she can't even prove *she* did it. She tries to put the stuff on us, it's her word against ours. What can she prove?"

"Nothing."

"So, all you have to do is give me the typewriter."

Cundo thought about it again. He said then, "You give me half the money, okay, *I* get rid of the typewriter."

"If I knew you better," LaBrava said, "if we were friends it would be no problem. But I don't know you. You understand? You give me the typewriter, you get half the take, and neither one of us has to worry. What do you say?"

Cundo thought some more and began to nod.

"All right, half the money. Keep your camera, I don't want it."

"When?"

"Maybe tonight. After I go-go."

"Why not right now? Three hundred thousand, you don't need to hang around here shaking your ass."

"I like to do it."

"Okay, then later on?"

"Let me think."

LaBrava let him. He looked at those cat whiskers painted on Cundo's face and said, "You know, one time I was as close to Fidel Castro as I am to you right now. It was in New York."

"Yeah? Why didn't you shoot him? Maybe I wouldn't go to prison if you did."

"What were you in for?"

"I shot a Russian guy."

"Just trying to hustle a buck, uh?"

"Man, is tough sometime. You got to think, is somebody want to kill me? You never know."

LaBrava, nodding, had to agree. "As Robert Mitchum once said, 'I don't want to die, but if I do I'm gonna die last.' "

The Cuban with the cat whiskers painted on his face stared at him and said, "Who's Robber Mitchum?"

*   *   *

Cundo Rey was back at the place on Bonita now.

The first thing he had decided: there was no sense in the picture-taker giving him half the money when he could give him all of it.

The second thing: he needed light to see it. Make sure it wasn't some money on top of newspaper; he had enough newspaper. He didn't want to go to the woman's apartment where, the picture-taker said, the money was still in the trash bag; he didn't want to go anyplace he had never been. He didn't want to go to a bar or a cafe or some all-night place where people came in. He didn't want to go outside, in a park, where there wasn't any light.

He went through all this before coming around to the place he already had, on Bonita, a perfect place. Nobody on the street knew him or maybe had even seen him. All he had to do was leave the picture-taker here, go over the Seventy-ninth Street Causeway to the Interstate, be in Atlanta, Georgia, tomorrow. Go anyplace he wanted after that with his bag of money. Somebody would find the picture-taker in a week, two weeks, they would smell him and call the cops and break into the place.

He couldn't get over the picture-taker being so simple and trusting. He had thought the country people recruited for the housing brigade in Alamar were simple. This guy was as simple as those people. Either he believed he could trade half the money for the typewriter, or he believed he could pull a trick, get the typewriter and keep the money. Either way he would be very simple to think he could do it.

Cundo could feel his snubbie pressing into his spine, silk shirt hanging over it. Let the guy come in. Make sure the money was in the bag—no newspaper. Then do it. No fooling around. Do it. Leave the guy. He could drive out maybe to Hollywood, California, see how things were doing out there. Sure, get some new outfits, go Hollywood.

He was getting excited now, looking out through the Venetian blinds to the street that curved past the apartment. Empty. It always looked empty, even during the day. He was getting anxious waiting for the guy to arrive here. He rubbed a finger under his itchy nose, looked at his hand and saw the black Magic-Marker on his finger, from his cat whiskers he had forgot to wash off, from being anxious and excited. It was okay. Take half a minute.

Cundo left the window, moved from the living room through the short hall to the bathroom. That snubbie was hurting him. He pulled it out of his pants, laid it on the toilet tank. Wrap a facecloth around it after he washed off his cat whiskers, try it that way stuck in his pants, so the hard edges wouldn't hurt . . .

A sound came from the front.

He ran into the living room, looked out through the blinds. The street was still empty. Right behind him then, a few feet away, someone knocked on the door and Cundo jumped. He moved to the door and listened. The knocks came again in his face.

"Who is it?"

"It's me," LaBrava said. "Guy with the money."

Cundo opened the door, stood holding it for the picture-taker and right away could feel a difference in him. Like a different guy . . .

Coming in like a Brinks guard, holding the round Hefty bag in his left hand and Richard Nobles' .357 Mag in his right, pointed down.

Cundo couldn't believe it. He wanted to feel the snubbie pressing into his back; it would have felt good now, but that fucking snubbie was in the bathroom. He said, getting amazement in his voice, "Man, what do you have that gun for?"

"Respect," LaBrava said. "You still have your cat whiskers on."

Cundo didn't like that big goddamn Mag. He said, "Listen, why don't you put that thing away?"

"Pull my shirt out, stick it in my pants?" LaBrava said. "Where've you got yours, in back? I know you bought one off Javier, he's a good friend of mine. Turn around."

Cundo said, "What are you doing?" as he turned around, wanting to show he was a nice guy, cooperating. He felt LaBrava poke the barrel of the Mag against his spine and then run it along his belt.

"Where do you keep it?"

"Man, I don't have no gun."

"What'd you shoot Miney with?"

"You mean that old man? . . ."

"Why'd you shoot him in the back of the head like that?"

"*Why?*" Cundo turned and stared at him, frowning, because he couldn't believe this was the same guy. This guy didn't sound simple and trusting. He was calm, but sounded like he didn't care very much, without emotion. What he sounded like was a policeman. "Who said I killed him?"

"Where's your gun?"

"I told you, I don't have no gun."

LaBrava was looking around the room. "You don't keep a very neat house. What do you—you don't like the news, you tear the paper up?" Still looking around. "Where's the typewriter?"

"All right," Cundo said, and motioned toward the kitchen.

LaBrava dropped the Hefty bag between the

green arms of a vinyl living room chair and followed Cundo through the kitchen to the garage, where he got to the trunk of the Trans Am and said, "Oh, I got to go back in and get the key. I forgot it."

LaBrava slid the barrel of the Mag over Cundo's hip, over tight knit material to his right-hand pants pocket.

"What's that?"

Cundo didn't say anything. He brought his keys out and opened the trunk—a clean trunk, nothing in it but a typewriter case.

"Bring it inside."

In the living room again LaBrava motioned and Cundo placed the typewriter case on the maple coffee table. LaBrava sat down on the sofa in front of the typewriter case and motioned again. Cundo moved back a few steps. LaBrava laid the Mag on the coffee table and opened the case. It was empty.

Cundo waited for LaBrava to look up. He said, "Somebody must have stole it." He began to turn then, carefully, saying, "Excuse me, but I got to go pee-pee."

He walked past the Hefty bag sitting on the vinyl chair, he walked through the short hall and into the bathroom, hand going out to that beautiful snubbie on the white tile of the toilet tank . . .

* * *

"Drop it in the toilet," LaBrava said from the doorway, "and put the top down."

Cundo turned enough to look over his shoulder. "Man, I just want to go pee-pee."

"Drop it in the toilet, go pee-pee and then put the top down," LaBrava said. "How's that sound?"

He brought Cundo, hanging his head, back to the living room. He lifted Cundo's face, the barrel of the Mag under his chin, stared at him with a deadpan eternal cop look and Cundo said, "Is in the closet."

LaBrava found the typewriter. He stuck the Mag in his waist, carried the typewriter over to the coffee table and set it into the case, then had to bring the carriage in line so the top of the case would come down and snap closed. He looked over to see Cundo sitting in the vinyl chair now, the Hefty bag on the floor in front of him. LaBrava sat down on the sofa; he had not yet decided how he was going to handle the difficult part: how to get out of here with the typewriter and leave Cundo, with the money, for the cops.

The cops would wonder what was going on, because Cundo would tell them a story and LaBrava would have to say to Torres, "Oh, you believe that?" The cops would give the money back to Jean and she would have to return it to Maurice and then answer all the questions about Cundo's story the cops would ask her at the station and all the questions the state attorney would ask her perhaps in a courtroom. He could protect her tonight; tomorrow she would be on her own.

LaBrava looked up as Cundo said, "Is this half or all the money?"

"All of it," LaBrava said. "Six hundred thousand dollars." The Mag was digging into his groin. He pulled it from his waist and laid it on the typewriter case.

"Something is telling me we not going to do business," Cundo said.

He sounded tired, almost sad, and LaBrava said, "You can look at it if you want. Imagine what it would be like."

"Why not?" Cundo said, and began unwinding the baling wire from the neck of the bag.

He could lock him in a closet, LaBrava was thinking, and call the cops. But he would have to stay here until just before they arrived or Cundo would bust out.

The boat-lifter was reaching into the bag now, feeling around. He brought out a handful of currency he looked at shaking his head very slowly. His hand went into the bag with the currency to stir it, feel it, sink his arm into it. His expression changed then, eyes opening a little wider. He drew his arm out and extended it toward LaBrava, his hand gripping a small bluesteel automatic.

"How do you think about this?" Cundo said. "You know, I say to St. Barbara I believe this is my day. Then I don't think is my day. Then I have to think, yes, it is my day. How do you like this, uh?"

LaBrava nodded—not to say yes, he liked it, but to confirm what he felt. See? He wasn't able to be detached, objective enough to take it all the way. When the boat-lifter reached for the gun in the bathroom that was the time to be detached and shoot the motherfucker and that would have been it; but he had even felt sorry for the guy, invited him to look in the bag . . . He had looked in the bag himself in Jean's apartment when he picked it up and had brought out a handful of bills, but it hadn't occurred to him to ask her what she did with the gun. He could pretend to think like a cop and he could put on a cop look with a gun in his hand, but he couldn't take it all the way.

Now it was turned around and now it was all right to be subjective about staying alive and having to shoot the guy to do it, *if* you could do it . . . with the .357 Mag an arm's length away on the typewriter case and the boat-lifter aiming the automatic from about eighteen feet away—LaBrava stepping the distance off with his eyes, less than six strides to the guy who had shot the old man in the back of the head, twice.

Cundo said, "You look at me like that . . . Now you don't have nothing to say."

"I got a question," LaBrava said.

"Oh, you want to make a deal now?"

"No, I was gonna ask, how do you know the gun's loaded?"

Cundo didn't answer.

"What is it, a Beretta?"

Cundo didn't answer.

"It's probably a Walther. Pray to St. Barbara it isn't a Saturday-night special and misfires on you. They always misfire."

Cundo, one eye closed, was trying to look at the gun and keep LaBrava in his sights at the same time.

"If it's a Walther you'll see some writing on it, in German. Unless it's a Czech seven-six-five."

Cundo was squinting, one eye closed, extending his head now, leaning toward the gun and turning it slightly to read the inscription on the side of the barrel . . .

And LaBrava thought, Jesus Christ, knowing he was going to have to take it all the way right now, before he started to feel sorry for the guy aiming a gun at him, if that was possible—right now all the way—and reached for the .357 Mag on the typewriter case, concentrating on picking it up cleanly . . . Cundo firing . . . and coming around and putting the Mag on him . . . Cundo firing . . . and squeezing the grip . . . Cundo falling back in the chair firing at the ceiling . . . squeezing the grip, squeezing the grip, and shot him three times up the center groove of his rib cage. After that, in silence, the little Cuban with the cat whiskers stared dead at him in the green vinyl chair and then hung his head.

LaBrava locked the Hefty bag in the trunk of the Trans Am, called the Miami Beach Police to report gunfire on Bonita Drive, just to be sure, and left with only what he had come for, the typewriter.

28

NOW HE WOULD STAY OUT OF IT as long as he could, or until it was settled.

He slept late. He didn't answer his phone. He kept very still when there were footsteps in the hall and twice during the morning someone knocked on his door. He did not look out the window at the view that was all ocean views. He did look at his photos and decided he didn't like any of them: all that black and white, all that same old stuff, characters trying to be characters. He said, Are you trying to be a character?

In the afternoon, which seemed like a long time after to him, there was a knock on the door and he opened it when he heard Franny's voice.

Franny said, "Where've you been? . . . Don't you know I miss you and hunger for you?"

He smiled because it didn't matter what kind of a mood he was in. When he saw her he smiled and knew he would not have to bother choosing an attitude.

Franny said, "What's going on? The cops were here again."

He told her he didn't know. He didn't want to learn anything from Franny that might be misinformation or only part of it or speculation. He wanted it to be settled and then learn about it in some official way, facts in order.

She said, "*Some*thing's going on and I'm dying to know what it is. I mean finally we get a little ac*tiv*ity around here. Live in a place like this, LaBrava, the high point of the day is some tourist comes in and asks where Joe's Stone Crab is."

"Or the mailman arrives," LaBrava said. "Let me take you to Joe's tonight, or Picciolo's, any place you want to go."

He put on the banana shirt after Franny left and looked at himself in the mirror. He liked that banana shirt. He looked at his photos again and began to like some of them again, the honest and dishonest faces, enough of them so that he could say to himself, You got promise, kid.

Who was it said that?

Who cares?

He took off the banana shirt, showered, shaved, rubbed in Aqua Velva—Maurice had told him, "Use that, you must have cheap skin"—put the banana shirt on again and picked up the typewriter case. It was now seven in the evening. It was time. So he went up the stairs to the third floor, walked past Maurice's door to Jean Shaw's, knocked and waited. There was no sound. He walked back to Maurice's door.

Maurice said, "The hell you been?" Wearing a white-on-white shirt with long collar points, a black knit tie; his black silk suitcoat was draped over a dining room chair.

Jean Shaw, in a black sheath dress, pearls, stood at the credenza making drinks. She was saying— and it was like a background sound—"Orvis, Dinner Island, Neoga, Española, Bunnell, Dupont, Korona, Favorita, Harwood . . . Windle, Ormond, Flomich . . . Holly Hill, Daytona Beach. There. All the way to Daytona."

"You left out National Gardens." Maurice winked at LaBrava standing there holding the typewriter case.

She turned saying, "Where does National Gardens come in?" Her eyes resting on LaBrava.

"After Harwood," Maurice said. "Look who's here."

"I see who's here," Jean said. "Is that my typewriter you're returning?"

"Sit down, get comfortable," Maurice said. "Jean, fix him one. He likes it on the rocks."

"I know what he likes," Jean said.

"Well, it's all over," Maurice said. "You missed

Torres this morning. Go on, sit in my chair, it's okay. In fact, I insist." He waited as LaBrava curved himself, reluctantly, into the La-Z-Boy; being treated as a guest of honor. "There's a couple a discrepancies they can't figure out. Like Richard was killed with the Cuban's gun and the Cuban was killed with Richard's gun, only he was killed *after* Richard was killed," Maurice said, moving to the sofa. "Which has got the cops scratching their heads. But that's their problem."

Jean came over with drinks on a silver tray.

"The cops found the money, we got it back," Maurice said. "Far as I'm concerned the case is closed."

She handed LaBrava his and he had to look up to see her eyes, those nice eyes so quietly aware.

"The cops can do what they want," Maurice said.

She handed him his drink, Maurice on the sofa now, and sat down next to him, placing the tray with her drink on the cocktail table. LaBrava watched her light a cigarette, watched her eyes raise to his as she exhaled a slow stream of smoke.

"You can't have everything," Maurice said. "I told your friend Torres that, he agreed. You got the two guys you want, be satisfied."

Her gaze dropped to the typewriter case on the floor next to the recliner, lingered, came up slowly to rest on him again.

"Torres said they always thought there was a third one. Only why didn't he take the money? Unless he had to get out a there fast once he shot the Cuban and didn't have time to look for it. Richard's gun—you know where it was? In the toilet. Listen, there was even another gun in there, in the toilet, they find out shot somebody else. You imagine?"

LaBrava said, "Maybe the third one will walk in, clear everything up."

Jean was still looking at him.

"I told the cops, be grateful for what you have," Maurice said. "That third one, whoever, did you a favor. Any loose ends—well, you always got a few loose ends. Who needs to know everything? No, as far as I'm concerned—" He gave Jean a little nudge with his elbow. "What is it they say in the picture business?"

"It's a wrap," Jean said.

He nudged her again. "Should we tell him?"

"I don't see why not," Jean said.

Maurice got higher on the sofa, laid his arm on the backrest. "Well, we decided last night . . . Jeanie and I are gonna get married." He brought his hand down to give her shoulder a squeeze. "Look at him, he can't believe it. Yeah, as a matter of fact we start talking last night, we couldn't figure out why we hadn't thought of it a long time ago. Make life easier for both of us . . . We're tired a living alone."

LaBrava didn't say anything because he didn't want to say anything he didn't mean.

The former movie star in her fifties looked younger, much younger, sitting next to the retired bookmaker, natty old guy who didn't know he was old.

"I'm gonna take good care of her," Maurice said.

"And I'm going to let him," Jean said. She said then, "It's not the movies, Joe." Looking at him with those eyes. "Maury wants you to be his best man."

He wasn't going to say anything he didn't mean or cover up whatever it was he felt.

What he finally said was, "Swell."

Then gave them a nice smile: maybe a little weary but still a nice one. Why not?

Read on for an excerpt from

ROAD DOGS

A NOVEL

ELMORE LEONARD

Available in hardcover in May 2009 from

wm

WILLIAM MORROW
An Imprint of HarperCollins*Publishers*

THEY PUT FOLEY AND THE CUBAN TOGETHER IN THE BACK-
seat of the van and took them from the Palm Beach County jail on
Gun Club to Glades Correctional, the old redbrick prison at the
south end of Lake Okeechobee. Neither one said a word during the
ride that took most of an hour, both of them handcuffed and
shackled.

They were returning Jack Foley to do his thirty years after
busting out for a week, Foley's mind on a woman who made in-
tense love to him one night in Detroit, pulled a Sig Sauer .38 the
next night, shot him and sent him back to Florida.

The Cuban, a little guy about fifty with dyed hair pulled back
in a ponytail, was being transferred to Glades from the state prison
at Starke, five years down, two and a half to go of a second-degree
murder conviction. The Cuban was thinking about a woman he
believed he loved, this woman who could read minds.

———

They were brought to the chow hall, their trays hit with macaroni and cheese and hot dogs from the steam table, three slices of white bread, rice pudding and piss-poor coffee and sat down next to each other at the same table, opposite three inmates who stopped eating.

Foley knew them, Aryan Brotherhood neo-Nazi skinheads, and they knew Foley, a Glades celebrity who'd robbed more banks than anybody they'd ever heard of—walk in and walk out, nothing to it—until Foley pulled a dumb stunt and got caught. He ran out of luck when he drew His Honor Maximum Bob in Criminal Court, Palm Beach County. The white-power convicts accepted Foley because he was as white as they were, but they never showed they were impressed by his all-time-high number of banks. Foley sat down and they started in.

"Jesus, look at him eat. Jack, you come back 'cause you miss the chow?"

"Boy, you get any pussy out there?"

"He didn't, what'd he bust out for?"

"I heard you took a .38 in the shank, Jack. Is that right, you let this puss shoot you?"

"Federal U.S. fuckin' marshal, shows her star and puts one in his leg."

Foley ate his macaroni and cheese staring at the mess of it on his tray while the skinhead hard-ons made their lazy remarks Foley would hear again and again for thirty years, from the Brotherhood, from the Mexican Mafia, from Nuestra Familia, from the black guys all ganged up; thirty years in a convict population careful not to dis anybody, but thinking he could stand up with the tray, have the tables looking at him and backhand it across bare skulls, show 'em he was as dumb as they were and get put in the box for sixty days.

Now they were after the Cuban.

"Boy, we don't allow niggers at our table."

They brought Foley into it asking him, "How we suppose to eat, Jack, this dinge sitting here?"

Right now was the moment to pick up the tray and go crazy, not saying a word but getting everybody's attention, the tables wondering, Jesus, what happened to Foley?

And thought, For what?

He said to the three white-supremacy freaks with their mass of tattoos, "This fella's down from Starke. You understand? I'm showing him around the hotel. He wants to visit with his Savior I point him to the chapel. He wants a near-death-experience hangover, I tell him to see one of you fellas for some pruno. But you got this stranger wrong. He ain't colored, he's a hundred percent greaseball from down La Cucaracha way," Foley looking at the three hard-ons and saying, "Cha cha, cha."

Later on when they were outside the Cuban stopped Foley. "You call me a greaseball to my face?"

This little bit of a guy acting tough.

"Where you been," Foley said, "you get stuck with the white-power ding-dongs, the best thing is to sound as dumb as they are and they'll think you're funny. You heard them laugh, didn't you? And they don't laugh much. It's against their code of behavior."

This was how Foley and Cundo hooked up at Glades.

———

Cundo said Foley was the only white guy in the joint he could talk to, Foley a name among all the grunge here and knew how to jail. Stay out of other people's business. Cundo's favorite part of the day was walking the yard with Foley, a couple of road dogs in tailored prison blues, and tell stories about himself.

How he went to prison in Cuba for shooting a Russian guy.

Took his suitcase and sold his clothes, his shoes, all of it way too big for him. Came here during the time of the boatlift from Mariel, twenty-seven years ago, man, when Fidel opened the prisons and sent all the bad dudes to La Yuma—what he called the United States—for their vacation.

How he got into different hustles. Didn't care for armed robbery. Liked boosting cars at night off a dealer's lot. He danced go-go in gay bars as the Cat Prince, wore a leopard-print jockstrap, cat whiskers painted on his face, but scored way bigger tips Ladies Night at clubs, the ladies stuffing his jock with bills. "Here is this middle-age mama with big *tetas*, she say to me, 'Come to my home Saturday, my husband is all day at his golf club.' She say to me, 'I give you ten one-hundred-dollar bills and eat you alive.'"

Man, and how he was shot three times from his chest to his belly and came so close to dying he saw the dazzle of gold light you hear about when you approaching heaven, right there. But the emergency guys see he's still breathing, blood coming out his mouth, his heart still working, man, and they deliver him alive to Jackson Memorial where he was in a coma thirty-four days, woke up and faked it a few more days listening to Latina voices, the nurse helpers talking about him. He learned he was missing five inches of his colon but healed, sewed up, good as new. When he opened his eyes he noticed the *mozo* mopping the floor wore a tattoo on his hand, an eye drawn at the base of his thumb and index finger, a kind of eye he remembered from Combinado del Este, the prison by Havana. He said to the *mozo*, "We both Marielitos, uh? Get me out of here, my brother, and I make you rich."

Foley said, "You thought you'd be cuffed to the bed?"

"Maybe I was at first, I don't know. I was into some shit at the time didn't work out."

"A cop shot you?"

"No, was a guy, a picture-taker in South Beach, before it became the famous South Beach. Before that he was a Secret Service guy but quit to take pictures. One he did, a guy being thrown off I–95 from the overpass, man, down to the street, the guy in the air, Joe LaBrava sold to a magazine and became famous."

"Why'd he shoot you?"

"Man, I was gonna shoot *him*. I know him, he's a good guy, but I was not going to prison for a deal this woman talk me into doing, with this dumbbell hillbilly rent-a-cop. I didn't tell you about it? I pull a gun and this guy who use to be in the Secret Service beats me to the draw, puts three bullets in me, right here, man, like buttons. I should be dead"—Cundo grinning now—"but here I am, uh? I'm in good shape, I weigh the same now as the day I left Cuba. Try to guess how much."

He was about five-four, not yet fifty but close to it, his dyed hair always slicked back in a ponytail. "A hundred and thirty," Foley said.

"One twenty-eight. You know how I keep my weight? I don't eat that fucking macaroni and cheese they give us. I always watch what I eat. Even when I was in Hollywood going out every night? Is where I went when the *mozo* got me out of the hospital, to L.A., man, see a friend of mine. You understand this was the time of cocaine out there. All I had to do was hook up with a guy I know from Miami. Soon I'm taking care of cool dudes in the picture business, actors, directors—I was like them, I partied with them, I was famous out there."

Foley said, "Till you got busted."

"There was a snitch. Always, even in Hollywood."

"One of your movie buddies."

"I believe a major star, but they don't tell me who the snitch is. The magistrate set a two-million-dollar bond and I put up a home worth two and a half I bought for six-hundred when I was first out there, all the rooms with high ceilings. I pay nine bills for another worth an easy four and a half million today. Both homes on the same canal, almost across from each other."

Foley said, "In Hollywood?"

"In Venice, California, like no place on earth, man, full of cool people and shit."

"Why do you need two homes?"

"At one time I had four homes I like very much. I wait, the prices go up to the sky and I sell two of them. Okay, but the West Coast feds see Florida has a detainer on me for a homicide, a guy they say I did when I was in Miami Beach."

Foley said, "The *mozo*?"

Cundo said, "Is funny you think of him."

"Why didn't you trust him?"

"Why should I? I don't know him. They say one time we out in the ocean fishing I push him overboard."

Foley said, "You shot him first?"

Cundo shook his head grinning just a little. "Man, you something, how you think you know things."

———

"What I don't understand," Cundo said, walking the yard with Foley, "I see you as a hip guy, you smart for a fucking bank robber, but two falls, man, one on top the other, you come out you right back in the slam. Tell me how you think about it, a smart guy like you have to look at thirty years."

Foley said, "You know how a dye pack works? The teller slips you one, it looks like a pack of twenties in a bank strap. It explodes as you leave the bank. Something in the doorframe sets it off. I walk out of a bank in Redondo Beach, the dye pack goes off and I'm sprayed with red paint, people on the street looking at me. Twenty years of going in banks and coming out clean, my eyes open. I catch a dye pack and spend the next seven in federal detention, Lompoc, California. I came out," Foley said, "and did a bank in Pomona the same day. You fall off a bike you get back on. I think, Good, I've still got it. I made over six grand in Pomona. I come back to Florida—my wife Adele divorced me while I'm at Lompoc and she's having a tough time paying her bills. She's working for a magician, Emile the Amazing, jumping out of boxes till he fired her and hired a girl Adele said has bigger tits and was younger. I do a bank in Lake Worth with the intention, give Adele the proceeds to keep her going for a few months. I leave the bank in the Honda I'm using, America's most popular stolen car at the time. Now I'm waiting to make a left turn on to Dixie Highway and I hear the car behind me going *va-room varoom*, revving up, the guy can't wait. He backs up and cuts around me, his tires screaming, like I'm a retiree waiting to make the turn when it's safe to pull out."

"You just rob the fucking bank," Cundo said.

"And this guy's showing me what a hotdog he is."

"So you go after him," Cundo said.

"I tore after him, came up on the driver's side and stared at him."

"Gave him the killer look," Cundo said.

"That's right, and he gives me the finger. I cranked the wheel and sideswiped him, stripped his chrome and ran him off the road."

"I would've shot the fucker," Cundo said.

"What happened, I tore up both tires on the side I swiped him. By the time I got the car pulled over, a deputy's coming up behind me with lights flashing."

"Tha's called road rage," Cundo said. "I'm surprise, a cool guy like you losing it. How you think it happen?"

"I wasn't paying attention. I let myself catch a dye pack in Redondo Beach, something I swore would never happen. The next one, seven years later, you're right, I lost it. You know why? Because a guy with a big engine wearing shades, the top down, no idea I'd just robbed a bank, made me feel like a wimp. And that," Foley said, "is some serious shit to consider."

"Man, you got the balls to bust out of prison, you don't have to prove nothing."

"Out for a week and back inside."

"What could you do? The girl shot you, the chick marshal. You don't tell me about her."

Karen Sisco. Foley kept her to himself. She gave him moments to think about and look at over and over for a time, a few months now, but there weren't enough moments to last thirty years.

Foley's conviction didn't make sense to Cundo. "You get thirty years for one bank, and I'm maxing out seven and a half for killing a guy? How come you don't appeal?"

Foley said he did, but the attorney appointed by the court told him he didn't have a case. "If I can appeal now," Foley said, "I will. If I have to wait too long, one of these nights I'll get shot off the wire and that'll be that."

Cundo said, "Let me tell you how a smart chick lawyer can change your life for you."

———

"I was told by the Florida state attorney, the federal court in L.A. gave me up 'cause I can get the death penalty here or life with no parole. But this cool chick lawyer I got—and I thank Jesus and St. Barbara I can afford to pay her—she say the reason L.A. gave me up, they have a snitch they don't want to burn."

"One of the movie stars," Foley said, "you turned into a drug addict?"

"Miss Megan say maybe because they like his TV show. Plays a prosecutor, busts his balls to put bad guys away. You have to meet her, Miss Megan Norris, the smartest chick lawyer I ever met. She say the Florida state attorney isn't sure he can put me away on the kind of hearsay evidence he's got. She believe he's thinking of sending me back to the Coast. They find me guilty out there I do two-hundred and ninety-five months, man, federal. You know how long that is? The rest of my fucking life. But Miss Megan say they don't want me either if they have to give up their snitch, the famous actor. So she say to the state attorney here, 'You don't want Mr. Rey?' She say, 'Even if he was to plead to second degree and does a good seven for you straight up, no credit?' Man, the state attorney is tempted, but he like me to do twenty-five to life. Miss Megan tells him she can get that out on the Coast where they have new prisons, not old joints full of roaches, toilets that back up. No, she sticks to the seven and adds, okay, six months, take it or leave it. She ask me can I do it. Look at me, I already done five years at Starke. It got crowded up there, the state prison, man, so they send me to this joint, suppose to be medium security, 'cause I don't fuck with the hacks or have snitches set on fire. Ones they can prove. Can I do three more less five months, all I have left of my time?"

"Standing on your head," Foley said. "What's the runout for the federal action?" He saw Cundo start to grin and Foley said, "It already has."

"They have five years to change their mind and bring me to trial if they want. But I'm doing my time here in Florida by then, safe from falling into federal hands. I said to Miss Megan, 'Girl, you could have made a deal, six years, I be almost to the door right now.' Miss Smarty say, 'You lucky to max out with seven plus. Say thank you and do the time.'"

"You get out," Foley said, "you're free, they can't deport you?"

"Fidel won't take us back."

"You glad you came to America?"

"I'm grateful for the ways they are to improve myself since I come to La Yuma. I respect how justice wears a blindfold, like a fucking hostage."

"Where'd you find Miss Megan?"

"I happen to read about her in the Palm Beach newspaper. I call her and Megan come to look me over, see if I can pay her. She like my situation, a way she sees she can make a deal. I tole her I pray to Jesus and St. Barbara. Those two, man, always come through for me. You ever pray?"

"I have, yeah," Foley said. "Sometimes it works."

"You want to appeal?"

"I told you one guy turned me down."

"Let me see can I get Miss Megan for you."

"How do I pay her, rob the prison bank?"

"Don't worry about it," Cundo said. "I want you to meet her. Ask what she thinks of me, if she goes for my type."

New York Times bestselling author Elmore Leonard is back, and so are three of his favorite characters, Jack Foley, Cundo Rey, and Dawn Navarro!

"*Road Dogs* is terrific, and Elmore Leonard is in a class of one. Not only does he have no equal, he doesn't even have a legitimate contender. He makes it look so effortless that if he wasn't the greatest crime writer who ever lived I might have to hate him. But he is, so I just tip my hat." —Dennis Lehane

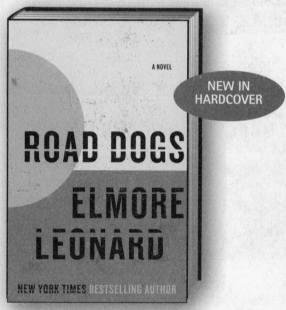

A NOVEL

NEW IN HARDCOVER

ROAD DOGS

ELMORE LEONARD

NEW YORK TIMES BESTSELLING AUTHOR

978-0-06-173314-7

"When you read Elmore Leonard, you enter Mr. Leonard's world. A trip like that is its own kind of vacation." —*New York Times*

"A superb craftsman . . . his writing is pure pleasure."
—*Los Angeles Times Book Review*

THE UNDISPUTED MASTER OF THE CRIME NOVEL

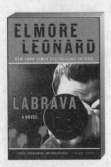

LABRAVA
A Novel

978-0-06-176769-2 (trade paperback)

Ex-Secret Service agent Joe La Brava gets mixed up in a scam involving a slew of eccentric characters.

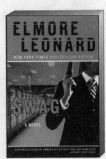

SWAG
A Novel

978-0-06-174136-4 (trade paperback)

Used car salesman Frank Ryan has a surefire way to get rich quick: armed robbery.

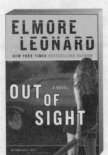

OUT OF SIGHT
A Novel

978-0-06-174031-2 (trade paperback)

Minutes after pulling into a prison parking lot, a Deputy U.S. Marshal meets a legendary bank robber—that's when the fun begins.

THE COMPLETE WESTERN STORIES OF ELMORE LEONARD

978-0-06-124292-2 (trade paperback)

This collection is a must-have for every fan of Elmore Leonard.

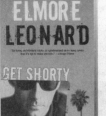

GET SHORTY

978-0-06-077709-8 (trade paperback)

A mobster goes to Hollywood—where women are gorgeous, men are corrupt, and no one can be trusted.

FREAKY DEAKY

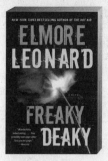

978-0-688-16096-8 (trade paperback)

It's only after he transfers out of the bomb squad that Chris Mankowski begins juggling with dynamite.

BANDITS

978-0-688-16639-7 (trade paperback)

An unlikely trio targeting millions of dollars is sure to make out like bandits—if they survive.

BE COOL
A Novel

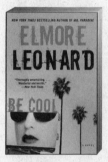

978-0-06-077706-7 (trade paperback)

Chili Palmer searches for his next big hit as murder blurs the line between reality and the big screen.

KILLSHOT
A Novel

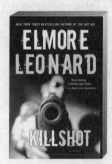

978-0-688-16638-0 (trade paperback)

After witnessing a scam, Carmen and her husband must outrun two thugs determined to eliminate any living evidence.

WHEN THE WOMEN COME OUT TO DANCE
Stories

978-0-06-058616-4 (trade paperback)

Driven by terrific characters and superb writing, these short pieces are Elmore Leonard at his economical best.